Journey through the Narrow Gate

Rick and Pamela,
 I am very blessed that you have read this.
 Blessings on your journey through these pages.
Denise [signature]

Journey Through the Narrow Gate

Dennis Stephan Cole

Journey Through The Narrow Gate by Dennis Stephan Cole
Copyright © 2017 by Dennis Stephan Cole
All Rights Reserved.
ISBN: 978-1-59755-439-8

Published by: ADVANTAGE BOOKS™
Longwood, Florida, USA
www.advbookstore.com

This book and parts thereof may not be reproduced in any form, stored in a retrieval system or transmitted in any form by any means (electronic, mechanical, photocopy, recording or otherwise) without prior written permission of the author, except as provided by United States of America copyright law.

Library of Congress Catalog Number: 2017945541
1. Fiction / General
2. Fiction / Christian / Allegory

First Printing: September 2017
17 18 19 20 21 22 23   10 9 8 7 6 5 4 3 2
Printed in the United States of America

Endorsements

I have just experienced an incredible Journey Through The Narrow Gate. As I was reading this book, I found myself drawn into the pages of the storyline. Dennis Cole writes in such a manner that you find yourself identifying with the personality of each character. Before you know it you're inside of a movie, experiencing the story with them! The imagery and transparency of his writings, cause you to do some self-examination as you're enjoying this journey. I would highly recommend this book for everyone. It can even be used in book clubs or small group settings so that you can discuss the different aspects of how people handle life. I can't wait for his next book!

Dr. Richard A. Mansfield, Senior Pastor New Beginnings Church, Albuquerque, NM. Member-at-Large of the Executive Committee of the Church of God Gen. Assembly

Journey Through The Narrow Gate will make you feel the brunt of your flaws, but also the full force of God's love, redemption, and forgiveness. I recommend it as a new way of hearing the old, old story of the gospel.

Lawrence Kimbrough, Editor, Lifeway Christian Resources

Journey Through The Narrow Gate is an incredibly imaginative story in which the profound experiences and insights of the Bible's greatest 'actors' and stories are shared with struggling New York actor David Cohen. Once you've devoured this book, you'll read the story of Jonah (and the other Bible actors) in the Bible with an entirely new perspective. You'll even know them more intimately than you've ever known them before. Dennis Stephan Cole has written a profoundly thought-provoking book, bringing the Bible's 'story richness' to today's modern everyday life. You'll soon consider 'Journey' as a read-all-night, can't-put-down experience! As a longtime Bible study group leader, I find the structure and presentation of this book to be excellent for both individual reading and small/large group study. The books regularly challenges the status quo of today's Christian life and thinking, and thereby provides great seed for group discussion.

James R Topmiller, Lay Leader and V.P. of an Albuquerque Engineering Firm

Journey Through The Narrow Gate is an imaginative journey that will help you face your demons, and look to the real source of Winning—in life and heart. In fact, Dennis Cole will lead you into your own soul-searching that will help you realize that "winning is facing your greatest obstacle and overcoming your biggest fear" and help you wrestle with finding how you can yourself come to that same conclusion. You'll be inspired, intrigued, drawn in, and delighted all at the same time. You will not regret entering this great story, by a great author, Dennis Cole. And if you are at all intrigued by Jewish culture and Jewish history, you'll get a bonus in this great story

Dr. Byron Spradlin, president, Artists in Christian Testimony Intl, Brentwood, TN. Founding Board Chair, and current Vice Board Chair, Jews for Jesus, San Francisco, CA. Professor of Worship, Imagination Arts, Williamson College, Franklin, TN.

It was my pleasure to read Journey Through The Narrow Gate. This well written book by Dennis Cole kept me wanting to read more and more. It was fascinating to go down the road and experience what the main character was feeling in such detail. The storytelling was compelling. This coupled with the theater style dialogue caused me to want to go back and read more to see where the story was taking me. Journey Through The Narrow Gate is not in your face but an adventure into the heart of Jesus.

Karyn Janiczek, DSLitt, Advantage Books

Dennis uses allegory and his own unique style of story-telling to bring the Gospel to life for both believers and those seeking to know Him more.

Julie Gwinn, Seymour Literary Agency

Dennis has a truly unique method of addressing Christian philosophy. I can hear his voice as I read the story.

John Glaser, MA (Master of Arts, Education Administration), meteorologist, educator, school administrator, teacher, and Christian.

I liked reading Journey Through The Narrow Gate. There is allot of depth and truth written in these pages. The book would make for a great live play or film screenplay.

Pastor Jim Timmons, Contractor's For Christ Ministries, Watchman on the wall.

Acknowledgements

My first acknowledgment is that this book came to me from the Lord. I was staying with a family on my Bible Acting tour in 2005. Upon waking that Sunday morning in South Bend Indiana I saw a 'new' New York City that I had never before encountered. It felt more real to me than a dream, and for a brief period that morning I was sure I was in another place and time. I had several other dream encounters like this over the years always visiting this heavenly city. It became my go-to place for inspiration in writing *Journey Through The Narrow Gate*.

Linda Topmiller was the first to read my early manuscripts. It was her heartfelt appreciation for the Jonah chapter that encouraged me she loved the allegory of the book. I knew then we had a book in the making. My wife Wendy and I will never forget her many kindnesses toward us.

I don't think I could have written this book without Lawrence Kimbrough, my editor friend from Nashville. He helped me to believe that my thoughts and writing could and should be a book. His affirmation and his editing of my early drafts mentored me about being an author. Lawrence also introduced me to Julie Gwinn who was my literary agent for one year. As my agent, she drew from her editor essence and had me write three crucial turning point chapters that without her influence would not have been written. A special mention to the kindly Pastor Wayne Barber from Hoffmantown Church in Albuquerque, New Mexico who introduced me to Lawrence Kimbrough. Also to Annette Garcia, a faithful friend. As president of Son Broadcasting, she arranged my trip to the National Religious Broadcasters Convention in Nashville where I met the key people who began the publishing of *Journey* for me.

The copy for editors was brought to the page by my friend Stephen Bockemeir. He edited my grammar, sentence structure and made it much more readable for the publishing industry. He was a great listener.

Kathy Darlington really 'got it' in a way that inspired me that there were others out there that were right for *Journey*. Brandon Campanella and Mike Sanchez added high confidence to me for their enthusiastic feedback on the book. Thanks to Pastor Bob Barlis' insightful read, My core Narrow Gate Actors, Ken Armstrong, Cindy Spencer, Mary Catherine Walker, and Kaitlynn Glaser are greatly appreciated for encouraging me in their reading the manuscripts and for being faithful actors that bear the name that is our book. The online teacher John Glaser gave it a blessed read too. To Dacy Stevens, my brother since eighth grade who profoundly spoke into this book. To Pastor Richard Mansfield my friend, counselor, and Friday morning prayer partner who made the book better and truer by being my friend. To Doug Roth my old new friend from Cleveland and now Espanola New Mexico. Steve Holdman was one of the first to read the entire manuscript. He is a steady stream of encouragement to me. Jim Timmons was my final and very significant read before publishing. Thank you, Pastor Jim. To Mike and Karyn Janiczek for publishing many books including *Journey* and loving the 'Truth' through Advantage Books.

James Topmiller cannot go unmentioned in any aspect of my life and indeed this book. He was there for every new endeavor of *Journey* being published. He is the alongside witness of the "friend who sticks closer than a brother." He and his wife Trish are a special blessing to our family. I want to mention Stephanie Cole because when I told her the book was to be published, she was openly proud of me. She loves her Dad, and I love her too.

My final mention is my most important one. My wife Wendy has been my constant inspiration in every word that was thought or written in *Journey Through The Narrow Gate*. She has demonstrated to me what a man can be by stepping away from the mores that appear to bring success, but in reality, bring unhappiness and stress. She has suffered and persevered through the greatest challenges of gain and loss. She has overcome them all, and her love has stood the test. She is greater than this book, but *Journey Through The Narrow Gate* is my testimony to how great she is to me.

Table of Contents

ENDORSEMENTS 5
ACKNOWLEDGEMENTS 7
1: I Begin 11
2: A SIGNIFICANT STEP BACKWARD 14
3: A NEW YORK STATE OF MIND 17
4: JANET VS. JOHN STEPHENS 21
5: AN ELEGANT MAN 28
6: CONVERSATIONALLY COMATOSE 34
7: ENTER THE BLACK WITCH 38
8: BACK TO CENTRAL PARK 43
9: MAKING A TURN AND GOING NOWHERE 46
10: MYRIAM'S NEW FAITH 49
11: BACK TO BOSTON 54
12: U-TURN 58
13: RIGHT BACK WHERE I WAS 63
14: A SIGNIFICANT TURN 65
15: AN OPEN DOOR 70
16: MEET JONAH 73

17: DAVID'S NINEVEH 90
18: MEET SOME OF THE CAST 95
19: MORE THAN A DOCTOR 104
20: PAUL IN PRISON 130
21: JIMMY 141
22: THE WRESTLER 157
23: THE MARY YOU NEVER KNEW 167
24: MYRIAM MEMORIES 181
25: THE HEART OF DEATH 191
26: INSIDE THE SCRIPT 205
27: BACK AT MOUNT OF BEATITUDES 209
28: AT TIMES SQUARE 215

1

I Begin

It's good to be back in Boston. I wasn't born here, but it's where things truly began for me. I have not done this walk in five years and it is good to be back again. It's perfect weather today as my skin feels the warmth of the sun and the humidity is just right. Humidity is good for the skin.

I often start at Northeastern University, which in Boston talk is *Back Bay*. This is where Mom and my brother Mansfield dropped me off at the dorm on Hemenway Street. It was the summer of '67 and I was a nervous freshman doing remedial reading as my final requirement for admittance to college that summer. Northeastern on Huntington Avenue is adjacent to the Museum of Fine Arts. I still love waltzing through those halls.

I will often walk to the Fens behind Hemenway Street and the private gardens people keep. It's a city-sanctioned thing as people really get into their gardening there. I will often notice some ball fields and an apartment building where a few roommates and I once rented a two-bedroom place.

As the walk continues I arrive at the doorstep to Fenway Park, home of the Red Sox (or *Sawx* to the locals) I am then on to Kenmore Square. I often will walk to the other side of Massachusetts Turnpike (Mass Pike) near the Beverly School of Music. I will then walk past Copley Square and that huge library. From there I walk to Boston Garden and the boat rides on the tiny city lake. My walking tour often takes me to the Commons, where squirrels eat right out of your hands. I will then work my way over to the Charles River. I love crew season with the college teams paddling in sync. Sometimes I will walk over the bridge at *Mass Ave* to MIT and Cambridge. I walk and walk. The aerobic feels good too.

I will often return to Kenmore Square, as it is to this day *central* to my Boston experience. In the 60s and early 70s it was a *center stage* for college students such as I. Perhaps this is a metaphor for my entire college years, but my memory of Kenmore is Walt Disney's ancient animated film *Fantasia*. In the late 60s it was a re release from many years before. It *seemed* every student in Boston put the anti Vietnam War agenda on hold. We took *Saturday night* off to get high on marijuana. As I remember and memories can do this, it seemed the long-running featured presentation at Kenmore Square for *every* Saturday night was *Fantasia*. The animation was *highly* (no pun intended) visual. The caption on the movie theater billboard read Walt Disney Is on Our Side. I doubt he made the masterpiece animation with marijuana on his mind, however we were certain the universe centered around us. Funny how my cat has the same problem.

I want to tell you about Myriam but first let me share about the Red Sox. Myriam and I had tickets to see the final two games of the major league baseball season in September 1967. It was the Red Sox versus the Minnesota Twins for the pennant that year. It was the first time in a very long time the Red Sox had the opportunity to go to *the World Series*. The Sox had not won the pennant since 1946. The 40s were the olden days. Well the Sox won both games that weekend—and the pennant. Carl Yastrzemski went seven for eight in the two games and also made some amazing plays in left field. He had perfected the charging of a bouncing ball into left field toward home plate and then throwing the ball on the run to nail the runner. YER OUT!

I love baseball.

Yaz won the Triple Crown that year. (That means most home runs, most runs batted in, and highest batting average.) He was simply the best baseball player on the planet. Baseball is a boy's game and I loved being there.

I was with Myriam, the most beautiful woman in Boston—no, in the entire universe. I was also at the center of *planet earth*. I was in Boston with Myriam.

The Yankees dynasty of forty-plus years was officially dead in 1967. It was odd to see the Yankees as a last place team and the Red Sox as the best. 1967 was for the Red Sox the *Impossible Dream*. It was based on the popular musical of those days about Don Quixote. *The Man Of La Mancha* and it featured the famous song *To Dream The Impossible Dream*. I was a Red Sox fan now, which isn't to say that if the Yankees were in town I would root for the Red Sox. No way! I also was living in a dream I thought was impossible to ever lose. I don't think I processed it at the time but as life took a different turn, I would look back and say to myself 'those were my best days.'

Myriam and I were exceedingly happy to be holding hands at the center of the universe. In those days I would often ask Myriam if she *really* liked baseball, and she would say, " I love baseball." On the night I proposed marriage to her, she confessed, "I was lying on that Impossible Dream date... and on all our baseball game dates. I was lying ha ha ha."

Oh how I loved her laugh. Her laugh caused me to laugh. There was no reason to laugh at her jokes. I was simply so happy to be with her *laugh*. She could always make me laugh. Her deep red brown hair and blue grey eyes. "Those lips, those eyes" Is what I often said to her. She had never been to a baseball game before she met me.

2

A SIGNIFICANT STEP BACKWARD

Why did I ever move? Historically the hardest part of this trip was that being in this *perfect place* is where good began. I would inevitably go through the pain that good ever went away.

There had been some trips where I promised myself I would never return. It *is too painful*. Life was cut off here.

On the other hand, I always come back no matter how my life is. Something inside me wants to check in with the *beginning*. Sometimes I love the trip and the walk. In these times I am inspired to live life again and go forward.

If Yankee Stadium was my *cathedral of prayer* as a child, Fenway Park became my new place. Fenway Park is where I could find what a religious man might find in prayer. Historically every time I come back to Boston I always make a visit to Fenway. It has often been lonely because Myriam was not with me.

I had become a kind of monk, as I would spend so much time alone. I often thought of that movie that starred Montgomery Clift called *The Razor's Edge*. The man said of Clift's character, "You are a religious man who does not believe in God."

I could afford better seats (or so I thought). On this particular visit to the cathedral I of course chose the bleachers. After paying fifty dollars for what I once paid only *one* dollar I thought to myself, *"I still can't afford more than bleacher seats."*

Often on Boston trips I fall into cynicism. In these times I seek the culture to awaken the vision I had for life. I seek the old life but the culture I knew is gone. I remember one former roommate of mine named Fredrick Schwartz who upon seeing me fifteen years after college said to me, "Dave you were so free, and now you are so stuck."

His comment *stuck* with me on one of my trips to Boston. It got me thinking of earlier days when I was *so free*. Always a walker, I walked right out of something that was so good.

I left Boston because I was enamored with a passion to become a star on the Broadway stage. We moved away from Boston that summer of 1971. Myriam and I left immediately after we both graduated from college. New York City had to be my starting place because we *had* to move to *the city*. My new wife and I had agreed to disagree on the move from Boston to New York City. One should not make deals agreeing to *disagree* on personal matters.

We agreed to get pregnant or was that a *disagree-agree too?*

To have a child was what Myriam wanted most, and the move to the city was what I had wanted. I was now *winning at the losing game. Winning at the losing game* was the game I played and lost. The paradox is it only appears to be winning. In reality winning at the losing game is the greatest loss of all. It's the loss that keeps on *losing. I lost* Myriam and our daughter Sarah.

I got my way, and it was the worst for all of us. Myriam was accommodating the ambition monster in me. Have you ever seen *Rosemary's Baby?* A horrible child is born of the devil. The ambitious actor husband is the accomplice to the crime. Was that me too?

On this given day sitting at Fenway in September the Sox were playing the Oakland A's. I observed the park did not appear sold out for the game. Maybe fans were showing up later these days. I sat back and almost fell over. I then remembered I can't sit back, these are bleacher benches. Sit up straight Davey I said to myself it's good for the abdomen. I then remembered the bleachers of '67' with Yaz and the Impossible Dream. I began to smile from the inside.

I had the whole day free. It was a Saturday afternoon. I turned off my cell phone as I had plenty of time. I was in the center of all that mattered, and all that mattered was absolutely nothing. I then thought of the Bible verse from Ecclesiastes that Rabbi Fishberg would teach us: "There is a time for every purpose under heaven . . . a time to kill."

He used to say that killing time means just what it says. A time to *goof off.* I never questioned the rabbi's interpretation, and certainly not now while I was reminiscing my rabbi's loveliness.

I was in the comfort of being where I wanted and needed to be. The walk for the day was over and it was time to sit and watch the game. Baseball—*the boy's game.* Shalom was now coming upon my heart and mind. I had experienced much peace in recent days more than the 1967 pennant race at Fenway. I am in these days at the center of the universe, yet I am not the center. I am not the star, but in the *center field* of peace.

Yes, it's nice to be here.

I was now seeing back in time without emotionally going backwards. I was not trying to fix my mistakes. A good counselor I once knew said, "A good indication of spiritual healing is to go back to the place of hurt and allow it to now be historical." My joke then and now is, "that it no longer be *hysterical*."

I have made my peace. One of my understandings in theater is that the audience is a real character in every live play. The camera is the same in film. The audience plays the part of the listener. Taylor Caldwell wrote a masterpiece book called *The Listener*. Her theme was God is the Listener. I remembered this in my personal sanctuary—Fenway Park—by myself again but this time not alone.

3

A NEW YORK STATE OF MIND

I then began to remember another walk. It was a walk I will never forget because it involves my life today as much as it does the past—my walk into Central Park about twenty or so years after the Boston years. It definitely was a nice day for a walk. It was October and I was in New York City. I was hearing in my mind the words and the melody to *I'm In A New York State Of Mind*. The fall breeze was blowing in warm air on an Indian summer day. The hairs on my arms liked the hand of nature's comb gently moving from my wrists up to my elbows. I was wearing short sleeves in October. My light tan colored lambs-wool sweater was over my shoulders. Yes, I was in a New York state of mind.

Great song I thought to myself. Central Park had become a more clean and safe place than in the New York City bankruptcy days of the 1970s. I say *safe* with caution regarding any complacency about places on planet earth. Having said that, if you've ever seen an aerial view of Manhattan Island you might think the Native Americans still owned it. A huge percentage of Manhattan is green and fully treed.

Well, at this point it was 1996 and I was a Manhattan guy again. I had just one year before moved back to *the city* after spending a number of years in Albuquerque, New Mexico. I was a partner lawyer from the successful firm of Sterling and Cohen. I ran our Albuquerque office. I was currently living off some previous financial success as I saw no need to be employed and I was tired of working in a field I had no passion for. As I remember this day I was a kind of lost in time. I was walking yet not knowing where or what I was walking to. Central Park that day was merely the starting point for 'memory lane'. It was by the way the nicest day in the history of the entire universe. Okay I'm exaggerating, but as I said the weather was Indian summer warm and sunny. It was a perfect day for a walk.

I then began to think. Thinking was a common pattern for me and thinking myself into a bad mood was a most common manifestation of my most common pattern. Often when I would begin to relax, I would re-enact bad memories. The more at peace I was, the more I saw life through the screen of bad times.

In the beginning of those years after Boston, Myriam and I were living near downtown Brooklyn. Many aspiring actors lived in restored town houses in our area. We were renting from a friend who had recently bought his apartment. Our townhouse had two bedrooms—one was for our new addition, Sarah.

My career was taking off. Television commercials and great parts in Off-Broadway plays were happening for me. I of course had attained actor's equity status (professional) for a Paddy Chayefsky play called *In The Middle Of The Night*. It had played on Broadway in the 1950s. I heard he was a very vulnerable person. Once years later driving my car in Manhattan I happened upon him. I knew him from his photographs. He was standing in the streets of Manhattan on a dark rainy day near a Bus Stop. He looked so sad and almost homeless. He didn't have an umbrella. Rich or poor suffering comes to us all. Manhattan has a way of showing how that works.

As years went by I would remember the vision of that day.

The part I played was a married man who was in love with his music and not exactly in love with his wife. His name was George and he was in love with himself. I came up with some clever idiosyncrasies for my character. I did this finger snapping of one hand into the other. He was a musician with lots of rhythm. It was a big success.

"The best George I have ever seen," I often heard.

My agent was happy because he saw future money in me. He was old enough to be my father and constantly was giving me advice. In a professional way he was like a father. I was happy he liked me but feared all he saw was future money in me. I liked him allot too but was mostly glad he was working my file. To *really* like people took too much of my time.

Myriam and I were not making many friends, as I was too busy building my stock in the '*the- a-ter.*' Myriam, not exactly an outgoing personality, was busy with baby Sarah. She was very insecure in those early New York days. I called her *the clutcher*. I was always in a pushing her away kind of way saying *you are smothering me*! I made this rather unfriendly comment to her often and in mostly non-verbal ways.

Her verbal and nonverbal response to this was, " I need you. *We* need you."

I heard her and at the same time didn't hear her. I was in and out in my communication with Myriam. I was however, in communication with the beat of my heart that said, "You can now be more than you ever dreamed you could be, so do not let anything or anyone distract you from *success*." I would however from time to time, become introspective.

The way I am today I asked myself, "Would I go to Fenway with Myriam?" Why don't we just take a Sunday walk over the Brooklyn Bridge into Manhattan? Can I see myself hand-in-hand with my love strolling the baby carriage over the bridge?"

I unfortunately was not introspective long enough to wait for my own answer. I was in a hurry to get famous and I was certainly on my way.

I cannot tell you how often I heard the word *talented* with reference to me. I only half-believed their compliments. The other half of me knew I was lucky. I was as they say, "at the *right place* at the *right time*."

I knew for instance that the actors I did scene study with at *The Acting Studio* were as good as me. They just didn't have as many jobs as I did.

Myriam by the way was the best of all the actors I ever worked with. Back at *Center Stage Theater* in Boston she brought reality to every character she played. Her leaving Boston was leaving something very personal to her. It was a sacrifice. She wasn't like me. She wasn't ambitious. She was a pure artist. For her working with the company and developing her craft gave her great pleasure. Pounding the pavement in the '*City*' and chasing stardom was my thing. She on the other hand sacrificed a great love in moving to *the city*. She gave up theater. I gave up theater too come to think of it. *Seeking stardom took its place.*

I could now hear horns honking through the trees of Central Park. I was getting closer to Columbus Circle and 59th Street. The ringing in the eardrum I punctured in a swimming pool accident was acting up. The buzz from the injury of so many years ago was a reminder to keep walking the park. I sometimes get light-headed and a ring in my right ear.

"I don't want the city sounds and stress just now. Today I'm going to walk Native American country. Yes, Native American land had more for me on this day."

I heard a ballgame just east, closer to 5th Avenue and I walked closer to see the game as my heart raced thoughts into my mind. " I can never get enough baseball, even if it's a pick-up softball game. If it's got bases, and it goes around it means getting home is the victory."

"Oh how I want to get home," I reflected. "But where is home?"

I knew where I lived, but my question was not, "Where is my house?" The personal loneliness I ignored was a sob within me that said, "I want to go *home*."

I was so unsure and insecure. "No Myriam is the insecure one, not me," I pondered as I walked past the answer to my own question. It was this other half of me—the *I am plain lucky half* that revealed my insecurity in a way that even I noticed. You see, Myriam's insecurity was for me to love her by giving her attention; my insecurity was

19

to be told I was a great actor. I needed to believe every moment that my agent wouldn't drop me if something better came along. That's intense to live with. With all that baggage I was not a very friendly partner. Let me get to the point. I was not a partner at all.

What I sometimes would ask myself is, "What is the criteria for greatness anyway?" My father was always saying with regard to himself, "I want to be great."

Once, in a vulnerable moment with Myriam, I sincerely asked her to answer me, "What is great?" She answered me. In another sense, she answered me once or twice every day.

"What greatness would you like to see in me?" I asked with my soft voice.

"Greatness," Myriam said, "Is to love your family and be content with what we had when we first met." She said this without vindication or bitterness. She spoke it with hope, mixed with a knowing loss and an intense loneliness for something that was *no longer there*.

4

JANET VS. JOHN STEPHENS

I had a habit that I was not about to share with Myriam. I was frequenting tarot card readers. One in particular was Janet. She worked for a tealeaf place in downtown Brooklyn that I heard about from an actor friend. He said her readings were accurate, so I *had* to know her too. I visited her once, and then again and again. Her thing was timing. I too was passionate that I be at the right place at the right time. She and I hit it off really well.

She was—as I was—very ambitious. Maybe she wanted to be a world famous psychic. What if my career took off and I gave credit to her? Our personalities jelled. I cannot say she liked me, but I am certain she liked what I could do for her. I found myself handing her one hundred-dollar bills at the close of our weekly meetings.

She had a very fair complexion with long blonde hair and was very short. I assume she was short. In all our meetings over two years, I never saw her stand up. She was always sitting at her table, saying, "Take a card, David," even before saying hello. Come to think of it she never said hello.

"Take a card David, it's good luck." She had these St. Francis cards she was always handing out. *The good luck saint?*

I referred to her (to myself) as 'The White *Witch.*' This designation showed I knew something was wrong, but I was a man with an open mind. I could not follow through with my caution. Let me say it another way. I refused to see signs of caution. I figured there was a white witch in *The Wizard of Oz* too. Come to think of it Mickey Mouse in Fantasia casts spells. Right?

She was not a beauty, but was highly spiritual. She had incorporated Catholic saints into her lineup of spirit aids. I do not mean to say she was a practicing Catholic, but that Catholicism was in her background. The occult was her career and her one passion was money. There was death *all* around this world of hers. I did not see this to the point of articulating this even to myself. *I just felt it.*

It's not that she was unpleasant or that the sun didn't shine through the windows of her tealeaf restaurant. It's what she said over and again that I knew was evil. The main caution she spoke of was Myriam. "Get rid of her. She is bad for your career."

"But we're *married*," I reminded the white witch. I thought those words "*white witch*" when she first suggested I leave my wife and child. I was offended by her demand. She said this so often that I got used to hearing it. "She's bad for you."

"Listen," I said the first time she brought it up, " I have a little girl too."

"I know about children," she said. "They get over things. They don't know much. And once you get out of the house, you can visit her on weekends."

The other thing she said was, "You see this card? It says she is against you. She is very bad luck." This is the kind of on going Myriam talk we had.

There was one other huge negative to our talks as well. But this second one was short-lived because I acted on it quickly.

"Get rid of that director, John Stephens," she said. "He should never have been listed in the *Thespian* auditions. My sister Natalie has had encounters with him. He is out to destroy the good work we do. He is bad. He is not interested in art, show business, or your career. He has his own agenda. It's bad luck. He is evil!" she said with a panic.

Ironically my agent, Murray Flagstein said, "Go to the audition. You are my client no matter what you do. I advise you to see what he's all about." He was currently doing a play about Jonah called *The Angry Man*.

I was aware of the Bible implications. Jonah had been part of my father's synagogue tradition. My grandparents were orthodox Jews from the Bensonhurst section of Brooklyn. I grew up in Scarsdale, Westchester County a suburb of New York City. My Dad became a reformed Jew, which compared to orthodox is modernistic within Judaism. He gradually became a non-temple-going *secular* Jew. I as a consequence attended synagogue less and by the time I was a teenager not at all.

How original, I thought to myself, to make the Bible relevant.

My artistic thinking was: "The Bible needs help." It was a famous piece of literature that I liked. Maybe some revision work can make it better. Jonah was one character I knew and I saw great theater in. I always loved this particular Bible story.

I had gotten to know William Mayer, who owned several Broadway theaters. He told me the Bible was classic and it had stories that were well etched into human psyche. He reminded me of the success of *Joseph And The Coat of Many Colors*. "The Bible is a mutual starting point with the audience. It empowers the audience's attention if done right," he basically said. "The Bible is classic literature and the artist can bring contemporary interpretation into a familiar story. If one adds some music, and hard work one can have a staple for international audiences that frequent the Broadway stage." So I explained this rationale to Janet but Janet was very against it.

I remember one crucial visit when Janet was extra-aggressive at her tealeaf table. She suddenly - shockingly looked into the tealeaves and said, "And now I see what I have been seeking for you. Now this very moment you have the opportunity to achieve the goal you and I have wanted for us!"

"You can see this?" I said. " I am always amazed at what you can see."

"It says here, across the river is the place."

"Manhattan, of course."

"Yes. Do you see this?" she said.

"I see tea leaves,"

"Yes but look at this!" she said.

I suddenly noticed for no particular reason I am sure; how uncomfortable these seats are. They are skinny wooden seats and the tables are only slightly bigger than card tables. My lower back was aching as I leaned over trying to understand these cards Maria was so happy about.

"Yes, yes. Pick a card—right now—now as I am speaking—it's good luck. Pick one now!"

"Okay. This one. What does it say?" I asked. Odd that my back would suddenly ache with sharp pains shooting into my head. I now had a super intense headache. Nevertheless, I was certain *this was a crucial* reading from Janet.

"It says Levy wants you, that you have made a good impression. Did you do an audition for him? He likes you? It says here he has clout, and lots of money too!"

"I am so impressed that you said his actual name. His name is Barry Levy and he is the executive director for the Broadway Theater League. He's also a super-agent with a huge company. That's absolutely correct," I said.

"Well, it says here he wants you for the lead in his company. It's a major new play on Broadway, and you can be the lead. He wants you. Now give me two hundred dollars right now! It's good luck. Don't write me a check—cash only. (I thought this odd, since I always paid her in cash.) You know how we do things here. We can talk real money later." Janet was on a roll.

Funny how one can process so much in a moment of time. As Janet was ranting about my opportunity with Barry Levy I found myself remembering my meeting with John Stephens the week before. He held interviews at his apartment. I thought this odd, but it was in a particularly nice neighborhood on the Upper East Side. There were no crowds, he was working by appointment only I assumed. My meeting time was 7:00 on July 7, and his apartment was on the seventh floor. His apartment was of course on East 77th Street. I was wondering if this was all "Janet-ized" because it was all those sevens. Maybe a *lucky number*?

In my walk on this day I was at Central Park facing Mr. Stephens's building at 77th and 5th Avenues. *It's not a coincidence that I am thinking about him this very moment, I thought to myself. I am right now at the very place we met just two decades ago. It is odd how time can be so timeless.*

I remembered John introduced himself to me at the door to his apartment. It was over twenty years ago, but it felt so like twenty minutes ago. I remember his apartment having lots of fine wood, walls, and ceilings. It felt like a cabin in the deep forest. The floors were hardwood and the ceilings very high.

He knew my name, but I felt it was more—like he *knew* me. He had the familiarity of a relative who was always asks about you. He was immediately friendly, welcoming, and oh so warm. I had unofficial parents from my friends families in Scarsdale that knew me better than my father did. I did over two hundred sporting events in four years of high school, and he didn't make it to one of them. So my friend's fathers became surrogate fathers. John Stephens was like one of those surrogates only more intimate.

He immediately was as Rabbi Fishberg had been to me. I found myself warming up to him. I noticed my hands were not clenched as they often are for long talks and especially at auditions. My knee jolting was not happening either. When I get nervous trying to make conversation my knees jolt. He also took the burden of being social away from me. There was something going on here that was greater than just shooting the breeze as they say. We talked for two hours but he drew me out of my ambition shell as no one had ever before done. We spoke about life, love, and things *careerism* cannot touch. He was very interested in Myriam and in our experience at Center Stage Theater in Boston. Sarah was now four years old, and he gave me a gift for her—an ancient looking doll. Her face was so human, real, almost super human. It was a most innocent face of a great woman. He called it his *Hannah* doll. He then reminded me of Hannah in the Bible—so faithful in waiting for a child from God and so sacrificial in dedicating her son Samuel to the Lord.

He told me, "Myriam is so like Hannah, and the doll is a blessing of direction for Sarah's life. The doll, I pray, will be an incentive for Sarah to be like her mom." I wondered to myself how he knew so much of Myriam to make that kind of statement.

On the other hand, I was going on and on about her and how we met. I was not only loving my shared moments with Mr. Stephens but I was loving Myriam while I shared about Myriam. I also suddenly excited about Sarah and how we all were starting out together as a family.

He then told me Mary the mother of Jesus was Myriam in Hebrew, and that Jesus name was Yeshua in Hebrew. He told me Bible things from the thirty-nine books of the Old Testament, which we Jews referred to as the Tanakh. He also reminded me of the law or Torah which are the first five books of Moses.

More significantly, my time with him was peaceful and so very pleasant. The audition for *The Angry Man* took no more than ten minutes. I was wondering how a man with his countenance could have so much time to just talk. I wondered to myself, "*where are the others?*" I was accustomed to cattle-call auditions from *Thespian*. I used to do these kinds of auditions before Murray became my agent. This was more private and exclusive than anything I had ever before received. I expected a '*cattle call*' abound with actors, but it was only me. *I really like this guy, and Myriam would too.*

John concluded that I should come to his theater on Sullivan Street in the Greenwich Village section of the city. "It's near where *The Fantasticks*, the world's longest running production at one location, is still playing" John said.

"I want you to meet some resident actors in our company, and "I want you to play Jonah. Congratulations, David."

It was that simple. He was spiritual as was Janet, but his spiritual was different. He wasn't appealing to my ambition. He wanted me as an actor, but never once told me I was talented. He never talked money either. The spiritual climate here was relaxing. He included my wife and child as part of who I was. He without having met them loved them. I could not articulate this, but I loved him too.

With Janet I had to be quiet about family or else get the warning, "Your career must come first." With Janet I kept Myriam out of the conversation. With John, I *wanted* to share personal things. I so wanted to share this experience with Myriam and Sarah.

In this moment I wanted to hold hands with my bride and embrace my Myriam. I wanted to stroll our baby and carriage across the Brooklyn Bridge. I wanted to sing a song with me doing harmony to Myriam's melody. I wanted us to sing the Jewish National anthem, or at least the unofficial version we used to sing when we lived in Brookline in the Boston days when we first walked the Charles River.

"Hope and faith are still within the Hebrew heart.
People of Zion do not drift apart.
Look now to the east the day of Zion dawns.
Fair Promised Land to Israel belong.
Cherished hopes of many years gone by.
Raise your voices praise your God on high.
Rise to new glory in your land of liberty.
Zion's freedom all the world will see.
Rise to new glory in your land of liberty.
Zion's freedom all the world will see."

"David, do you hear me? Hello?" Is anyone at home?" Janet's words charged at my heart. "What gets into you? How can you drift off again at such an important time as this?"

"No," I said. "I mean, yes, I was drifting."

"What were you thinking about? Are you aware you do this—this drifting—especially when I am getting good cards for you?" she said. "You have to stop this. It's bad luck, and it says here (pointing to the cards) you have to stop doing this."

I then thought it wise to lie to Janet.

"I was just making plans for this big break with Barry Levy, that's all."

"Well, you can't dream anymore. You need to get to work. It says here—you see it? It says come back on Friday. My sister is going to be here! I want her to read your cards, and your hand, and of course the leaves. There is a lot of power coming from this today. Bring a thousand dollars in cash too. Bring ten $100 dollar bills. We want to make sure he casts you. And one more thing. Do not go back to that religious director. It says here, stay away from him!"

Suddenly it was as if my meeting with John Stephens never happened.

"Oh him, yeah, I don't know how he got onto *Thespian*, my agent should have never let me go there. I thought he was very weird and not at all professional. Definitely a stall for my career."

"He could do much worse than that, David," said Janet. "It says here to throw that script away. No! It says burn it up. Do this as soon as you get home. Do you hear me? Evil spirits surround that man and his script. There are bad spirits in this play of his."

"Yes, I understand."

As I said this, I seriously wondered to myself, why, with all these possibilities, would I waste two hours talking religion with this guy anyway? This guy is a big stall.

"Okay," Janet said. "Leave right now. Come Friday at 10:00 am before this place gets busy. Also in addition to the cash, bring a special gift for my sister. It says here you will know what it is. In fact, it will tell you before you get home."

Janet's appeal to me was never greater than that Monday morning. I was believing her more than ever.

"Thank you, thank you so very much, and tell your sister I will have the cash and a very special gift to commemorate the special occasion this coming Friday morning." I said this with a gusto of enthusiasm.

As I walked out the door into downtown Brooklyn I noticed my countenance was tense and my thoughts were nervously planning my every move. My body tensed up as I noticed my lower back was now aching. I pondered for one moment, I don't want to share this opportunity with Myriam. She might discourage me. I shouldn't have told Myriam about John Stephens either as I regretted I ever got her hopes up.

Maybe if I never bring him up again she will forget about him, I thought. "Yes, I can't take any chances now. Timing is everything. And luck, yes luck is everything!"

5

AN ELEGANT MAN

When I woke up the next morning, I was surprised to hear a voice message from John Stephens on my phone machine, "Please come by my apartment this morning if possible. Thanks. *John.*"

What a coincidence, I thought to myself. Here I want to talk to him and he contacts me. That makes what I want to do so much easier. I know Janet would say, "Don't go near his apartment." I could only imagine all the superlative reasons she would give for my staying away. Still I wanted to see him. *Why?*

Hearing the echo of her anxiety was hard to take. Sometimes I wondered to myself, "Is she my kind of person? Where in my education was I prepared for the likes of her?" Again introspection came to me more often than I would admit to myself, but introspection never lasted long enough for me to act on it. I would maybe react to thoughts, but never *act on a strategy*. Finding myself at his apartment my final thoughts were: "He's a nice man just irrelevant and that's nothing personal."

The doorman had announced from downstairs that I'd arrived and the elevator took me up to the seventh floor. Knocking on his door I thought to myself, *"David, make this short and sweet."* All of a sudden the kind face of John Stephens opened the door.

"Hello, Mr. Stephens," I said. "I got your phone message. Did you get my return call?"

"First off call me John and yes, I did receive your call. Thanks for coming."

"Well sir, your story line to *The Angry Man* was, well, really good writing, sir, quite good." I had the script in my hand extending it to give it to John.

"Thank you. Please sit down. I want to talk with you for a few—" I was literally standing in the doorway. My back was stiff as if I were standing all day doing factory work. My upper torso was leaning left so that I must have appeared to be five feet tall instead of my normal five feet nine inches.

"No," I interrupted, "no thank you. I have to run actually. Your storyline is good and the characters are well defined. I always knew Jonah was a runner but never so *deep*. (I decided to play act with John, exaggerating the obviousness of *Jonah And The Whale*.)

My thought was John is very bright and elegant. I wondered to myself, *"Why is it I can joke with him and be myself?"* I saw him as twenty years or so years older than me—forty-five-ish. Wearing a white shirt and perfect fitting dark blue jeans he had good taste in clothes. I especially liked that I could not quite see *Ralph Lauren* labels on his clothes. He had sophisticated casual down to a T. It wasn't pretentious either. *"A poor guy would feel at home around John,"* I thought to myself. "John in his brightness picked up on my Jonah joke."

"Why not swim on in and have a cup of tea?"

"Yes," I heard myself say as I walked through the corridor and into what he referred to as his family room. John then walking toward his wide-open kitchen began to heat up some water for tea.

"So, you see Jonah as deep? Or just in deep waters?" he probed.

"Yes. Deep and conflicted. Indecisive too," I stated

"Kind of trapped and confined?" he asked

"Yes, swallowed up." I shot back.

"Entangled? And we thought we had problems." I said

"Running problems? Or problems from running?" I was on a roll of words.

"Oh," *John said, seemingly impressed I was getting it.* "So you saw how Jonah was trapped?"

"Yes, suffocating—and much worse than flying first class on an Eastern Airlines all night *Red Eye*. [There is no first class on these all night flights.] Really trapped and in a very... small... space." I was having fun hearing my wit so well received by John.

John was now with an animated face. Showing a man holding his throat. Now with a faint voice,

"Gasping for air! Help?" David how do you like your tea, milk, cream, lemon?"

"Hot" I said "and wet," we then *both laughed*. We were now in the family room sipping our tea. I allowed the heat of the teas water to reach my throat. Funny with me I always like hot tea even in a heat wave. I then continued.

"Yes, and even more so than the baggage space underneath the aircraft. Your script doesn't mention this, but I hope Jonah didn't have vertigo. You know, the pukey kind of vertigo?"

I knew about *pukey vertigo* all too well. *Pukey* has happened to me when flying red eye flights.

It was truly *fun to be with John* again. I was sitting down now, even though my intention was to leave. *"He is irresistible,"* I said to myself. I was glad to be with John. My neck was relaxed. I could also feel my stomach muscles as the center of my body. When my body feels centered as it did just that moment, it underlined to me how relaxed I was with John. He was beyond a doubt the best director I had ever spoken to. Even moreso he was a friend. I was even more relaxed with him in this second meeting.

"You know," he said, "when an actor can see where the writer is going with the character the actor can then make better choices for the character he plays. We call this the *actor as author*. What do you think Jonah was running from?"

"As the fable goes, from God, right?"

"Yes, but that's not what I'm asking here. Why was he in such a hurry to go out the door?"

I thought John directed this last question directly at me. *He knows how much I want this play and this part.* The conversation had now switched to being serious. He knew I really did like him. He also knew I wanted out—out that door where my eyes just glanced. *How does he know what I know? Is he trying to be parental? Well, I do fine without a father, thank you, Mr. Stephens.*

"You did say Jonah was indecisive," he continued.

"Yes, he didn't have a grasp on who he was." I said. "He was, you might say, tangled up in what people say about everything."

I began to process how quickly I was entangled too. Tangled up in this grungy world of spiritual seaweed. It's the Janet world that is my big fish isn't it. I'm caught. *"I know Jonah,"* I thought to myself, because I'm the same way. I avoid what I know to do. I then thought of Shakespeare's great insight. "Oh the tangled web we weave when first we practice to deceive."

"Yes, David," John replied. "Jonah was tangled up in what others say about everything. Entangled by opinions and theologies that were *concepts only*. He lacked the faith that comes from truly relating with *Truth*. He couldn't and wouldn't act on faith. He was intentional in his avoidance and yet still saw himself as original. That's a lot of self-imposed pressure. He was indeed influenced by his culture, which was training him into a way inconsistent with what he said he believed. Why would he run from who he really was?"

Those last words—*run from whom he really was*—were autobiographical. It was me! I didn't believe in a God, but I knew intuitively that to know God was related to a person knowing himself. Maybe through Jonah I can see my own inconsistencies and hypocrisies. Playing Jonah could maybe help me see life better than I do now.

I then began to value what I had with Myriam, and what I was letting slip out of my hands. "Am I running from the *real me*?" John is spot-on here. John Stephens is offering me more than a part in a play. *He's offering me my life back*. My life as better than ever before.

"So," John continued, "you're saying the Jonah character was being driven from his true self. He was internalizing the public's opinion that represented the spiritual norms of his times and of his culture."

"Yes. Swallowed up by it," I said and I wasn't joking. I was now gliding with words easily flowing from my heart "Convincing himself he was an original he was really following the ordinary, predictable, and mainstream mindset. Running! He was not running *from* the norm but running *into the norm*. He was sprinting into the web of normal's confinement. He was boxed in even before he was in the belly of the big fish. He was afraid even to take a risk on what he knew was right. He wanted things easy and justified a 'theology' that would endorse easy and convenient."

John sat back, his expression sighing into a satisfied grin... "David... I want to say it again... I want to cast you as Jonah."

"On Sullivan Street?" I blurted with a rookie's enthusiasm.

"Yes!" he said.

"Yes, and you know John, my career is at an apex for great things right now." I was in effect *asking him for help* as one who was drowning and John was my lifeboat.

"I know very well the time of life you are in, son."(He smiled ever so gently.)

He called me son. I heard my voice echo his words to me. *"Son."* I loved my father, deceased and *uninvolved*, but why bring up my father at a time like this? Father? Family? Wait! This play is a career thing. Family?

I began to process, " Is this a Mom and Pop operation? What is Stephens running here? Is he running from reality? Things like work, job, and career? Maybe we're getting too close for comfort here." Son? God? "What's this got to do with my life, job, and career as an actor. Even family! What good is family without a goal? WHO IS THIS GUY?"

I now found words coming out from my mouth. Speaking to John I said " I want to be pragmatic with you, okay?"

"Yes, of course David. I thought we were being *lots* of things—certainly pragmatic—but please, tell me, what's on your mind" as John spoke ever so gently.

"Who is this play for? You know, who do you want to reach?" I asked with sternness.

"Humans actually."(John was being happy and victorious with these words, using humor to make his point.) "All humans. I hope all kinds of humans will come to our production. Animals don't need attend unless they bring their human pets."

"We," he then said in a most sincere way, "want to reach mankind. All of mankind, as long as time permits. We want to reach you."

"We want to reach YOU?" Those final words were now ringing in my ears. I now noticed my tea was no longer hot. I saw John in the corner of my eye indicate that he could heat more for me. I indicated shaking my head saying in effect *"no I do not want tea or talk"* What kind of a producer wants to reach his performers? My thoughts were running, no better yet, my thoughts were *racing* from this conversation. I wanted to hear why he wanted to reach the audience.

When he says, "reach me," does he mean I don't have talent? He never did tell me I had talent. Maybe this whole thing is, you know, to get me some *religion*.

He knows I'm Jewish. Doesn't he know this is insulting for a non-Jew to proselytize a Jew? He said the word *son* to me too. Well, one thing I know from my father is that I am a Jew. My father, God rest his soul, got that through to me. "You're a Jew, David. Know this. Know who you are and where you come from."

John is skating on thin ice here. I don't want to be in the temple play. I want a career. Let's face it. I want to be rich, and famous too. Look he's very nice, but he isn't serious about my career. Not serious about my need to make a living. Nor would he care for the unusual opportunity I now have *with Mr. Barry Levy*.

John, you are bad luck, at least for me. I wondered if my feelings showed on my face. I am SURE there are some humans out there for you, but I am not that human.

My self-examination finally came to an end.

"I... we want you, David," he was saying. "You are the lead man we . . ."

"Look, John. I don't mean to cut you off but—well, I have a career, an agent and, well, I . . . we . . . my family . . . we have plans for me. This whole ethos you've got, well it's really not for me. I also don't want to typecast myself into, you know, this kind of—of a play. I don't want to be confined into such a small space. This play is just not mainstream, and frankly, John, your whole vision is too confining. Okay? Do you understand? I don't want to hurt your feelings but *it's for religious people*. I really don't see people coming to Greenwich Village to hear about God. Do you know what I am saying? I really got to go."

"What are you afraid of, David?" he answered, not digging but with kind compassion and pure empathy in his face.

"Look, it's a GREAT play, and thanks for the offer. I gotta run. Bye bye. Thanks for the tea."

I walked across Central Park to 72nd Street. It wasn't the shortest subway route to Brooklyn. But I needed to, as they say, *"unpack."*

Okay, I began to process. I had just walked away from a lead part on Sullivan Street and the theater center of Off Broadway. How many big parts, or *any* parts, have I turned down lately? Have I ever turned down a part?

Why can't I have Jonah and Barry Levy? Why can't I have Myriam AND Janet? Why can't I have it all?

DENNIS STEPHAN COLE

6

CONVERSATIONALLY COMATOSE

I got on my train but was huffing all the way to the 72nd Street and Broadway station. It was not due to poor conditioning but a heart full of regret. My anxiety then channeled into a kind of observation therapy.

Have you ever been on a subway in New York City? Nowadays if you say *subway you* think of a sandwich, but never in New York City. It's always '*The Subway.*' This *was* the underground home of today's morlocks a la HG Wells *Time Machine*. This morlocks thing was a common joke for Myriam and I. The subway for me was a dirty underground train system that in the 1970s was horrid. New York City as I said before was literally bankrupt in those days.

The subway culture is a sub-culture. The people that enter the subway world are non-stop talkers. They are feelers of *feelings*. They go to therapy to talk. They have *bar mitzvahs* to celebrate and talk even more. They have Holy Communion so old and young *can talk*. There is no one people on the earth that talk as much as New Yorkers talk. *They use their hands* as a talking instrument. Yes, New Jersey people do it too. New York City is very ethnic.

Richard Nixon once said of New York City, "When I am in New York, I see New Yorkers, I see America, and I see the world." His statement is so true. New York has a way of making people feel very ordinary and for some that is intimidating. Celebrities can get lost in the crowd of New York City. If noticed they do not necessarily get the *star* treatment. They have "other things to do in New York" the stars will say. "But in Boston, there is no privacy for a celebrity."

It's not that the city is so impersonal. It's more that there are so many people. You cannot, as Frank Sinatra sings, '*make it*' in New York City in the big picture, but in the small you can you get your piece of the pie. In New York City one needs to make his own *small pond* and then be a *big fish*. That's the secret to making it in the *city*.

Specialization was what I was learning. My specialty was theater and from there to film, to stardom and to celebrity. As celebrity maybe I could run for mayor of New York City. Maybe I could run for President and win. The key is to be focused and do one thing at a time. To just survive in New York City is its own success. There are many failures here. I thought to myself, *"I do not want to be one that failed."*

Now these same residents and visitors Mr. Nixon spoke of, are laughing, crying, and yelling. There is lots of yelling here just so to be heard. Maybe all the noise is what makes New Yorkers so deaf? Excuse me. "What did you just say?"

I was joking! I do believe living in New York, particularly Manhattan, has made me hard of hearing. *"Whatcha say?"*

These same people, who ride on a subway, do not normally have an introverted side. Perhaps thanks to the subway system New Yorkers can now have an introverted side. Perhaps two hours a day, or say five days a week one can cultivate a time to be quiet. There is unofficially *no talking allowed* on a subway.

Ironically if there were anti-talking laws, New Yorkers might talk incessantly on the subway.

In all my time and years in *the city*, the only place where there was and is no talking is on a subway. The silence is weird. I call it *comatosed silence. Conversationally comatose!* People on a typical subway ride are cramped as one body onto another, and like sardines in a can. Faces are squished up one to another and onto the overcoat of another subway traveler. In the summer it's sooooo much closer. Especially in the 1970s so many people saying nothing, giving nothing, and staring into oblivion. *Caution watch for strange subway smells during summer heat waves.*

It would take me almost an hour to get to my stop in Brooklyn. On this day thankfully I did not have to stand up for that whole trip. In other words, I got a seat. Luckily for me it was not rush hour.

In my staring time I began to think of Myriam. She has one sibling, a sister named Marianne. She and Marianne had a bond. They grew up in Scranton, Pennsylvania and had to fend for themselves. Their Dad was gone from them from the time Marianne was 4 and Myriam was 2.

Their Mom was a Jewish Italian immigrant whose birth certificate reads Giaquinta, or in English Hyacinth. Like the flower, my mother-in-law was so very sweet. Her last name was Locantore. It's the Cantore part that may have showed her Jewish? The *cantor* is the singer in the synagogue. Her Mom had a great voice. Myriam and Marianne sang beautiful duets. Just another talent my wife had.

Their Mom throughout Myriam and Marianne's childhood never healed from the shock of divorce. Her Mom was so very graceful like Myriam. Myriam always held to a kind of sadness from her Mom. It was a sadness that showed in her extraordinary empathy toward people. Myriam understood rejection in a way that made her a nicer person than she might have been if things were easier for her. I benefited from Myriam's compassion. She was so very patient with me.

People today think of divorce as common. Well it is, but to a child it is not common. The divorce just happened for the child whose parents split up. The child has not known any other way for him - no matter how many of his or her friend's parents are divorced. It is devastating.

Myriam and I had divorce as a common bond. My parents were divorced too. As children in our homes we saw our parents go from silence to yelling and then a deadlier silence. Finally, to no life together at all. In our household Myriam was now learning this again - this time from me. It was a *deadly comatose*.

In my subway ride, or shall I say my *conversational coma*, I was empathizing with Myriam's sadness. She had no father. She leaned on me for this, yet I hardly had a father either. Rabbi Fishberg had a great influence on me, yet I had not seen Rabbi Fishberg since I was twelve. Here on this subway ride I was all of 24 years old. "*I am alone*," I pondered. Myriam is too.

"Myriam has Marianne now," I thought to myself. Marianne had recently moved to our apartment in Brooklyn from Scranton. She was single and knew Myriam was so very lonely. Their bond was deepening and I was now becoming more and more conversationally comatose to Myriam. I was giving Myriam the vacant stare treatment people on the subway give to each other. On a subway with those you do not know the vacant stare is not rejecting. In a marriage conversationally comatose is *rejection*. It's one thing to get the stare from someone you do not know. It is something else to get it from your closest friend who is no longer that friend.

It's not that I was feeling guilty about these things on the ride home. I was numb because I was *comatose in my heart*. My comatose was a cold heart, much like *a dying body whose body parts were shutting down*. I was shutting down to Myriam's grief over my change.

I thought of my life as that of a vampire. I was making life a death with Myriam and Sarah as my victims. I saw this as if I were watching a movie about someone else, *only it was me*. I was amazed that I felt little blame or guilt. New York City is a tough town and I *had* all my plans in *order*. Like a shot of Novocain into the gums of my mouth I was getting used to it. I liked the *numb*.

I was going to visit Janet's sister Natalie and we were going to see into this Barry Levy thing. I still had a good amount of cash from my father's inheritance money. In this city you understand that you pay for services. I was alright with that as I was certain, soon enough, others would be paying me for my services rendered. My Dad often said, "You gotta be tough to make it here." I was tough, and on this subject my thoughts toward Myriam were, "She is not tough. She's not making it in New York."

I then heard in my mind the melody, harmony, and finally as we came to my stop the words to Sinatra's famous song *New York, New York*. "If I can make it there, I'm gonna make it anywhere, it's up to you New York, New York." *I was suddenly very lonely, but in my comatose I did not take notice.*

7

ENTER THE BLACK WITCH

I do not remember much regarding the rest of the week. It was part of my being numb. Friday morning came and I had $1000 dollars in cash in my right front pocket. I walked two miles from our now being *restored for us* neighborhood brownstone. I was never comfortable with the *uncool* downtown Brooklyn *vibe*.

I had to admit not many of the tealeaf clientele were college types like me. On the other hand, I didn't really care what they were. I was not as impressed with my education as I was aware that if my father had not paid for my college I might be like Janet's other clients too. I was not friendly toward the tealeaf people, but at least I wasn't a snob.

As blonde as Janet was, her sister Natalie was black haired. Her skin however was as refined and white as *Janet's*. I thought to myself, "*the black witch*." My palms, the very hands she might look into began to sweat. I noticed this because my two hands were soaking wet, and it was ten am on a dry summer day.

"David!" she exclaimed with a booming voice. "Yes hello," I said as my hands were now trembling. "David it is very important you being here now. We have much to do," she commanded. *There was nothing quiet about this sister*. Of course what the two did have in common was she got right down to business. She was about 5 ft. 6 in. and she was standing. Janet of course was sitting.

Janet getting down to business said to me, "Quick take a card. It's good luck." Natalie said quickly, "Do you have the cash gift?"

"Yes" I said. "Here are ten one hundred dollar bills," and I put them into her hands one bill at a time, then I wondered, "Why did I do that? I usually pay for services *after the service is rendered*," I scolded myself.

"Here's the card," Janet said again. "Take it now right now or it's bad luck."

"Have you cut off the friendship with that director man?" Natalie boomed at me.

"Yes I have," I said. "It's a done deal."

"Good! He is an evil man. I have known him to destroy great talent and ruin many careers."

Natalie in her standing was like a preacher. I might call her a kind of prophet. Definitely an activist. This fortune-telling thing was for her more a means to an end. It was I was certain her *day* job. Making contact with whatever resource she had for seeing into things was her passion. I could see how she might be aware of John Stephens because as mild-mannered as he was, he too was also more of a prophet than a director. They both were much more in life than their job titles might indicate.

John and Natalie were more like characters of the Bible. I for instance was aware of the story with Elijah and the prophets of Baal. A good versus evil conflict. They also reminded me of great classic works, such as works like Ebenezer Scrooge and his partner Jacob Marley and his words from hell!

"*John Stephens Versus The* Witches" I chuckled to myself complimenting my *ingenious new title* for a chapter in my life. Truth is, *both good and evil were appealing to me*. I thought this funny and odd. I had never been interested in *religion* and yet here *I was in a place with all kinds of preaching*.

In no way am I saying that Natalie and Janet were religious the way John Stephens was. I was seeing, in the two the classic *opposite* story. Certainly Janet and Natalie were not Jewish or Christian. They were like the Baal prophets and John Stephens was Elijah. I now saw evil and good as opposites, but *equal in power*. The winner gets the power. *I wanted power and I wanted to win.*

I finally understood the word surreal. Surreal has to mean something bigger than life and yet it's really happening in the now. Surreal to me was not symbolic. What was happening here was a kind of super-real. *A heightened reality on steroids.*

Was I in someone else's morality dream? A play of good versus evil? I was reminded of a play I once studied called *Six Characters In Search Of An Author*. A strange entity of a play that suggested we are seeking to be in someone else's mind for a play not yet written. In today's interplay, I thought "Is this what I am doing?" I want to be under a power that will get me what I want, don't I? Hollywood has this kind of star power. Of course there is the power of the press to create news, money, fame. Yes, I want it all!

I suddenly saw my two witches as one side of media and John Stephens as the other side. Bad news versus good news? I thought of the golden rule: "Do unto others as you would have them do unto you." The truth is, when decision time comes, *one needs to choose what is best for himself*. Clearly John is good and these witches are, well, they are witches.

I thought of another play we did at Center Stage Theater called *No Exit* by Sartre. This play truly was religion for atheists and agnostics. Here they dealt with life as hell. When they get a chance to get out of hell, they say no. They stay miserable and stay in *hell*. Milton's *Paradise Lost* came to mind and it's the devil again. This book features the famous quote from Lucifer, "I would rather *rule in hell* than serve in heaven."

Surely John was good. Janet and Natalie let's face it, were evil. I doubt they give to charity. I would believe they stole from charity before they would give anything to charity, especially money.

"So why am I in both camps?"

I was certain I was no longer in the camp of *Good*. I left the Jonah Play and here I am playing cards and tea leaves with a couple of witches. Which side would Myriam choose? No doubt John Stephens.

Am I somehow wiser as a neutral? Yes! Neutral is seeing both. A greater knowledge was upon me. A knowledge of good and evil.

"Yes, Yes!" I am neutral. I thought to myself, "Let's come up with a clever saying here. *However, which way things may seem, the answer lies in the in between.*"

"Wake up David!" Natalie shouted in my ear.

"Hey!" I shouted back. "That's my punctured ear drum." I was *kicked in* the *ear* as a fourteen-year-old boy at the bottom of the YMCA pool while we played a co-ed game where you carry someone on your back. I was now angry and angrier than I like to be.

"My sister Janet has warned me you go on these *hikes* somewhere - just when the spirits are waiting for us to go to work."

Natalie was now standing over me as I was slouching in my chair. Good thing for me she wasn't a boxer because she sure did sucker punch me. I now wanted to fight back.

"Yes," said Janet. "My sister is a very busy person. She normally does not have time for people who are like you, …"

I was more than angry now. I don't like anger because I do not like to lose control, but I was now *very* angry. I was in a peeve and then my voice shouted "You are saying people like me versus some other clients more, ah more famous, and endowed with prestige? People such as Al Capone?"

I was surprised to be so sarcastic and showing it too, but I was seeing how seedy this whole place was.

"You think you are better than us don't you," Natalie said. "Well we have real power here, and maybe you can't see it. Seeing is what we do and we see that you have a block! You are passive David, and passivity is a curse that comes to people who seem nice but are very indirect. Myriam is passive and evil too. You stay with her because you are just like her. *Passive!*"

Natalie was now holding cards in the air the *way a preacher* might extend the Bible out and upward to make a point. It then occurred to me. All this talk about Barry Levy and how they can help me? The truth is, I do not need these witches. I already have an appointment with his office next Tuesday. The only goal I now had for this meeting was to get my money back and leave.

"I want my money back. Nothing personal, you are professional and this is not working out."

"It's very bad luck to give money back," Janet whispered with the intensity of a scream.

"I will take my chances with $1000 back in my hands," I fired back. "Sorry Natalie but there is not good chemistry here." I was polite.

"If we give you the money back, we cannot control circumstances for you anymore. It's been two years now. Janet tells me you've had good luck in your career since you and she met," said Natalie.

"I am willing to take my chances on my talent which you do not place a high degree of importance on."

"Get Out of Here!"

I was stunned by the element of surprise. I did not expect such a violent and direct response.

Natalie then threw ten bills at me as they floated into the air of the seedy tealeaf room floor. She watched me as I crawled on the dirty floor picking up each one hundred dollar bill. We were in a private room or there might not have been such histrionics. Natalie murmured with a haunted directness to her voice. "Things are going to go very bad for you."

Janet in the background was saying, "Bad luck, very bad. All my cards for you, David, are bad cards. Very bad. Today is a very bad day. You did not bring my sister Natalie the special gift. It says here bad things will come to you now."

"Oh I just remembered." I said to myself, "I forgot the gift. *Good!*" It would be harder for me to get my money back on a gift.

Finally, when I had all $1000.00 I looked up to make nice. "Thank you." I was about to wish them well when Natalie interrupted me one more time

"Get Out!"

This time I was not surprised. I was frightened however. Something inhuman was happening here.

Natalie's shrill voice in the background sounded like shrieks from a horror movie. "*Are there acoustics for sound in this hole?*" I wondered, "Did I actually hear those sounds?" I had never before been in such a situation. I was sure to not speak even one word aloud "Maybe they *really are witches*," I thought loudly.

"Many years of bad luck, very bad David, very bad," I heard again in the background from Janet's voice. "Bad luck, very bad luck, is coming your way. Very bad luck."

I was so glad, I thought to myself with a thrill. What luck I thought to myself *to never have to hear Janet's "bad luck - good luck again."* The thought of never seeing her face was also very appealing to me. I then managed to get out of that tealeaf hole and began my walk back to our apartment. As you might imagine as sunny as it was at ten o' clock now at eleven o'clock a major rainstorm began as soon as I opened the door into the downtown Brooklyn streets. Those familiar streets never looked drearier than they did that ugly morning when I last encountered the witches.

8

BACK TO CENTRAL PARK

It was starting to get colder on this October afternoon some twenty-two years after my final meeting with the card readers. Reminiscing in time was *taking time and taking its toll*, too. I was very tired and not inspired by my memories of my twenty something years. Forty something is hard enough. To be drained from my twenty something nightmare was now adding a new nightmare to my forty somethings.

The sun was still out. It was about three o'clock I guessed. "It's been 3 hours circling Central Park," I thought to myself. I was now walking along Central Park West near the place where John Lennon was shot dead. Horrible thought that he was murdered right across the street from where I was. My recent pondering was horrible too. It's been fifteen years since he was murdered on Central Park West and yet time was like the song, *Time Stands Still*, and its words "I think it always will since I don't have you on my mind." I wasn't pondering John Lennon in this song.

I was pondering Myriam.

It was not long after all this that I approached Columbus Circle again. The city noises were increasing with rush hour traffic in full. I again walked past the exit and decided to stay in the park one more time around. My mind again took the exit called *The Past*.

In my mind I was in Brooklyn again. My life was so like the book that I had attempted to write in those days. It was called *Lost in Brooklyn*. My fascination with marijuana and unwillingness to deal with who I really was prevented the book from being more than a statement about a period of time. The term *'lost'* however was a perfect description of a life that was far from perfect. The New York City Borough of Brooklyn was more than the fourth largest city in America to me. It was something that was too big for me to grapple. My life in the most vital areas of what is really important did not go as planned. As much as I spoke of being a big fish in a small pond I was after all a small fish in a big pond. In the things that really mattered I was overmatched. I was lost in a pond that I could not swim in. *My big pond* was a life that was out of my reach and a life that was passing by.

With Marianne nearby, Myriam now had a companion. Marianne being in the area showed the contrast of real love versus my extroverted form of passivity. Ironically, as good as Marianne was for Myriam, she being around triggered my leaving home sooner than it might otherwise have been. Marianne like morphine to a terminal patient speeded up the process of the death of my marriage. *"What a frightful thought."* Then I would quickly change the *pain channel into dreams of fame*.

Myriam said to me, "You are leaving our child. Our only child. Why? What good reason can you give? You are doing to Sarah what your father did to you and mine to me. You are making it so we both have to go through divorce again. For what?"

Of course this was not one conversation but the essence of many. Something cold happened in me. Something cold in a season of ice and winter. Why and how in the face of Myriam's plea did I take the action to walk away?

Something broke out in me that week. The fateful week I met with John Stephens and the witches, I made a clear decision. I decided to be *neither good nor evil*. I also decided to not be me anymore. In a weird way, I was fascinated to discover this non-me making my decisions for me. In addition to losing my family, I was also losing my creative drive. This creativity loss made me even colder toward my family. The kinder side of creative was being replaced by a colder narcissistic side.

I was losing interest in what I was sure was my destiny. I was losing my love for acting, theater, set design, costumes… you name it. It was all gradual but quick too. Like a marathon march into hell, I was no longer struggling with moral issues. I crossed over to the colder side of the pond. I could actually see myself pick up and walk out on the marriage. This shocked Myriam. She was deeply wounded by my numbness, yet also stunned that I was losing my grasp for wanting her love. *I looked forward to being alone and it showed.*

My meeting with Barry Levy was a dud. He thought I was someone else. He thought a relative referred me to him. Once he saw that I knew nothing of his family, he said, "I am sorry David, but I have another appointment."

A few months after that fateful week I also visited the theater on Sullivan Street to see how *The Angry Man* was turning out. There was no show. There was no indication there ever was a show either. I asked the theater workers "What of the Jonah play?" You know, *The* Angry *Man*? They said they "we don't own the theater our boss rents it out ask him."

My first reaction to this was, "Good, I am glad I did not get involved." When I told my agent Murray about the non-play, play, he said he did not ever know about the play. He said "look I'm your agent if you go on these stupid for the public *Thespian* auditions why, do you expect good results?"

"You gave my going on the audition your blessing" I pleaded

"I hardly remember the conversation David I have hundreds of clients do you understand?"

Did I imagine this? Am I going crazy? No wait. John gave me a Hannah doll for Sarah? Sure enough we had the doll. It was such a nice and unique gift. Sarah held to her doll dearly. The doll is as pure as I remember John to be, and as pure as Sarah too. This unfortunately did not trigger any life from me. I was glad Sarah loved the doll. The doll was as pure as a child could be, yet with a face of a woman tested by life's challenges. The doll showed who Myriam and Sarah were but I was now from a different family. In reality I changed from *David to Numb* aka *Dumb*.

I was however glad that I did meet John. It was a sad reminder that even though his play did not play I still walked away from what I once valued. Our meetings overtime felt like a dream, and not a fantasy. They were so real and so deep. I saw him and I turned him down. The facts are I was with him; the truth is I spurned all he offered and said. Facts and truth are they the same? *I wondered.* No they are not the same are they? Truth is greater than facts? *"What is truth?"* "Someone in history said *that. Who said that" I pondered.*

I explained to Myriam that I was moving back to Boston and to Northeastern for their law program. "Acting was a boys dream and I had to go on with life," I stated. I took what I would need for school lodging and living. I wanted school, but no side jobs. I would live in the YMCA apartments on Huntington Ave near Northeastern and do three years in two years. The YMCA was the equivalent of living the life of a monk. *A religious man who did not believe in God.* I often meditated on the reality of being a materialistic Mother Theresa.

I took what I needed from my father's inheritance money and gave the rest to Myriam. "Please no alimony," I said. I gave her one hundred thousand dollars and kept some for myself. I promised her more and when I graduate to become the best lawyer in New York City. I still wanted to "make it there."

Dennis Stephan Cole

9

MAKING A TURN AND GOING NOWHERE

It was 1996 when I did this Central Park walk. I had lived in Chicago and its vicinity in the 1970s. I even tried living on a cornfield for a year in a former parsonage of a church in Cassopolis, MI. It was not practical but living in a cornfield among pigs was a novelty. The church, by the way was still active, only the house was for sale. I bought the huge farmhouse for 25 thousand dollars. I tried commuting to Chicago for my first work as a lawyer. I worked for legal aid. I had many poor clients and I loved going to court as it satisfied the actor in me.

The church, as I said, was on a pig farm and let me tell you the smell was not always so sweet. They sometimes tried to get me into church services but I told them I would not attend because they were "casting their pearls before swine." They would laugh. I was encouraged because I was trained that Christians, aside from being idiots, were also bigoted and hateful. Of course, I knew who was bigoted and who was hateful. I knew the worst person of all. I knew that man was me, but knowing this didn't change me.

I would wake up in the middle of the night trembling with fear. Sometimes when I was unguarded, I would call out for Myriam. I kept sending money, but I did not want to see them. I hired a professional company to help me be sure Myriam and Sarah were safe and taken care of.

I asked to not know anything else. I walked away from my family when I was 25. It was in August of 1974. It was the same day Philippe Petit walked the tightrope across the Twin Towers. It was also 2 days before Richard Nixon officially left office as he resigned as President on August 7th and waved goodbye at his helicopter on August 8th. Do you remember that wave?

A lot happens around you at the same time a lot happens to you. The big world is a small place when all you know is gone and when you know it didn't have to happen.

I was the cause. I could have stopped it but I walked off *the set*. I did as Richard Nixon did. I resigned. He had to, but I wanted to.

I met Robert Sterling in Hartford Connecticut in 1983 while working for another Legal Aid firm in Hartford. He was a New York lawyer and he invited me to move back to Manhattan where I would live and work. He liked how my mind worked and convinced me that I had real talent for courtroom drama. In other words, "David, you can be a trial lawyer for rich clients who have money. You can make real money for yourself. You have the *talent*."

Way down deep I like that word *talent* when applied to me even if it had nothing to do with acting. I as you may have noticed worked hard to have nothing to do with acting. My inheritance money from Dad was also beginning to wear thin too.

We became partners and I was glad to be back in *the city*. He needed a junior partner like me because he had stage fright in the courtroom. I was never intimidated by New York City or as we say *the city* or the *big apple*. I was however intimidated when I pondered what I had let slip away. On the other hand, I did little to get my family back. My past was like a sad movie that could make me cry, but it was still somehow someone else's story.

So I kept myself with busy-ness and courtroom success. The courtroom for me was time off. I was an actor wearing a mask. It was a role I played that did not affect my emotions. Waking up in the middle of the night *did affect my emotions*. The 3am wake ups were *work*.

Sterling was a perfect partner for me to hide out even while in the public. I hardly knew him, yet we were partners from 1983 to 1995. He apparently hardly knew me too. He thought he did, and in some antiseptic way he did know me. He, however, did not love me. I knew the difference. Myriam loved me and she knew me. Robert could not hurt me. The only one that could hurt me was someone who loved me and someone I loved. I did not love him either.

So when Robert told me one day he was sick of my sentimentality and *meekness*, I was not offended. He meant nothing more to me than a lot of money I could make and forget about.

He had formed a merger with a team of trial lawyers who, "Do not live as mystics like you, David. My new partners are those who live in the real world." He then went on a tirade of hidden anger now exposed for me to hear.

"I never met a person more out of touch with who he really is than you. You are not funny or fun to be with. You are out of touch with yourself. You live inside your head. You made us some money, but you have no life, so we don't really make the money we could make. You lack imagination. You are a good actor in court but a bad actor in life. Therefore, you are a bad actor."

"Your opportunity to be an actor is, well, passed. You missed it long ago old man. You are so out of touch with who you really are. Frankly, I'm tired of trying to figure you out. It's not that what's in you is interesting. There is nothing so *not interesting* as a person who tries to be what he is not. I am finished trying to figure you out."

"We will give you a good settlement and I know one thing about you. You will not contest. You are passive my friend and I have no idea what you will do with your waste of a life. I am only glad I will not have to see you again. Maybe you will move back to the YMCA or another pig farm. Maybe you will save all your settlement money and give it to your daughter or ex-wife. Maybe you will join the Peace Corps or, God help us, become a street preacher whom we can all spit on. Congratulations to a stupid and wasted life. Get Out!"

That *Get Out* was something I had heard that before. His voice had a similar shriek I heard when Natalie screamed at me at tealeaf place.

The same voice?

10

MYRIAM'S NEW FAITH

The remark about the street preacher was an insult to Myriam. What she had become, she explained to me, was *messianic*. He was referring to *Jesus Is Yeshua*, and the reference was that I would join them in their version of street preaching. Years before when she first became a believer I called her *Masonic* by accident at first, and later on purpose. I hurt her feelings, but I still do have trouble with her being Christian.

She was messianic, or a Jew who made Jesus her Lord "because He is Jewish too," she explained to me. She was not part of the organization but she was a Jew who believed in Jesus. I however even as a non-believer was insulted by Sterling's remarks. Myriam had been a believer for about twelve years when he fired me.

"Jews and gentiles need the same savior," she explained.

It's not that her new faith was absolutely sudden. In the late 70s Myriam and I tried to get back together. She was living in Brooklyn and I was now an activist lawyer in Hartford Connecticut and working as a Legal Aid. I now wanted to be closer to Myriam and Sarah, and Chicago was too far away. It was an easy job and I was transferred to the office of the same group of lawyers in Hartford, Connecticut. The money was ok too. It was an easy career choice because it did not affect my choice to continue being neutral. I had trouble with loves or hates, but not with neutral. Neutral had become my mantra. It was my way of avoiding the extremes that bring so much disappointment. If you met me in a social situation you might think me as a well-adjusted man.

I stayed in Hartford and rented two houses in Woodstock, NY - one for me and one for Myriam and Sarah. The two houses were on the same street. We used it year-round for holidays but also for weekends and many vacation days in the summers.

In 1979 it had been ten years since the famous Woodstock Festival. There was a media buzz in Woodstock around the 10-year anniversary of the Woodstock Festival. It was those summers of '79, '80 and '81 Myriam and I began acting, writing, and producing theater endeavors in Woodstock.

Life Acting in Woodstock became a catchall phrase, and the tiny media in Woodstock picked up on it. I of course had hoped it would catch fire everywhere. Woodstock and the Woodstock generation was bigger than a lovely small town in the Catskill Mountains. I was its figurehead leader and Myriam and I were partners. I liked being together with my family and Woodstock was still neutral territory. Woodstock was known as a place where married couples would move to start a new life and then get divorced. We did the opposite. "We already are divorced," I joked. Myriam did not laugh.

"When will you be serious about what is real, David? Look at me! Wake up! You have a child too?"

Sarah grew up around this in those years from '79 - '81. She loved seeing Mommy and Daddy together. She was eleven years old in 1981 when Myriam and I gave up on our experiment in Woodstock.

Myriam eventually moved to Israel after her messianic change in 1983. She trained me not to say *conversion* because Jews are not converted as much as completed. I said to her,

"Well you *have* changed quite a bit. Completed or not you *are* different."

Yes, she explained. "I am now born again - this time born of the Spirit of God. That's what everyone needs to be. Jew or gentile, we humans all need salvation. *Hell is a real place* David. All humans need to return to God's perfect original plan for us. When you truly want this you will know how much you need this. You will know how much you need Him. Then He is yours."

When she said "*human*," I remembered John Stephens saying the same thing about his play *The Angry Man*. "We are seeking to reach humans David," he said referring to me.

I was so offended by that. Why? Here Myriam is saying the same thing to me. On the other hand I really did not give much energy to Myriam's change even though it was apparent she had new vulnerability and new strength. However, when she said to me she was moving to Israel with Sarah, *that got my attention.*

I was moving back to Manhattan, New York City, and she was moving to Israel. She said there was a school and ministry for artists there, Ruach Adonai, Israel Leiber a Chicago man and now a long time resident in Israel was the leader. His wife, Esther was his partner. I was instantly jealous and more than jealous. I was grieved that I was not invited. My *family was* involved in life and my life was a living death. Suddenly although it had been years, Myriam was now a past thing. In all our separation I had not internalized that life goes on for her too. *It does for everyone but me.*

I so hated these encounters with what was missing in me. Myriam of course knew this. She exploited my missing link by loving me and caring for me even when she criticized me. She wanted for me to *come home* in more ways than one.

Now however, she was no longer waiting. She was leaving. Leaving me for another man. For Jesus? "The man Christ Jesus," she said to me. I was later apprised that she was quoting scripture when she said that. She had a whole new dialect too. A new way of expressing herself.

I again was out of my element of what I could control. I so wanted to have control. I thought of the days when I had my conflict with John Stephens and the witches.

My career, my talent, *my, my, my, my,* and all that was mine was being threatened all over again. My family, which I left, was being taken from me. The consequences of my bad choices were catching up to me. I was in a time warp. I had at this point in time left my family a long time ago almost 10 years. All these feelings of loss were not *really* real to me until *now.*

"David it's your own doing. You are doing this to you."

Myriam said these words to me often and in various ways always trying to call me *home.*

I had so little in life, but ironically I still *had ambition.* My ambition was to keep things as they were. *Mystical secularism* was my way of controlling things in much the same way seeking to be a star was my way before. I just switched addictions. Now Myriam my one staple in life is leaving me for another man.

Somehow religion and theater were the same as it was with the John Stephens offer. The difference here was, Myriam is getting the offer I once got. She was now living out what I was offered then.

"Israel Leiber reminds me of John Stephens," Myriam said to me. Israel was also a Jewish Christian. "He has a vision for God that demonstrates faith and courage. I have heard enough talk about God but now want to see Him and be in His Presence. I want a community that wants this too. I so want to experience a demonstration of the character of Yeshua. Theater is a God thing you know. We ask will it play 'on earth as it is in heaven?' He, Jesus, is the missing link not only to the arts or religion. He is the missing link to our humanity. He is the link to what I want and what I need. No one else can do this for me. In our best days, not even you could do this for me, David."

I was jealous again. I was jealous of Israel Leiber who inspired my Myriam to leave and move so far away. I was familiar with *Jesus Is Yeshua* because they were very visible to me in Manhattan and in Boston. They were famous for handing out humorous tracks into the crowded downtown areas explaining the Jewishness of Jesus. Now Myriam was one of these and Sarah, a teenager, would be one too.

"Sarah is a young believer, David. It's so exciting for me to see this."

I *was jealous* yet again. My daughter is Jewish and she is now gone from me too. "I have no one now," I said to Myriam.

"You gave that up a long time ago David. What do you expect anyway? I feel for you but I cannot help you. Only God can, and even He cannot if you will not."

What was missing in me from when I was seeking stardom was still missing. *I lost my soul.* I thought of *The Devil And Daniel Webster.* A man who sold his soul to the devil for some success. I was not a visible horrible distortion of myself, such as *The Picture Of Dorian Gray*, another kind of sold to the devil story. Certainly if I had sold my soul, I had not attained success. I was simply *numb.* I was not really caring. I was certainly not creative, or colorful. I would have passion but it quickly was subdued on the inside of me. My outside was neutral. I was like an undecided voter. Occasionally *voting* but never choosing to change or have *passion.* I definitely was committed to *middle of the road* in all important choices. Someone once said to me "the middle of the road is where you get run over." I due to my own choices felt personally *beat upon* as if I were someone else's slave. Life continued with or without me. I cursed the day I chose to be neutral. I could feel pain but could not act. No! I *would not* act. I was cursed, yet unwilling to explore how to get out from under the curse.

"I love you David, but you do not have a clue of you. You used to be so decisive and now, unless you are defending a client in court, you give nothing of concern. You lack urgency. You are discouraging me and I cannot wait for you any longer. Good bye."

I heard that before. At least it was not good riddance. Bad joke, I know, but jokes can numb *the pain.* My heart was wrenching. I did not show feelings, but inside of me I was well aware of what I was losing. I simply could not act on it. I would not act on it.

I knew what I wanted but apparently did not want it enough. Something in me was breaking but still I would not act. I remembered an essay I once read. The title described how I felt when Myriam and Sarah left for Israel: *I Have No Mouth But I Must Scream.*

In my Central Park walk this day I then remembered one other conversation with John Stephens. I just let it pass at the time but I was now *re-remembering* it. "Acting was a calling" John said. "It was more than a career or talent. Art and theater are from God and divinely meant to be holy and personal. Hollywood exploits the holy and makes it crass and immoral." These words *holy* and *personal* were now all these years later reaching something in me I had not gone to in years.

He said to me, "*real acting is* giving compassion. Compassion based art is from God and for people. The word in the Bible to describe mercy is bowels or intestines. It literally means *inside skin*. When one feels his greatest grief he feels it in his or her lower intestine. Jesus acting is His real compassion and He has empathy for all people. This is how He loves. When He gets inside your skin you can know He's there for you in your pain. When you allow yourself to go where you hurt you meet Him there. Through personal, spiritual death one discovers new life. He feels your pain inside *His skin because you let Him into your greatest fear. Inside skin is where one's emotional intestines are. People fear real pain but God has gone into your feelings center and this is where He heals. He will heal all your pain when you feel His pain for you. Then you are with Him as He is. David He will make all your secret sorrow go away. He will go inside your skin where the pain is and make something beautiful of what was most unhappy.*"

In remembering John's words I was taken back to a little known story of myself. Little known because I *locked it* from my mind and heart. It began just after I left Myriam in August of 1974. I was living in Boston at the YMCA and doing three years of law school in two years. These were years of grief and great loneliness.

11

BACK TO BOSTON

Even though I gave up acting after I left Myriam and Sarah I still got calls from my agent Murray Flagstein in New York City. He referred me to his associate agency in Boston and it seemed they never stopped tempting me back to what I gave up. Over and again I would say, "I am not interested," but he and his associates in Boston ignored my plea. Sometimes others can know you in some specific way better than you know yourself. Murray was one who knew my deep passion for acting. He would say to me, "Listen David I have had many actors who get divorced and then get discouraged." My reply was "yes, but I did not move back to Boston to act but to change careers. I am through with acting Murray, do you understand?"

My room at the Huntington Street YMCA was hardly exotic. No paintings on the walls. It was absent of culture. Not quite a jail cell but very plain. Light grey color walls, and one single small bed. There was one window with basic white blinds. There was a chest of draws and a bathroom with a shower too. Of course it was better than a concentration camp. My Jewish brethren in Germany did not have a choice but I could afford better. I just did not want better. Down deep I was feeling sorry for myself with much self-indulgence. I never did justify myself in leaving Myriam so I am sure it was a kind of *penance* I was under. It was a kind of *"I am not worthy to continue in what I had a passion for."* So I built up a wall of self-pity and imprisoned myself with more denial. This denial was "I never want to act again" *when really I did*. I was absolutely going against something that was so basic in me. Ask a fish if it likes to swim. In the same vein ask a dying man if he wants to breath. His answer is more profound than *"yes I want to breath."* He simply breathes if he can. Ask David Cohen if he wants to act and he acts. Only I was working against basic instinct. My agent knew this about me. I was a younger son to him in a professional way and he was my professional mentor. He kept offering me auditions for commercials and calls from filmmakers in Boston. I kept turning him down. I saw these acts of offerings as *temptations*. It was getting harder to say no as everything *in me* me wanted to act. In the meantime I was cloistering myself in law books. I used *law as means for self-imprisonment*. Ironic wouldn't you say?

There was one notable audition that I did go on. It was a national commercial for Garnet. I had a kind of Americana but slightly ethnic look about me. In those days I was compared in looks to Michael Landon the famed Little Joe from the Bonanza television series. *Little House On The Prairie* a new Michael Landon TV series was just starting to capture America too. I figured if I went on the audition and I got the part it would air on its own. *One theatrical shoot and I am done*! I could get lots of exposure and let's face it I was not opposed to making lots of money. I pondered that "this *could not hurt Myriam and Sarah*" and my guilt for leaving was somewhat assuaged by the prospect of getting the job? So the shoot was on a Monday. It was a Presidents Day holiday in February and aside from that, all classes at Northeastern were cancelled. I showed up at the executive suite of hotel rooms where the auditions were held. It was at the Parker House Hotel in downtown Boston near Government Center. The Center Stage Theater Myriam and I were part of was not far from the audition location. I noted as I walked into the Parker House that Willy Loman the fictional character in *Death Of A Salesman* by Arthur Miller had his *Waterloo* or pre *death* encounter at the same hotel. "Willy Loman is fiction and I am in the real world," I thought aloud to myself. "Yes," I pondered, "If I am going to somehow continue in acting I am not going about it as I did last time in Boston. Willy Loman was a dreamer, and a procrastinator. I am no longer doing irrelevant plays as I did at Center Stage. Willy Loman is fiction. I am real and today is reality." There was hardness in my thoughts and chills up and down my spine as I took the elevator to the third floor on that cold, damp and foggy February morning. My hands began to sweat. "Why sweat on a cold day?" I thought to myself. I used to love the Willy Loman character because he was real and now I only saw him *as a loser*. It was an ugly February day and I was in an ugly mood. Time passed and suddenly in the Garnet studio it was my turn to register before the camera, lights and... *Gulp my turn*

"David Cohen with Murray Flagstein Agency"

The audition went well. *I was also amazed at how irrelevant the script was.* They must have liked my Michael Landon like smile, but I was just happy to get a good shave. I was not trying to act in the audition. My audition was to shave my face. The camera must have picked up on my liking the shave as I put off shaving for three days. I wish I could tell you what it is I said in the script, *because I cannot remember* the script. It was a *stupid script*. I cynically repeated this *stupid script* dialogue over and over in my mind. I asked myself "was I doing this job as a kind of addiction?" The commercial I thought to myself exploited "*my need to act the way cocaine exploits an addict's need for drugs.*" It was like junk food for the body instead of good nutrition. A wave of pomposity was overcoming me and I hated my time there. The Garnet representative was a nicely dressed businessman in a dark colored three-piece suit. He began to rave about me as he and the film director were both congratulating me on my reading.

"Such great expression and so real David. Very, very good work! We want to contact your agent and advise him that you are the new Garnet Man. The next Marlboro Man? We hope people will identify the act of shaving with *Your Face*. You can be the '*Face*' of Garnet for the next twenty years. Congratulations!"

I was shocked. I hadn't had a compliment said to me in such a long time. I forgot how much I liked being complimented. I also heard the '*T* ' word for *talented*. "David you are a top talent. This opportunity will catapult your career and you can name your price for the next twenty years." I was flabbergasted and was enjoying the excitement generated by my audition.

Then I got to thinking again, "*what did I do to deserve all this praise*? I mean I shaved! So I shaved but I looked like Michael Landon shaving and so they say I am a talent? *I used to be a talent but I lost my talent when I lost my passion for life?* These people are nice but are not very smart" I thought to myself. "The actors at Center Stage just a few blocks from here have talent. This here *is a joke*. On the other hand, why look a gift horse in the mouth?"

Odd how I had never been to the racetrack in my life, but this Garnet commercial seemed like gambling to me. Oh, I longed in my heart for the good scripts we had at Center Stage. Ironic how just minutes before I was thinking that Center Stage was stupid. I was losing who I was. It was scary to lose me and in those moments I was aware I was losing me. *I was scared. My mind was now racing.* Like a lawyer I was building a case for my client? Against me? I remember thinking "I am not making sense to me." Some actors think acting is lying so having no sense of yourself can work by playing other people. For me acting was finding truth. Acting is where I want to be real but I was now losing grasp of who I was and why was I here. I was scared. I was losing confidence in any and all of my decisions. I was afraid and when afraid I say stupid things. No, "*I just want to hide,*" I thought to myself. "I lost my talent to act when I *lost knowledge of who I was.*" I look back at that Garnet day as a waterloo where significant fabric *of self* was gone from me. I was *lost* just as Willy Loman was in the same Parker House Hotel in *Death Of A Salesman*.

Much of this was not cognizant to me at the time. I only knew on that audition day that I had crossed over a personal bridge to somewhere very lonely. The audition was merely a catalyst to show how far down I had fallen.

Abruptly I asked the director if she would show me the tape to my audition. The executive from Garnet was smiling at me nearby as he could see and hear me talk with the director.

"Do you see my face I said to her."' Yes', she nodded." Well I am moving it too much. The shave cannot be upstaged by the actor being too busy moving about. I should be more still. Also my eyes are too wide open and it tends to show over acting. Do you see that? "I said to her.

"The smile after the shave is also too big." She was speechless and I can remember her looking at me and saying without words, "why are you doing this?" She was also insulted as I was critiquing her abilities as a director. The Garnet executive and the director were quickly losing confidence that I was their *Garnet Man*. Timing of criticism is crucial in one deciding if one likes a talent or not. My critique of myself and its timing were ruining their excitement for hiring me. That the critique came from the same actor they admired moments before was eerie to them. They lost confidence in the person who was their actor. I saw into their faces as one face and the one face showed they were as confused about my audition as I was confused about myself as a person. I used my ability to communicate to bring my audience to where I was. Simply put I brought the director and the Garnet executive into David Cohen's personal disorder and pure misery. "Yes" I heard the executive say "yes well, we will get in touch with your agent in a week or so after we have auditioned many others. Thank you David and goodbye."

I walked home back through the Boston Commons, Copley Square, and passed the Midtown Motor Inn one half mile from home on Huntington Avenue. I was severely rejected, but it was all my doing. The February fog never lifted that day and I was frozen to the core of my bones. I entered my *prison* literally shaking and shivering. I was never in my entire life more alone than I was that February night. "*Why?*" I stated this aloud so many times. It was a kind of chant or prayer that I said miserably, into my sleep. I had a heart, but did not know how to make it work.

"Why live?"

12

U-TURN

It was in those two years at the Y where I splurged and bought a car. It was a Volkswagen Bug. Maybe you remember those? Well I had one and garaged it too. Garaging my car was as expensive as rent for the room at the YMCA. My purpose for living at the YMCA was not for saving money anyway. I had money. My purpose? Quite frankly I did not know what my purpose was. My misery threshold was reaching its high point in those days after I suddenly left Myriam. That's why locking myself up in the room and attending a rigorous study schedule at law school could decide my day for me. It was easier for me to face than that I walked away from my family.

As an undergraduate I was the envy of my classmates because I *knew where I was going*. There was no equivocating for me. Regarding careers I was an actor. With regard to love, I loved Myriam. I was a happy go lucky kind of person who was very certain about things. These days I bordered on clinical depression and exhaustion from doing a three-year law study in two years. I was not so much in a hurry, as I was not simply not wanting to engage in anything that would cause me to get well. "I'm sick," I screamed out into an open window of my Bug to passersby on the Massachusetts Turnpike.

I would often drive the Mass Pike down to Newton; pay the toll and head back to the city. I enjoyed my drives to Sturbridge too which was west of Boston, especially in the fall. Sturbridge is the home of Norman Rockwell the truly great American painter. I had no friends in Boston this time around so I walked the city and drove my VW for *date nights*.

There was one date night that actually included other people and my car. My agent had finally given up on me. He said something like "David you are a schlemiel." That word is a Yiddish expression for being a big loser.

"You are the worst client I ever had. You think you are a good actor but you are a bad actor and the worst kind of bad actor. You are the kind that cannot be trusted.

You quit on me and embarrassed me with Garnet just as they were going to make us big. If you ever want back in the industry I assure you I will destroy you and your name will be as rotten as the eggs you left out on your kitchen table in the YMCA cloister you live in. Did you think I didn't notice the smell when I visited you? I felt sorry for you. I did more for you than any other client I ever had. You deserve all the bad luck you get because you know it's really not bad luck with you. It's karma. Your karma is very bad. I do not want you and your karma around me not anymore. You contaminate my business. I did so much for you. I even cared about your personal life and you turn down Garnet and insulted them too. *Schlemiel!* I will track you down if you dare to enter the industry again. You have made me your enemy and now YOU have to pay the piper. I already have."

I was stunned that I hurt him so much but he did have a point.

Only "Murray please stop being so subtle."

As I was saying I had a date night with my tan colored VW. By the way I decided to give my car a name that summer evening so I called her V. Well V and I had a long date planned as we were driving the 212 miles to New York City and Manhattan. Lizzy Mable's a long-standing high school girlfriend stayed in touch with me. She may have liked me as an adult too. She was a casting director for *Changing Times And World* the most popular soap opera on daily television doing live shows five days a week. We were friends in the industry, but Myriam was always an obstacle to our connecting in any kind of personal or business relationship. It was an obstacle for Lizzy, not me. When the word got out that I left Myriam then Lizzy became extra friendly. She had my Boston information because we had a coffee date the last week or so from my Brooklyn days. She now *held out a carrot*. She said "I can cast you in *Changing Times And World.* We have a six-week role for you. If the viewers like you then you are in the main cast, which lasts *forever.* My boss loves you. He saw you in one of your plays and he has seen your many commercials. He told me point blank "Lizzy if you want David, he's our man." "The show needs a new strong good looking actor with real talent. You are the guy David," she said emphatically.

I explained that "I just did my bar exam and passed it the first time." I further explained "there is a law firm in Chicago that wants me. I gave up two years of life for this and now I walk away?"

"Yes walk away David," she said to me "and come back to who you really are."

It surprised me but she got to me. She got me in touch with me as I am? She knew me in a way I used to know me. She knew me as a confident man and her words reminded me I was once very confident. She knew me as free and *talented* before I got ambitious meeting tarot card readers every week. Does a fish have to learn how to swim? Does a horse take training for galloping? Why I asked myself "do I not just be what and who I am. *Ok I lost Myriam so do I have to lose what I do so naturally?* Law is work and acting is fun." I said to myself. "Does one have to plan his every breath when breathing is natural? Acting is breathing and law is planning because law work is unnatural to me. It's not as if the craft of acting does not have a plan but doing law was never my plan but my escape."

This in essence was what Lizzy was imploring and I liked hearing it.

"Yes Lizzy! I want this and I want the part. I want to go back to what I do and to who I am. Thanks for staying with me on this. I don't care about law or that I spent two years leading up to my bar exam. It's time well spent if the time I spend brings me back to who I am. When do we start?"

"It starts at Taborn On the Green next Monday for lunch, "she said "and soon after you will be permanently added to the show."

The character s name was Sudden. I liked the name as I saw good symbols in this. All of a *sudden yes* all of a *Sudden* I was on my way back to being me.

So five days later V and I were racing down the Mass Pike. It was June and the weather was perfect in fact it was June 21 and the 'longest day' of the year. We passed Newton and Sturbridge heading south and west. We then started south onto route 84 and down to 91 and Hartford Connecticut. I was now about half way to Manhattan. It was a nice drive in that I felt *clear direction*. I felt I was taking my life back again. I was very excited and my countenance was happy, as it was becoming sun-setting time in Hartford. My appointment was for noon the next day as we were meeting at the elegant Taborn On the Green in Central Park. I also had a bed and breakfast place set up for me to stay on Central Park West. The one night at the bed and breakfast paid for by *Changing Times And World* would cost more than three months rent at the Y.

Then without warning I *suddenly* I had a most unpleasant encounter.

It was as if once I saw the Hartford Insurance building I got very sleepy and lethargic. "Why am I doing this trip will you remind me?"

Suddenly I could not go further. If you drive to the very end of 84 at 91 you cannot miss seeing the Hartford Insurance Building structure. It comes very close to the Freeway. Once I was there I wanted to turn back.

"I can't turn back," I *shouted aloud*. I pulled over after taking the exit. I was at the side ramp for several minutes it seemed. I was losing my purpose for my travel to New

York. I started to yawn. I thought of the witch in Wizard Of Oz when Dorothy and company fell into a sleep along the yellow brick road.

I then found myself driving off the ramp and now heading east on 84 to Boston. It was all very *sudden*. It was as if I could not control the car, as if the car had its own life and destiny. "Where am I going!" now screaming aloud. I was experiencing a kind of frustration I had not known for years. It was happening now! *It was a new kind of pain. Where is my car taking me?* I was now to use a *guy* description being *emotional*. Well I will tell you I was *violently crying. I was like a poor man* losing all he had for a loved one who just died in his arms. When in high school chorus we sang classic *Negro Spirituals.* They were songs of pure suffering. I was now purely suffering and I was not resolving my grief. I had never grieved like this before. I was in a sobbing wave of loneliness. Extra lonely because there was no hope for a way out. So now as the poor guy I was wailing at the loss of life. I was at my own funeral and full of grief. My life is a waste of time, energy, and purpose.

"Why can't I change?" In these moments a huge wave of guilt was coming upon my soul. I was driving 70 miles an hour in the wrong direction to where I had an appointment to where I wanted to go. I could no longer however steer my car correctly. The date with *Changing Times And World* was a significant change back (if not back to Myriam) to who I really was. "Oh to be breathing again! I so want to breath! Why am I heading back to Boston?" My heart was pounding as I kept repeating, "Why am I heading back to Boston? I CAN'T GO BACK."

I left my would-be law practice to begin a new life. Others have been organizing something very nice for me and I can't let them down again. Not again as I did with Garnet! I can't do this! "WHY AM I DRIVING THE WRONG WAY?" The pedal to my Bug and my feet were on the same page. The high calling of my right foot and pedal were determined to crash my life and tear it to shreds. The car was taking me back and I could not stop the car! "THIS HAS GOT TO STOP!"

I had been driving east toward Boston for about an hour now. I was in total turmoil. Intermittently I would cry out. I was crying openly, groaning at times and calling out to Myriam. Then finally called to God? GOD! Why God? Whenever I mention him it's in a vulgar way. To put it plainly his name was one of my favorite swear words. *Why call him now? Why?* When not swearing in God's Name I would mention his name in Passover Seders every year. This time it was different. My head was then slowly lifted *to pray?*

It all happened in a moments flash but I now realized I was NOT looking at the road, but for how long? My head suddenly came up and I saw in a panic. I was headed for a wide trunked tree on the side off onto the service road.

I then had an unexpected thought.

"I can crash into that tree ahead! Yes, I can crash and really take a trip."

It's amazing how much a mind can process in a matter *of a moment.* I was now strategizing a plan. I saw the tree and I was going sixty miles as I saw the speedometer out of the corner of my eye. So I headed for the tree to take me out of my misery. *"Yes" If I had planned this I would not have the guts to just crash.* Yes of course crash! The car suddenly now off the service road reached soft grassy ground and many bumps. My lower back feeling every nuance of strain. My head hit the top of the Bugs roof. My Bug was so now so very low to the ground and its shock absorbers were so weak. I saw the tree forty feet away! Thirty feet! "YES, YES, YES... NO!" I quickly I turned my Bug to the left. V and I missed the tree by three feet as I slammed on the brakes. My heart was pounding loudly. *How close*! *Did I really survive*? It was ten pm now and it was very, very dark outside on Route 84. I pulled over and finally turned the car off. Thank God!

"I am alive." I then thought about being alive for a time. I must be alive *I am driving my Bug V and we are on a date.* I then began to process that I had missed my chance to die. "I would have to live," I thought to myself. I was becoming morose pondering I could live with such a dread for life. I was pulled over at the road feeling numb for an undetermined amount of time.

I then began to slowly and consistently push all philosophical questions of existence aside. I then continued my drive back to Boston. It was odd but even before reaching Boston I no longer had remorse about turning away from *Changing Times And World.* By the time I reached the YMCA I felt nothing in the way of feelings or emotions. I was back to being neutral. I did see the irony in the name of the opportunity I walked away from. *Changing Times And World* as my world *turned* at the Hartford exit.

I U-turned back to existence only. It was a *sudden* and significant turn. The *Sudden* I would never be. I would begin my law career one month later at a legal aid firm in Chicago. I turned my life back to *existence only.*

I was a body breathing without the oxygen of hope.

13

RIGHT BACK WHERE I WAS

"Here I am walking Central Park today and it feels like this happened yesterday" I mused in thought. In a way it did happen yesterday because I completely blocked it out of my mind. All these thoughts were now racing through my mind but more like a marathon jog.

I then remembered some other restful words John Stephens shared with me.

"Think theatrically with me David" John said. "Think the whole of life as a play. Theater is fun. Its play. You have been cast in Jesus play, but do you want to play? Wouldn't it be fun to show up to practice? In His play worldwide there would be a community that produced products that were founded on mercy, love, and sacrifice. Most people are *consensus minded*. We all often think ourselves as original when we really follow trends. Afraid to stand out we play it safe. I have to tell you a story now.

I have a friend who drove the narrow roads in the Colorado Rocky Mountains. He then saw what prairie dogs do.

He noticed all traffic was slowed down due to the many dead prairie dogs in the middle of the road. What happened was a prairie dog got run over by a car. Another prairie dog seeing a safe and easy meal in the middle of the road went to eat the dead dog. While eating the dead prairie dog another car came along and ran over the new prairie dog. Dog number three then saw two dead dogs in the middle of the road thinking it was *playing it safe* went for an easy meal and was run over too.

"There is a Jesus quote in the Bible, which gives an application that is rarely understood. 'Wherever there is a dead body that's where the vultures gather.' The prairie dogs show how deadly the middle of the road is. Playing it safe, wearing a *safe* mask, and following trends only appears to be safe. In real life people are doing the norm thinking the norm is safe. Unfortunately the norm is aggressive self-centeredness merging into the mind of a vulture. This causes a bad normal that appears moral. The cost is a *dog eat dog* world. *Surviving*, in the middle appears safe but its death. It's masks death and makes it look like life. Each person by divine design is endowed with uniqueness from Our Creator. Life comes from the *heart of God.* 'God is Love.' If Love is played out in life, its acts of expression transcend common thinking. People process old tapes and call it new. Consensus thinking causes a kind of numb which follows a trend creating unhealthy norms."

"*When that guy talks people listen*" I further mused in thought. I was reminded of those commercials where someone from E. F. Hutton was whispering financial advice and everyone got quiet to listen. John's words, were now giving me over twenty years later an insight into the identity of what masters me. *I* certainly *do not want to be a slave to trends and I know now that I have been. I then remembered E. F. Hutton went out of business. John's words will certainly not go out of business.*

"Our uniqueness," he said, "could blossom from the foundation that feeds humanity's true hunger. Jesus by divine design desires to play alongside us. We can be His actors and collaborators. *Doing from God and not for God* is where one finds his uniqueness."

"I hear those words, as I walk Central Park." I mused.

I received them into my mind but *they are so far from my heart*? Did I have a heart? I walked away from John less than two weeks after that conversation.

"I *have regrets about so much in my life*" I pondered, "yet in this moment *I have only good thoughts* about John Stephens. I feel somehow I have not burned all bridges of what he has said to me."

I then remembered that one day when I wanted to crash my car. I was saved by a *rush* of hope. Even back then I swerved to miss the tree. I want the same today.

14

A SIGNIFICANT TURN

I was now back at the Columbus Circle Exit in my walk of October 1996. I was remembering Myriam's exit to Israel from 1983. I was now at yet another beginning having been ungraciously un-partnered by my law office in recent days.

The city noise now beckoned me. It was time to enter Manhattan 1996. It was a good year to be a Yankee fan. We were back in the World Series. Luck (Janet would be so proud of my saying *luck*) was on the Yankees' side. The Yankees rookie, Derek Jeter, would hit a homerun that was really not a homerun but a bad umpire call that went in the Yankees favor. The ball was stolen out of the Orioles right fielder glove by a 12-year-old boy who was in the right field stands. It turned the American League Championship series in the Yankees favor so that they could win the pennant and get into the World Series. They would win the World Series too.

As I exited into the city traffic it was now 6 o'clock. I pictured myself taking a diagonal walk from 59th and Columbus onto Broadway and 52nd street. I used to, in my 20s, walk Broadway all the time. I would envision my name in the marquee lights. David Cohen in *A Streetcar Named Desire*. I still had found it hard to read a theater review. I often regretted that I just quit. If I had failed *trying to succeed* it would be so much better than not having tried at all.

It's been over twenty years since I walked away from Broadway. Today I wanted to literally walk back. I wanted my life back somehow, too. This walk is more than a *walk in the park* as they say. I just had my walk in the park. That walk was the past. This walk is the present. No more theory. I want results. This walk into the streets of Broadway is an exploration into me as I am now. I cannot wait for a mood change; besides it's been *twenty plus years of a bad mood.*

I was breathing some of my former bravado. The world according to Cohen, I thought out loud. I loved the book and the movie *The World According To Garp*. Ted Turner in *American Dreams Lost And Found* says, "Everyone is the star of his own life." Garp called it what it is but my life is about me. David Copperfield, who begins saying, "I begin" is fictional. I, David Cohen am real.

Garp was a wrestler and so too was I in high school. Wrestling is so like life. It's a grind. If you finish without being pinned and still do not win it's devastating. It is also exhausting. I won many more than I lost as a wrestler, but I won out of a fear of losing. A true winner cannot be afraid to lose. That was my liability as a child and teenager. Is it still? Am I so afraid to lose that I choose to not play at all?

Today in my journey I had been walking for five hours straight. I had been drinking a one-gallon jug of water and it was now finished. "A one gallon walk," I mused. It's *good to drink water*. It always gives me physical strength. We need strength to get through a day. Today however I was wondering if my water was *miracle water*. I was not tired. I was full of energy. My personal power was now something more than physical.

The city noises were if anything louder than usual but it did not matter. Even the smell of car exhaust poison into the air was not a bother to me. Breathing disgusting fumes did not bother me, not *this day*. I was focused. I had never felt this way before. I wanted to walk Broadway for the first time since my time with John Stephens and the witches. "Hey," I laughed to myself. *John Stephens And The Witches*.

I wanted to walk to Broadway so to head south and east. I never was one for counting street numbers but for traveling as a *crow flies* as they say. I just wanted to *get there*. I was working my way over to 8th Ave and the high 50s and east to 7th Ave and the mid-50s. Of course, the theater district is more than just Broadway and more than one Avenue. It's Times Square, too, which is famous for New Year's celebrations and many movie theaters, and the many dysfunctions of the world *all sold at retail*.

I was always fascinated by the live theaters on the side streets such as 52nd Street and Broadway. So in my mind on this day that was my goal. To see what's happening on 52nd and Broadway. I remembered my Mom had lived in a homeless shelter near there years after her devastating divorce from my father. People do not often understand that homelessness comes from life devastation more so than the economy. Post-traumatic stress disorder, PTSD, is for more than just soldiers. Ironically, homeless shelters were also for the conversationally comatose. There is great shame for its residents and therefore the extreme lack of conversation among its residents. Mealtime at a homeless shelter has a very sad kind of quietness to it. It's a total lack of sound. I had gone there to see Mom once before. I understood within the first five minutes that Mom's severe discouragement led her to the mission. I considered it *was a safe place for her shame and discouragement?*" She had invited me to see her. She was the mission's chef. It was hard for her to share this part of her life with me, but I had been her confidante during Dad's affair and after he left us. I only visited her there once. I stayed for about 60 minutes. It was all I could take. I'd like to see what the place looks like now. Why not! It's just a good day for a walk. Right!

I had always loved Louis Armstrong and his most famous song, *What a Wonderful World*. "...I see skies of blue red roses too, and I think to myself, what a wonderful world." I do not know what came first, the hearing of Louis or the change in the city of New York, but change happened. I started to actually hear Louis Armstrong. *Am I hearing this in my mind or is it audible to us all.* I said this aloud because the music and its words were reaching my soul and my ears.

Suddenly and without warning New York City was different. The crowds were there, but the smell was different. It smelled like Woodstock but it was the city. Woodstock was pure country featuring the full pure mountain air of the Catskill Mountains. The Catskills were also known as the *Jewish Alps*. I started to *laugh a happy laugh* thinking my joke thoughts were hysterically funny. The smell of trees was enveloping my entire countenance but this was Manhattan and New York City? "How can I smell trees we are not even in Central Park?" I thought to myself.

I was now on 52nd and Broadway but it was not the same. It was a different city. "A new section in the city?" I thought? The buildings were older but grander and they were new buildings. It was an older style from another era. "How did I miss this before?" I never saw this section of the city. "I love it here." My thoughts revealed an enthusiasm I had not had in, oh, so very long. I instantly wanted to live here. I want to buy an apartment here. I want to study acting again. *How did I miss this place, this part of the city? I wish Myriam could see this too.*

New York is a grind. If you love New York, you still hate the grind. Here the city was not a grind but quiet. Activity was all around. There was quietness instead of noise like the first city snow in December. All cars were gone. It was a walking mall. What a great idea I thought. The crowds were there, but they were very friendly. No vacant stares too. "*No comatose,*" I joked to myself. I again was hearing Old Satchmo singing,

"I see friends shaking hands sayin' "How do you do," They're really saying, I Love You."'. I was looking for where the music came from. Others in the streets were singing the words to the same song. Picture a musical and we are all just break out into song. That's what was happening here. They were singing and acting out, "friends *shaking hands* sayin *how do you do.*"

What I next noticed was the same song was playing to as a soft sounding orchestra was nestled in some trees. "*Terrific acoustics.*" I said aloud. Old buildings from the 19th century were surrounding the crowds. People were simply happy. There was no stress. There was no performance pressure or being singled out. Each of us was uniquely endowed with his or her part in the walk. We were being filled with purpose and the lack of any personal expectation. I was in the center, but I was not *the center*. I was in total peace as was everyone else. I had forgotten what it was like to not be *self-conscious*. I then began to do something I often did as a boy as a joke when we visited White Plains New York to go bowling. I began to skip. I began to sing a made up song that went something like this "*Walking is good... jogging is too... I like to run especially for fun!* But *Skipping Is Slipping Into Somewhere Over The Rainbow.*" Then I heard a chorus from *Somewhere Over The Rainbow*. Judy Garland's famous song from *The Wizard Of Oz*.

I was now at my destination on the corner of 52nd and Broadway, but the shelter I sought was gone. There was now a theater where I thought the shelter was. It was a ranch style building. It was color white with beautiful red panel siding in key places that offset the white. The marquee said, *Narrow Gate Theater - Paul In Prison - 8pm*. The theater also had a red door in its center. It looked like someone's house. I couldn't see how this could work as a theater as the building had no height that I could see. I was merely drawn to it and I wanted to go in.

I looked behind me. There were crowds but it was still quiet in the street. There were happy people waving. Did I hear someone shout out "*Hi Davey?*" I thought to myself. I had a plan but getting to my destination was no longer my purpose. There was no agenda. The walk and now the skip was the journey more than a means to the destination. The song played over several times. "I hear babies cry. I see them grow. They'll learn much more than I'll ever know. And I think to myself, what a wonderful world, what a wonderful world."

In my mind I was flying over the rainbow.

"I so received that song." I thought to myself, "When was the last time I saw the world as wonderful?" I continued in awe. "It is wonderful and I am alive." These were my feelings and thoughts.

I was now seeking for the box office to buy a ticket for the show. "I don't know who Paul is but I like the title," I said to myself. I could not find the box office. It feels corny but maybe I should knock on the door? I know this is a public place and I can walk in and find the box office, but it feels like we are in the country and visiting

Farmer Bill Barney. Bill was one of our staff of writers at the Woodstock Wood Journal. He and his effervescent, kindly, wife had a house in the woods. I turned around one more time to make sure I was in the city. Why would I do this? I was in Manhattan all day. I live here.

I turned around anyway just to be sure this wasn't a dream, but there it was. It was a Manhattan crowded city. I literally saw *friends shaking hands sayin how do you do* then a kindly old man and an angelic faced woman by his side pulled me on my arm. It was his wife I presumed. I was surprised I was not afraid to have physical contact from someone I did not know. He was ever so gently pulling on my arm in the streets of New York City. He then said to me, *"Hello sir my wife and I just want to say we love you."* Satchmo's words rang in my heart, "They're really sayin' *I love you.*" I found myself giving a hug and without saying words I said, "I love you grandpa and grandma." I was in a walking mall and there was no noise, only a series of mellow songs from street musicians all in conjunction with *What A Wonderful World*. I was as happy as everyone else. I then knocked on the door.

15

AN OPEN DOOR

Immediately, upon opening the door there was John Stephens. Bearded, older, and more distinguished, he said, "Davey, great to see you." My first response in my mind was, "He never called me Davey before." My second one was again to myself, "Why are you here? I cannot believe what I am seeing." My third response, which I stated aloud after he spoke, was "Wonderful to see you too." I wanted to hug him but restraint won over. My fourth response was also stated aloud "I see you are still wearing that same white shirt and perfectly designed dark blue jeans." We laughed. "I was just thinking of you all afternoon when I walked Central Park" I exclaimed with a Little Leaguers enthusiasm after *hitting one over the fence for a home run.*

"Yes, glad you noticed my attire. Your timing is perfect as last night I did my first wash since I last saw you." We laughed even more. There was oddly for me at least no self-consciousness with regard to our last meeting. *The meeting where I turned him down for the role of Jonah and then insulted his vision for theater.* So what are you doing here?" I am sure I said something like that. I was, however, surprised that I did not make a bigger deal in meeting John after all these years. " It was a theater. I should not be completely surprised," I said to myself. What I have experienced this last hour on Broadway was not the New York City I know the city to be. So why does John show up in this context? I just accepted it and let it be for now. I was just *so glad to see him.*

He then showed me around the theater. I noticed unusually high ceilings and many rooms not offices. I guess I just did not see that the building was so tall. This was hidden somehow from the outside. I then saw designated names that were wood stained with sculpted letters over the doors of various rooms: Jonah Room, Moses Room, King David Room, and Elijah Room. I could hear ever so softly in the background words being spoken. Like monologues, then another voice answering the monologue. The inside wooden walls were a creamy white almost tan color.

He showed me the big theater where *Paul In Prison* was playing tonight. He explained that he wanted me to sit with him as his guest. "Of course with a complimentary ticket." I asked,

"Who is Paul?" He smiled saying, "You will see."

He explained that he has been the director and producer for Narrow Gate Theater for several years. That had I joined his play, *The Angry Man*, that he would have had me join his ensemble acting company. "How," I blurted abruptly, "can you explain what is happening in the theater district? The walking mall, the singing, the atmosphere of peace. It's ... I can't explain it. It's happy, wonderful, fun, heavenly," and John merely smiled.

He explained that he was forced to leave Manhattan soon after my audition for the Jonah play. "The building owner of the theater on Sullivan Street suddenly reneged on our lease. He read the script to *The Angry Man* and did not approve its content. There is an ever increasing passion to legally outlaw our kind of theater by making new laws to prosecute the way we are" he said with passion and sadness.

"As a traveling troupe, audiences vary in the numbers of attendees, but the impact on the audiences was building momentum. Our plays draw people into a kind of transformation. The most common commentary we receive is "I was there" or I tell you? I came to see a play but I feel *I was in the play!*"

"When the audience breaks through the negative media about God it begins to form a *good news media*. The news media we refer to is Narrow Gate News and it's the signature of what our theater company is. It makes the news personal, as God Himself is personal. On the other hand the mainstream media is more powerful than news shows. It's in a government controlled non-religion *religion* so that its *religion* supports government agenda and Hollywood is its spokesman. It's in an emerging worldwide governing financial power seeking to know your personal information and control economies worldwide. It's The New World Order seeking to make the entire world into financial slaves working for the controlling powers, who own and love money. The plan also is for the sexual revolution of the sixties to become a worldwide Sodom and Gomorrah. Its endgame is for pure hostility among people to people. It's all planned by the powers that be for hostility to happen worldwide all centered around one's sexual and racial identity. It's designed for people to be on edge and against one another.

"Satan is the ruler of this world" and Satan knows his time is in short supply. His crazed panic against time causes the great stress and anxiety we see today. We see our company as a team of actors, journalists, and storytellers. We want to give *story* and the inside story in a way that slows people down from Satan's "hurry up offence."

Finally, John had a surprise for me.

"How would you like to meet Jonah?"

"You mean the actor who plays Jonah?" I said.

"OK, sure, just let me warn you… we get real close here. He may draw you in. Remember it's play, so have fun and I will be right back."

"Ok, I will." I said.

I then waited for the actor who plays Jonah. I wondered why John did not ask about Myriam and Sarah. He gave her the doll. It's not like him to not ask. Why didn't I bring them up?

Why? Because it was a nice day for me. To explain my failures to someone I respect would be embarrassing. *That's why*. Maybe he knew just by looking at me. He never asked why I gave up acting. We spoke of my career as a trial lawyer for a brief moment. I think he was being nice that's all. Who is this Jonah anyway?

As I waited for Jonah to enter the conference room, I was beginning to lose the purity I had just before. Cynicism was taking the place of childlike purity. My defenses were going up again. I remembered the last time I saw John. I had never known one better at identifying problems and so quickly to offer up solutions. *Too quick for me*. I was not a young man anymore. I had changed even if John Stephens was still John Stephens. I never thought of this until that very moment but why isn't John married? I doubt he was ever divorced. I should ask him what the single life is like. Maybe he can help me there too. *Why am I thinking about this?* I was in a small room that did not have windows. I was curious of what was going on outside because I was feeling cramped here inside. The wicker chair I sat on was old and needed a new cushion. I was not comfortable. The table before me was clean but it had cup stains. Suddenly I was tired and wanted to put my feet up on the table to rest my tired feet. Is it rude to put my feet up? It was probably all the skipping I did. Why did I skip anyway? Am I going crazy? I remember when Myriam and I went for a skip in downtown Woodstock. It was never done there either, but in Woodstock it was normal to be abnormal. Here I am an adult and why was I skipping? Was I happy when I was skipping, because I am not happy now? Why did I skip? I wish I had never skipped or sang songs in the street. I am getting vertigo now and this wait is taking too long" I was murmuring aloud.

The emotional wall I built up after my last meeting with John Stephens was coming back up. "Why am I raising up the curtain to my heart?"

16

MEET JONAH

I was sitting in my chair waiting for Jonah to enter. Of course it's the actor who plays Jonah. I was beginning from my talk with John Stephens to understand the Narrow Gate culture. They were a bit like the life actors we had in Woodstock. The *weirdoes in Woodstock had trouble delineating reality too.* They of course have a *God* influence at Narrow Gate that we didn't. I had a leadership problem, as I did not know how to steer the ship. If I had God maybe I could have led? Of course, you have to believe in God for that to work. My hands were beginning to sweat. My head was aching and I wondered if I had had too much sun. My lower back was starting to have pain. I was increasingly dizzy.

My father was always telling me that we as Cohen's were the priests of Judaism. Because of this I was called to be a leader. It's not that I was even the leading Cohen in my family. My brother and father had the same first name. My brother Mansfield was the *main* man, no pun intended. I did not feel like a leader. I did not feel a call to God, to my brother, father, or to my priestly role "Why am I thinking about this now anyway," I thought this over to myself.

I did notice that John Stephens seems even more intentional with his faith than before. I liked him but I also resented him. "That does not seem fair," I thought to myself. I was so happy outside in the new Broadway. "*I hate it here"* were my feelings, which became thoughts that raced into my head.

Suddenly almost abruptly, Jonah entered the room. He was tall, lean, bearded with red brown hair. He stretched out his right hand and said, "hello David." I thought to myself, "Well I would have been a different physical type for Jonah if I took the part 22 years ago." I stand at about 5 ft. 9 in with dark black hair. This Jonah was a big six feet two inches? "This guy looks like a reddish version of Jethro in *The Beverly Hillbillies*," I chuckled to myself sarcastically. Then I became even more stressed and very rude.

Jonah: "So we finally meet."

David: "It's not as if I have been waiting to meet you."

Jonah: "Hello David. I want to be helpful. You seem annoyed at me. Do you think being cynical will help creativity?"

David: "Listen sir. (This guy is kind of forward even aggressive I thought to myself) I was an actor on the rise at one time and I turned down a part. I gave up on creativity a long time ago."

Jonah: "You mean you ran away."

David: "Look, is the pot calling the kettle black? Besides, I don't know you, and how do you know me?"

Jonah: "I know you because I know myself. I ran from all that I was and had when I ran away. I did not stop to think. I did not navigate life's choices. I reacted."

David: "Listen, Mr. Jonah. I just took a walk down Broadway and I stumbled upon this theater. I don't know you. Am I on some kind of audition?"

Jonah: "This is not an audition. I do however know you love acting and I want to help you to know your part. You cannot really play any part until you know your own part. Your part in life and in *The Play*. I could say the *big stage*. The stage I refer to is more than a script, building or screenplay. It is very personal. Close up and small too. It's harder to play yourself because most of us are usually trying to be who and what we are not."

David: "Can I be excused please?"

Jonah: "You mean go somewhere else?"

David: "Do you mean go to Tarshish? My personal Tarshish, you might say?"

Jonah: "Well, now that you bring this up, yes. You are running away to Tarshish… but what is Tarshish? A place where one might feel like they are accomplishing something when at the heart just running away."

David: "Are you aware you used *they* or *their* two times in two sentences? I notice religious people refer to they and them quite a bit."

Jonah: "Tarshish is an actual place but its meaning is greater than any one town. In my time, Tarshish was my self-justification. It is however a mistake that is repeated in time, over and again, by the many *theys*. Are you one of the theys?

David: "So you are saying, when I walk out of this conversation, that I am running as you did and that I am justifying it?"

Jonah: "Yes, that's exactly what I am saying. Just like you did when Mr. Stephens offered you the lead part in Jonah. Listen to me. I want to encourage you. You are blaming me and for what reason? It's all my fault in your mind. 'Just get me out of this conversation with this guy,' you think to yourself. *Me* who is a someone you do not know."

David: "You are crazy."

Jonah: "I once was, but I figured out my own hypocrisy. I like it better being sane. David, do you want to try sanity? It's a lot more fun than the other way?"

David: "I am leaving!"

Jonah: "David, you walked out on us over 20 years ago and have you benefited from this? You were all worked up about by your career and how the Jonah play would ruin your life. Well, how's your career? How's life? Maybe, just maybe, there is something to this God thing. Maybe it does relate creativity into life's real *happiness*. Maybe, just maybe, you can enter into a scene with me. Maybe you can learn about yourself from my mistakes."

David: "You are right about one thing. I am crazy! I am talking to someone who thinks he is Jonah."

Jonah: "Yes but it's a good crazy. Some might call it foolish, but some call it wise."

David: "You mean the crazies think it wise?"

Jonah: "It's a good crazy!"

David: "I am going to stay awhile, at least long enough to see what I missed the last time I met your director and now you. You are a convincing actor."

Jonah: "Good Davey! I appreciate your… your…"

David: "Your willingness to be with a true nut?"

Jonah: "I know we are different here, but our show is the longest *theatrical revival* of all time. We want you to join us Davey. We like you."

David: "Only my mother has ever called me 'Davey'."

Jonah: "Consider us family."

David: "Mish bu kah?"

Jonah: "You got it son. *Mish bu kah* and real family. Life was never easy for me. It was full of expectation and disappointment. I felt I never measured up to what my family expected of me. I myself became an overachiever. All I knew of God, as a man of God, was some kind of ideal but not a *real*. I was absorbed in responsibility and order. I knew the way to God, but it was not a walk with Him. It was, instead, a map to a treasure that was not mine. It could not be mine until I found the destination on the map. So I was leading people to a place I had not yet gone to. Do you know what kind of pressure that was Davey? God was as real to me as a GPS signal? God as a relationship with Him was not even part of the challenge or discussion."

David: "I remember Rabbi Fishberg from our tent synagogue at the bungalow colony in the Catskills. We were talking about him, that is, me and my friends. I think I was eight years old. We were making fun of his preaching and his favorite song, *Zum Gali* ...gali gali zum gali gali! It was a fun song and he was actually reaching young, old, and all the many families on summer vacation. *Zum Gali* has to do with poor families enjoying life in the early days of Israel in the land of Canaan. It was fun and Rabbi was great at making God stuff fun stuff. I will never forget this but this grown man came out from the bushes where we could not see him and he was crying. 'You don't like me' he said. I had never known grownups to act like eight year olds. I mean being loved was something we cared about. Here he is, acting like eight year-olds do and to the point of tears. He was like a Charlie Brown character. I was devastated with guilt."

I was being mean, yet if he had not interrupted us with his pain, I would have never known something of who Rabbi Fishberg was. A God guy being like us. He valued what we said and that's why he could feel the pain of our harsh words toward him."

Jonah: "God is so like what the good rabbi showed. The rabbi was having the humility to be wounded by those he loved. Even if they were children. Your rabbi was very rare. You see I was not like your

Rabbi Fishberg. I was always in control. I was intimidated by my position. I was a leader and a man of God. So I wore my position as prophet the way a man might wear clothes, a kind of statement that I was a holy man."

David: "My Dad was in the garment business on the famed 7th Ave here in *'the city.'* He always spoke of *dressing the man* to play the role. Clothes were a statement that spoke of 'where you are going in life,'" he often said.

Jonah: "Yes, to know where you are going is important, but to not know *who you are* is tragic. The way to factor to knowing *who you are* is to *know who He is*. Lose yourself in me."

David: "Who said that? Freud? Sounds psychological."

Jonah: "Jesus said that."

David: "That's not a Jewish thing. You are Jewish right?"

Jonah: "One finds who one is when one finds God to be personal and available to him. This happens in the process of living. The choices you make will reveal what you believe much more than what you say. That's when we discover if we are believers or atheists. When I was in the body of that big fish, don't ask me what kind of fish it was, I only know it was big enough to store me *inside its mouth*. Inside the fish is where I found my belief."

David: "You don't expect me to believe that you were inside the mouth of a fish and survived?"

Jonah: "I do not want to seem rude here, but reality is not dependent on your belief. You can believe it or not. Facts are still facts. Of course I believe I was there. It challenged my personal atheism. In other words, I was an atheist until I was in the belly of the big fish. I went to Tarshish against God's will for me, the One whom I had heard speak 'Go to Nineveh,' but I did not believe the One I heard from. I did not really believe, certainly not functionally. People always separate function from theory, but in heaven it's not done that way. It's not done that way at Narrow Gate Theater either. If it doesn't walk like a duck, it is not a duck! This is how we think at Narrow Gate Theater. The way one function shows what he or she believes."

"People today say of themselves, 'I believe this way, but I act that way.' This way of thinking is non-belief. So too, I also didn't believe God was involved as in *really alive*. How could I? He was always just an ideal way but never *real to* me. He was to me a Bible story fantasy."

"Most faith you see today is in reaction to one's training. I was reacting as a believer who did not believe. My culture was 'belief' but my training was unbelief. My actions, ironically, did not go against my training. My training was to talk about God but not necessarily to believe him. That's who I was. That's how I was trained. *That's exactly how many who have training in God are trained today*."

David: "Well, my God training was Yankee Stadium. I mean the Yankee Stadium that Babe Ruth played in. It was called the *House That Ruth Built*. My Dad was not around very much. He was always trying to make a lot of money. It's as if I had 12 conversations with my Dad as a child, and 10 of them were at the stadium. Our Judaism, which was my main conversation with Dad, was training in a horizontal god. I do not remember prayer, for instance. We were Jewish, at least Dad kept telling us. So I would ponder 'but where is God in all this?' Except for Rabbi Fishberg there was no training like you had with God or the Bible. Being with Dad at Yankee Stadium and hearing how I was Jewish became my religious training."

"It's probably why I love the Yankees no matter where I am in life or where I live. I always love the Yankees. It's kind of spiritual to me. It's where I had my best family time. I was with my Dad. Rabbi Fishberg was gone from my life after age twelve. So too was my God training, but I still had the cathedral of ballparks. I had Yankee Stadium. Bob Sheppard was the public address announcer. I always assumed Yankee Stadium had the best acoustics. I was wrong. It was Bob Sheppard. It is often said Bob Sheppard is *The Voice Of God*. His voice was the high priest of my religious training. "Ladies and gentlemen, batting 3rd and playing *centah field numbah* 7, Mickey Mantle *numbah 7*."

"Dad left Mom after my twelfth birthday. He went on a business trip or so they told me. Later on my older brother Mansfield and Mom clued me in that my parents were splitting up. It kind of put a spin on my 12th birthday for life. This birthday was when Mom and Dad split and Dad never came back. Mom and I would sing 'Daddy's home, Daddy's home to stay' but he never came back."

"Aside from his passion for money was his passion for his girlfriend. Before he died he cried in my arms how he regretted leaving Mom. Her childhood sweetheart my Dad, left her for someone in the garment business that could understand his passion for success. He knew his failing in the end, but it was too late for his life on earth. He simply missed out."

Jonah: "When I was in the big fish I finally spent time with my father. It was dark. It was a very dark and small space. I thought I was blind. I assume you had a comfortable seat at Yankee Stadium? Well in the big fish it was hard to be comfortable. It's here where I believed in God for the first time. In the fish's belly is where I finally met my Dad. I first '*believed* 'when I realized I was *not being eaten*. When I realized this I prayed to God and discovered my new found father."

"People over time, since my experience with the big fish, have said,

'How is it possible that Jonah could survive in the fish's mouth three days and three nights?' The answer to this is how God became personal to me. Who but God sovereign over all creation could have caused that fish to go beyond its instinct to eat what it caught? God shut its mouth and its urge to eat. Simple!"

"I was, however, literally sick to my stomach. That poor fish eventually ate what I could not hold in. It was a pukey mess. I prayed and I promised my Father and my God that I was going to Nineveh. Nothing would stop me and my new faith."

David: "But you failed again, didn't you?"

Jonah: "Yes, of course I did. I want to talk to you about the Ninevites, but before I do, it is important for you to know how I really did change when in the body of the fish. I of course was a hypocrite after the fish experience, but in the fish God finally *became personal* to me. When I turned against God the second time, I did so as a bigger rebel than before. This second time is when I knew it was my Father I was betraying. I went to Nineveh on a crusade as an overcomer. I succeeded at this mission on the outside but on the inside I wanted more. When in the body of the fish, to live was all I needed or wanted. After Nineveh and all the success I achieved, I wanted more than what God had to give. God gives life. God gives all of life's benefits too. Peace, contentment, humility ... these are all God perks. If His benefits are not enough, then God is not enough."

"I wanted to get the credit for the revival in Nineveh. They came to me. I was the only preacher. I was *the one* people saw so I wanted more. I had been so very close to death myself that I now had a new understanding of life. I could never have known this except by having already suffered through the consequence of being so close to my own death."

"As I preached, my personal being was immersed with memory of my experience in the big fish. I was in the *big fish again* but this time the *life* and death I witnessed was not my *death* but *death* to the Ninevites. I saw Sheol (hell) as the Ninevite destiny. My big fish experience came to life again when I said to the Ninevites "repent." When I gave that threatening message to the Ninevites, I knew it was God speaking through me. Even so I was still holding back. I down deep did not want them to receive."

"I had a plan for three days in Nineveh as that was the time it would take to go through the city by foot. It turns out my work was done on the first day. I spent the two other days in Nineveh observing the results of my preaching there. It was a kind of three-day thing just as was my time in the big fish was a three-day thing. They must have seen a magnificent display of power come out from me. I myself as a death survivor had no middle of the road to my preaching. For me there was no in between. The Ninevites ironically were also as I was in a big fish, caught in a trap without an exit. My preaching was making them free to choose life or death. There was no in between choice offered. My message was greater than me as it was directly from God. When they received the warning however and chose life, I was very disappointed."

"I was suddenly lost. I was clearly *on my own* and now without God's fellowship. Alone again and more so than in the fish's belly because this time God was not with me. I was working against Him even while obeying Him in my preaching. In Nineveh I was loving my power, my voice, my body. By being a 'friend of the world' (hating Ninevites) I was at enmity with Him. This is the worst of hates. It's the kind of hypocrisy that causes divorce. God was my competition now. I could do war, but peace was my issue. I hated the refugees. I despised those murdering baby-killer Ninevites."

"My preaching was the worst kind of theater. It was *an act*. It appeared very real but my heart was hard. The worst kind of acting too. You see Davey people think acting is about adding up new things like stardom or success with talent as an extra add on. God's acting is about subtraction where less is more. The heavy weight of being a success can be a heavy weight to carry. It is repentance that releases burdens and makes creativity fun and easy. At Narrow Gate we are raising up God's *Acting Company*. How far and deep he or she will go into ground zero is as high he or she will transcend into the joy of having no agenda. I performed for God, but did not relate to Him. God was my *duty* all over again and seeing those Ninevites rot in hell was my goal. I had gone back into the ideal of God, which was yet another legalism and I again avoided the real. If it were real, *my preaching would have caused me to repent of my hearts hardness*. I was one of many who preach a '*they*' message - but not one for me. How quickly had I lost the reality of my personal Nineveh! My own big fish! I was playing God and would not allow Him to play me."

David: "Paul Harvey, the radio columnist, says, 'now for the rest of the story.' In giving your inner monologue, you gave me the rest of your story. Thank you."

Jonah: "I am an actor. I am in God's theater. As actor I share news stories in the first person. That's what acting is, being in the first person. That's how the gospel is shared in God's media. This is The Bible, The Living Word of God. *The Good News* and His show is real. His story causes one to be in His Story. We call it history or His- story. It's a real and supernaturally imaginative world. He reports truth publicly to all but at the same time personally for one's hard heart."

David: "I remember visiting Mt. Vernon near Washington, DC, with Myriam. I remember our getting into a conversation with Martha Washington. She told us about all her children. How the father of our nation, George Washington, never had biological children of his own. He had adopted all four of Martha's children and watched each one die before he or Martha died. We conversed and cried together. Her performance was so real. You are that kind of

	performer. I say *bravo*. Thank you."
Jonah:	"What you got at Mt. Vernon was a fantastic use of theater. It drew you into the play and you went beyond observing and into participation. We at Narrow Gate Theater do the same. The only exception is at Mt. Vernon; you spoke with someone who identified with someone else. With me, you are talking with that very person. I am Jonah and I am me. God is alongside and playing me *Jonah* right now. I used to play God and failed miserably. I don't know if you have ever done a Bible study but you are in one right now and the Holy Spirit is the producer. That's how *The Script* the *Scripture* is played out. It's fun David. That's why they call it play. Thats why its children who inherit the kingdom of God. I finally overcame excessive *adultitis*. You see how children can make words up along the way."
David:	"Ok, this is the crazy part of the conversation. So let's not get bogged down in details … let's continue our conversation. Okay? Jonah is one of the common stories in our synagogue. I remember Rabbi Fishberg bringing us to the end of the book, I mean play. There is more to your story isn't there?"
Jonah:	"Yes. I have to tell you Davey, this has been a wonderful interview. We have on our staff the top interviewer of all time, Dr. Luke. I want you to meet him after I finish my story. He, and now you, show me how a sensitive listener can draw so much out of we humans. Thank you."
	"The Greek word used in the New Testament to describe mercy is *inside skin*. Inside skin is an actor's word for one who learns the character he or she plays. Performers do this to ace the part. 'How am I doing,' he might say. This is the Hollywood model for acting, i.e., 'Look at me.' Jesus way is the *Holy-Wood* model, i.e., 'Look at you.'"

David: "Years ago John Stephens at his apartment went on and on about this very concept. Today in my walk at Central Park I was re hearing his words on this very subject and now you are talking about this too."

Jonah: "Yes David it's a compassion based approach to theater, acting and to life. It takes performance pressure away and makes the theater experience fun, creative, and compassionate. Acting this way is empathy and feeling the pain and the joy with those you are with. It's more than a play you are cast in; it is a way of living life. Off stage is real life and the real play."

David: "This has been nice. Jesus sounds nice too. My Dad never said much about him only that he wasn't Jewish like us. Dad said, Jesus was Jewish, but not the way we Cohens were. How is it that you know Jesus anyway? Jesus is not in the Old Testament the Tanakh as we call it. Also does this '*inside skin*' have anything to do with your closure with God and the Ninevites?"

Jonah: "Yes. First understand the Bible is eternal and it lives on its own time. You enter its time when you engage with its content, which is live and happening now. Because the Bible is happening now, this what I am saying to you is now. Jesus is alive and the God of the living and not the dead. I know Him apart from human history because I know Him from eternity. I was waiting for Him when He entered paradise and opened heaven for me and many other Old Testament saints. I know now that He was the same God, Yahweh, I prayed to then. I met Jesus when Yahweh became personal to me in the fish. I know this as the Holy Spirit has revealed to me that Jesus is God."

"God's final words were, 'Should I not have compassion on these 120,000 who cannot tell their right hand from their left?' Now I did not see God but I heard Him. I heard His feelings for each of these 120,000. I felt His loneliness for them and His pain. I tell you

Davey, I heard in His Voice His cry for each one of the 120,000. I heard 120,000 cries in Him, and His One Voice that spoke to me. I got inside their skin when I heard God's passion for them to be made right. He was doing this for me by getting inside my skin and finally causing my heart for them so that I got inside their skin."

"He took me to a place I had not known and to where I did not want to go. I saw that if I wanted God I had to follow Him. I could not say I love Him and not follow Him. If I did not follow Him then I was not His. I could not be one who separates His Love from His actions. He loved the Ninevites… every 120,000 of them… 120,000 thousand stories and He was in every one of their plays. He made Himself a character in 120,000 stories as the One who cared. If I wanted God, then I could not separate from where He was going. I again struggled with what I thought I was healed from. I thought I was healed from my personal atheism. I had to go with God back to Nineveh and give love but I could not. No, I would not."

David: "I don't understand. You saw the issue and your problem, why not just follow? It's amazing to me how you saw so clearly what was needed. So many times the many mistakes I have made were because I could not see the obvious."

Jonah: "No David think… have you ever seen the obvious and ignored what you knew was right?

David: I was stunned by Jonah's remark. My entire life's choice in the last twenty-two years have been ignoring the obvious. How could I even ask him that question? In my life it was not a question of could not but would not. I was and am a victim of my own choices.

Jonah: *Jonah then responded with kindness, "We* humans know more than what we allow ourselves to accept. We call it denial. I was not, however in denial this time, not after God's appeal for the 120,000.

I had to act on what I feared the most. You see Davey, fear, hate, and anger are closely related. I hated the Ninevites for what they did to me, to my wife, and to my family. They invaded my home city. They stole our son and made him a sacrifice to their god. Baal or Molech, does it matter? It's all to the same devil. It did not matter to me which disgusting demon raped my hope and heart."

"When I call them murderers, I say this from personal experience. They stole my life when they stole my son. They ripped my unborn son out from his mother's womb! I now hated them with every fiber of my being! The hate I had for what they did infected my whole being as a metastasizing cancer to a body, yet God loved the murderer of my son."

"For years, I would *not outwardly* resent God for loving my captor. Instead I became a religious robot and a mannequin for Him. This religious mask I wore was masking my resentment for Him and for all Ninevites. I was being indirect, and denial always causes indirect activity. What I could not accept, until my all out sin at Nineveh, was that God knew who my murderer was. What I heard that began a change in me was His Voice of deep sorrow for me. Me! He was not giving justice to my murderer's evil act against my family. It was in His compassion for me, that He deplored their actions because of what it did to Him and to me. Their evil was destroying me and He had compassion on me. He was not endorsing their evil. He had compassion on me for what their evil was doing to me. This inside skin is God's revelation of Himself and in Jesus we see this in action. We see its fulfillment. I did not know Him as Jesus then. I knew Him then as He reveals Himself to me now, as God who saved me then. He is the same to me then and now. He is the life from death that is the hope of all mankind. Jew, gentile, Old Testament, New Testament or zero testament knowledge. He has His signature on all humanity. He understands death, loss and the recovery of both. I in effect sought Jesus before I knew His Name."

David: I was stunned to hear all this and how it relates to Jesus. I never considered Jonah as a resurrection story and parallel to Jesus. John trains his actors very well. Certainly this man who plays Jonah has solid inner monologue.

Jonah: "I was the last Ninevite, the final human being in His Nineveh outreach. He was now appealing to me and I saw His love for me. He was showing me the kind of passion I had for Him in the belly of the big fish. *He was making Himself vulnerable to me.* He wasn't *'playing God'* as the boss giving orders. He was giving empathy by showing me His compassion for my murderer. He was causing me to revisit my pain. I still wanted Him to hate that one Ninevite, but He was forcing me to face my greatest fear. It was my personal pain and its extraordinary hate that was making me so sick. He caused me to face the avoidance of what my captor did to me, to my beloved wife and to my son. He gave me His greatest gift. He gave me empathy over what was done to me. He got inside my skin and revealed His love for me to be healed of hate. I was being offered deliverance from pain. He whispered into my ear 'blessed are the merciful for they shall receive mercy'. My giving mercy could be my final release into healing. *No I cannot let go of my hate!*"

"I was facing pure revenge all over again, and it was making me sick. Then suddenly, *He held me.* I knew it was Him. *'Underneath are the everlasting arms.'* Bigger than the big fish, Nineveh was my darkest tomb. It also was my personal resurrection. It was the place where I saw His hand. He again pulled me up out of my tomb as He did in the big fish. He rescued me. In His appeal to my enemies, He was doing to me what He did for me in the tomb of the fish. He was pulling me out of an even bigger fish. This time it was my metastasizing unforgiveness. While pulling them out of *their big fish* I too was *The Catch* of His harvest in Nineveh. *My tomb Nineveh had become my womb* and entrance into a new life."

"He was pulling me out of darkness and into the light of His

Forgiving Presence. He was also forgiving my captors through me. My smile to Nineveh showed my forgiveness and this caused God to shine more healing through me as I was being healed. I then went looking for *that one. All of the 120,000 were now one person to me.* I was ready to love him. I never saw this happening to me, and yet if it did not happen that very moment I could not have lived another day."

17

DAVID'S NINEVEH

Suddenly Jonah was gone. It was as if air itself was swallowed up into a vacuum. "Man that guy feels everything. How did he just vanish like that?" I thought to myself. "Did I fall into a sleep?" The color of this room is a kind of diamond white that draws me into tranquility. Is this what is giving me peace? If this is some kind of audition, I tell you they know how to do it here. I am *very relaxed*. I put my feet up on the wooden table of stains and age. I noticed a mirror and saw my face. I thought for a moment that I was twenty-five again. The lines of my face were so clear. The makeup department could not recreate me as an ingénue as well as nature has here.

I began to think through things I forgot I knew, such as people I had met when I first lived in the *city*. The strangest sensation to being a New Yorker, and when I say this I mean Manhattan, is that there is always noise. It is never without noise. The other sensation is that the ground shakes. There is a vibration to the atmosphere and it is always shaking. It's not the same as an earthquake shake. This city is all about its intensity. Had I always lived in New York City perhaps I would not notice. Manhattan is different from any place or city I had ever lived in.

I say all this to say that this place, this Narrow Gate building I am in is not the same as New York City. Where is the noise, the vibration, and the cabs honking? There is no vibration causing the ground to shake. I know once I walked onto Fifty Second Street and Broadway it felt like 'the country.' When I walked into Narrow Gate Theater it felt partly bed and breakfast and partly a mansion home. I still cannot hear any noise. Is this like that song *Silent Night*? Now that my talk with Jonah was over I could go outside the neighborhood to all the noise New Yorkers seem to thrive on, but "I did not want to go outside," I thought to myself. "Not even a little bit."

I was so relaxed, even more so than Willow Woodstock in the Catskills. This experience here at Narrow Gate Theater was beyond natural. It was similar to a word I had not used in years. This was *shalom*. I was there, here, and no need to be anywhere else. It was also to use another word I had not used in years. It was *groovy*. It was a fulfillment of the song "Slow down you're movin too fast gotta make the morning last sitting round the cobblestone havin some fun and feelin groovy. How corny," I thought to myself.

It's odd that in being relaxed one can begin to allow new thoughts to occur. In being at peace one can be available to open himself up to something that mattered so much once before. This was what was happening to me. It was soon after Jonah ended his conversation that I was finding myself exploring his issue with the Ninevites. To Jonah, Ninevite meant a murderer of children, namely his child.

A certain chill went through me as he spoke of this. His former hatred for them was very convincing. I was still in my comfortable wicker couch chair, in the room where he and I met. In my peace I began to process a difficult time for me.

My law partner, Robert Sterling, had introduced me to a woman almost young enough to be my daughter. He hired her to be our receptionist in part because he wanted me to meet her. I was divorced and did not want another marriage. Sterling wanted me to at least be in a relationship. Margo was not what I thought she would be. She was quite attractive. I cared for her and I was like a father to her too. She would share with me all about her life. She trusted me. I even encouraged others in the office to befriend Margo, who I sensed was quiet. I was her *older person* confidante. At one point after working for us for about two years she got involved with a man. In the early part of that relationship she confided in me quite a bit. I felt in helping her, I was doing for Margo what I failed to do for my wife in my 20s. I was a friend.

It happened rather suddenly but Margo stopped speaking to me. I was careful of our age difference as we were both adults, and she was very attractive. I would not cross the line on romance. Maybe in my diligence to not cross the line, I replaced a desired romance with her by giving her parental care. The truth is, I cared for her and gave the relationship energy. Finally after not speaking personally for months, she broke down and asked for help. I took her to a local place for coffee. She finally opened up.

"I am pregnant, "she said. "What should I do? My boyfriend does not want the child and says he will break up with me if I do not have an abortion. David please help me."

I, in this instant, was ill equipped to handle this. I was aware I was being thrust into being more than a role model. What was needed was more than a bastion of goodness and philosophical words of human wisdom.

"Do you want the child?" I asked. Her answer was, "Yes and no."

"I want the child and my boyfriend, too. What should I do David? Whatever you think is right I will do."

With that question I was oddly back into my comfort zone. All I had to do here was to give good advice with care but strangely not be involved. In that instant I heard Myriam say to me,

"Always words with you David - but never passion, never involved."

"*Shut up!*" I remember saying in my mind to Myriam in that freakish moment of anger and revenge. I often thought I was a decent man to this young girl as a kind of father and friend. I felt I was somehow undoing years of un-involvement in marriage. Now ironically I heard the voice of Myriam, "*You still have not changed.*"

"What of your friend?" I said to Margo. "Has he made arrangements for the abortion that he says he wants you to have?"

"No," Margo said, "he put it all in my hands. He warned me have an abortion or we are finished."

My mind was now clear. "Well Margo, I will take care of you. I will personally take you to the doctor and make sure you get A-1 treatment for the procedure. We will get you two weeks paid leave, too."

Two weeks pay was very generous as the abortion industry was promising in and out same day service. Ironic I thought, they call that procedure '*a service.*'

"We want what's best for you. You should break up with this boyfriend of yours. I however will take care of you."

She of course thanked me for hearing her need and for being responsible. I believe it was the very next day in the morning that I took her to the place for the abortion procedure.

I took her into the clinics admitting room. The place looked normal in that there were people, mostly young women in their twenty's waiting for their doctor. I sat next to Margo. I was surprised in being uncomfortable with Margo for the first time. Was I her father, or boyfriend in the minds of those in the waiting room? "What are people thinking of me and my role in this?" A not so slight embarrassment came upon me. I was hoping Margo *did not notice just how uncomfortable I was.* Again as it so often does in tense situations my hands began to sweat even to shake. A migraine was slipping into the forehead of my temple. Gratefully her name was called within five minutes of my personal torture. She looked back into my eyes and smiled faintly as she walked into her procedure. I smiled back nervously. In an emotional way I for the first time was really not there for her. "*Does she know?*"

She then closed the door behind her. Suddenly a man approached me and asked, "Are you the father?" I replied, "No I am not."He then said, "Are you the father of the woman (referring to Margo as he motioned to the door she had just closed behind her) having the abortion?"

I was stunned. Maybe it was his particular way of being abrupt. He actually grabbed me as his nails pierced my right shoulder. The same sensitive area going back to my broken collarbone speaking loudly into the same ear I punctured as a fourteen-year-old. Maybe it was that I did not know if he worked for the hospital or was merely a busy body. Maybe it's that he said that ugly word '*abortion.*' His attitude seemed to me to be inappropriate. I was also embarrassed in front of several others in the office waiting room.

I did notice my fists were clenched. What was so rare is that I was not a fist-fighting kind of guy. Tense and irritated I blurted out with a loud voice, "It's none of your business. Who do you think you are... *you buffoon*!"

At this juncture what I remember was another very large man coming over to us, and he said, "You have to leave this place immediately." I said, "I am waiting for my friend and I am taking her home." His right arm was now squeezing my right arm. *A quick pain* was then lifted into my right broken collarbone. His reply was, "No, you are not taking her home. Leave here now or I will have the police escort you into jail. We will make sure the person you are referring to will be given a taxi home. Someone on our staff will make arrangements. Leave right now or you will be very sorry."

I did not say another word. I was humiliated. People in the waiting room saw the skirmish. I walked into the corridor and into the city streets. I did not look back. My hands and knees were shaking. My body and entire being were out of control. I also got dizzy with a kind of *pukey* feeling of vertigo.

That was 10 years ago. Margo never came back to work for us. Had I not offered the two weeks off, we might have seen her again. I heard over time that Margo is '*extra quiet*' *these* days. I thought of the words "conversationally comatose" but did not find it funny. Something distinctly Margo was gone from Margo. In leaving her baby to die, she lost more than her own child but something of her soul. She, over the years had various jobs and relationships - some with men and some with women so I was told. She had lost whatever stability she once had. I saw her once at a restaurant and could hardly recognize her. She did not see me *or did she*? This was about two years later. She lost her beauty. I do not refer to her good looks as much as a vibrancy now gone. My lawyer partner was very disappointed about my relationship with

Margo.

"You blew that relationship David. Why is it so hard for you to see what is plain to see? If you had had an affair with her, she would be better off."That remark was kind of typical for Robert's way of resolving conflict. I was as stated not a religious man but Robert was a moral derelict. I would think to myself "*what if Sarah met a guy like my partner?*" How can I partner with a man I would fear for my Sarah? So after some introspection I did what I so often do. I did the middle of the road thing. We had been negotiating adding a new office in the southwest in Albuquerque New Mexico. We remained partners but I got out of town. Way out of town. I was Cohen without Sterling but still his junior partner as Sterling and Cohen Southwest.

I forgot all about this unpleasantry until just now at the *Narrow Gate therapy clinic for crazies*. I hate this place! I finally got some peace of mind, and then I *reexamine* my life and all its *horrid stories*. That's what I get for shalom. I will remember in the future not to get so involved in my auditions!

"Why did I come here anyway?" I screamed but in a whisper. Then I sobbed, "Why?"

I now found myself standing, feeling as if in a locked soundproofed room at a police station. I began to slur words.

"I am not a murderer! I was trying to help a young girl who was in trouble. Why am I responsible? I do not want this! I want out. Do you understand? OUT!" My violent whisper now audible words. "I want out of this crazy house. Get me out of here. I did not do it!" *I felt all alone*, but I felt others were listening in. These others were not just listening but *dissecting my pain and staring at me. It was* a nightmare right out of *The Twilight Zone*.

Then my shouting stopped and *reality stepped in*. There was nothing but *tragedy and death* connected to this. I was now in my mind and heart in a dark chamber of death. I thought of Jonah's early moments in the mouth of the big fish and it too was so dark here. I was so without hope. I thought I was in hell because I had never in my life felt such loneliness, guilt, and despair. "She would have done whatever I wanted for her." I said this aloud as I needed to hear it. I said it again. "*She would have done whatever I advised her to do." I sobbed.*

"I did it!" I said aloud. I had not thought about this in all these years. "Is there anyone on the other side of that wall? I want the wall to come down. I want out of this, please, it's too confining! Do you hear me! Please... help... "

18

MEET SOME OF THE CAST

"It is hard to gauge time here," but I was certain time had passed. I heard a knock at the door and I was startled. "Who, what is it?" I pleaded to the sound behind the door.

"It's John Stephens. David can I come in please?"

"Yes, of course come in," I replied. I was not calm but I was no longer distraught. In looking into John Stephens' eyes I was now experiencing a normalcy. I needed normal but I also needed to climb out from the tomb I was in. The tomb of my memory with Margo and her child. *"My child" I* thought to myself? All these years I in effect had been in this tomb of personal guilt. I was a murderer. My mind repeated over and again *"murderer."* I was however through John's presence slowly being released from that dark memory. My mind now went *inside the skin* of my friend Jonah. Jonah is a nice man I pondered as I was enjoying that my muscles were less tense. The physical centeredness in my abdomen is something I love to experience from walking. This centeredness was now coming upon me emotionally. *Spiritually too?* I was finding some new energy that wasn't hyper energy. I felt taller, calmer and my hands felt strong and dry. I was *being quieted.* I began to process that, in all this confrontation that it was having a good effect on me? I do not know exactly why, but *I was now happy to have stepped back into my former life.* I did not understand what was happening but *"It's okay,"* I said to myself. I then smiled into the eyes of the kindly John Stephens.

John: "So David. What did you think of Jonah?"

David: "Well, he was a lot of things. He was expressive."

John: "Yes, he is one of our favorite cast members. He is a constant reminder to us all of the passion it takes for real change to occur.

With Jonah, we all know repentance is real change. There are tears and joy in this place of real change."

David: "You know when I met you, what is it twenty two years ago?"

John: "Yes, exactly to the day in fact."

David: "You mean you keep track of these things?"

John: "Yes we do, but it's not like we work hard at it. We just know time and eternity as one and the same. We do not make too much distinction. So what did you think of Jonah?"

David: "I thought I expressed that."

John: "Well, an elephant is expressive too, (John *was not sarcastic but with straight faced black humor*) but what of Jonah's character? Character development is crucial for our company."

David: "I never met anyone like him actually. Sometimes he sounds crazy and sometimes courageous. I think he liked me though. That's what I got from him. Is that ok?"

John: "That's fine, David. You saw his love and his love for you?"

David: "I wouldn't put it that way, but as you explain it, it helps me to understand. Yes, I guess as much as you can love someone you do not know, yes. In that respect, yes, I guess he loved me."

John: "Perhaps he knows you better than …."

David; "Better than you know myself you were going to say?"

John: "Well, David, that is a very profound question you pose." (John was clearly joking with me).

David:	"I am not proposing a question about myself or Jonah, just a statement about how he communicates."
John:	"It's so good being with you again David. Jonah has told me you are to see Luke. Would you like to 'improv' with Luke?"
David:	"First off, are these improvisations I am doing, or just conversations?"
John:	"David, we are an acting troupe. We have never denied this. We love what we do. Of course we are improvising either on script or off script. Improvisation is the lifeblood of conversation, relationships, and prayer. I hope you are having fun. We like you David."
David:	"That's what Jonah said. He said we want you to join us too."
John:	"Yes, precisely."
David:	"Ok John."

I was now noticing how comfortable the chair I was sitting on was. It was wide and soft too. I was now stretching my legs outward. I then began to fold my legs in what we used to refer to as Indian style. I was now in the zone for good conversation.

"I get it about your location here in New York City and being on Broadway. I get it about your being an alternative to the typical play. I do get it. But I have another question for you? What's all this Jesus stuff I hear. Jonah was a Jew? I mean Moses and David are fine, but this Jesus is throwing me for a loop. Don't you know it's insulting to speak of Jesus to a Jew? I do not mean this in an offensive way but you make it easy for me to share thoughts with you."

John: "Have you ever just said, '*Jesus Christ,*' these same words frivolously or in anger or part of a cursing frustration?"

97

David: "Well, yes I have, we all do. What's that got to do with my religion and your insult of my Judaism?"

John: "Why are you calling out to Jesus when you swear? Why, when angry or frivolous why don't you call out to Buddha, Confucius, Molech, Baal or Allah?"

David: "I don't know why. Maybe it's just vernacular. Just a way to speak?"

John: "Maybe it's the wrong way?"

David: "Okay."

John: "It's just that when I speak of Him in reverent terms it's considered aggressive religion, but when you swear in his name it's considered vernacular. You on any given day might talk about him more than I do. I am not offended by your constant proselytization of '*Jesus Christ*' as a casual curse word. Maybe you should seriously meditate on why, you a Jew, call on him so often? In our theater we are expressing ourselves and offering a point of view. When you were a student at Northeastern, and you read Tennessee Williams, were you insulted by his plays regarding the homosexual lifestyle?"

David: "No he was a great artist giving a message."

John: "And so are we. Listen David, would you like me to give you a tour of our theater? Maybe we can catch some of the actors developing their characterization."

David: "What about my appointment with Luke?"

John: "I can show you around on our way to the Luke room."

David: "Ok, whatever you say."

John then opened the door for me and I was entering the world of The Narrow Gate Theater. "I will show you around?" John said.

The place was huge with very high ceilings, long wooden staircases; and paintings were everywhere. The paintings were interactive. For instance, there was a painting showing the parting of the Red Sea, but the waves were moving. The waves were not overflowing onto our family hardwood floors, but continually moving in circular patterns as the Israelites were walking alongside the high wall of moving waves. It was not a *cheesy* automatic loop either. It seemed to *show story* as a kind of Bible without words. It felt like chapters were demonstrating Bible stories and drawing me into its scene. I did not hear audible dialogue in the paintings, but my mind had pronounced thoughts showing the faith and the struggle of Israelites crossing the Red Sea.

The place was also a house and not an institutional building. As big as it was, it felt small too. Throughout the house were various sounds and words being spoken and songs were being sung. The music was live, but I couldn't see any musicians or choir. I then heard a beautiful male voice singing with a baritone resonance the words,

"Sing for joy, O heavens, and exult, O earth, break forth, O mountains, into singing! For the Lord has comforted His people."

"David, meet Isaiah," said John. Isaiah was now walking out the door to the room that had his name above its door. "Hello sir, you have a beautiful voice," I muttered not knowing exactly what was expected of me. It was the clearest and most penetrating voice I had ever heard. No, better yet, the most finite voice I had ever experienced. The notes from your song were a resounding wave of presence. A presence of something pure and cleansing." "Thank you, kind sir," said Isaiah.

He had the eyes of a small boy, say five years old. His body however was old, but very strong. I wondered if he walked 40 miles a day or at least 4 miles a day as there is not time for 40 miles, I chuckled to myself. Again his eyes were sage-like and his smile disarming. He was taking what I would call a great emotional risk in showing me, a stranger so much vulnerability.

"I love what you are singing," I replied. "The sound, the voice, it's, well, it's like nothing I have ever heard. You are speaking and singing at the same time. It's like, it makes me want to sing and I can't sing a note without going off key. Your words are like spoken jewels and, well for me someone who cannot sing, I feel I can sing along."

I was surprised I showed so much feeling. *He probably thinks I'm a moron.* I cringed hoping I kept a poker face.

"Yes Davey, sing along with me." As Isaiah shared, his eyes were looking into mine and his eyes were saying, "Welcome Davey. We like you." I was about to say I don't sing ... I don't know the words... I... ahh. Then I found myself in duet with Isaiah singing, 'Sing a new song to the Lord! Sing His praises from the ends of the earth.'"

We sang something like this over and again with slight changes here and there. I noticed that I was not the least bit *self-conscious*. I also noticed what I had just realized. I was generally not aware that I was *generally self-conscious*. I wondered how did I know the words to the songs we sang? My voice sounded really good, too. Mostly, I had a good time just jamming with some guy named Isaiah. 'Isaiah?'

"Isaiah is one of our singers. Most things he says are in song," John enthused.

"Is he practicing his lines?" I asked.

"Oh yes David. He is constantly developing music and song while practicing his lines."

"Is he practicing for a new show?" I asked.

"Yes David, he is always practicing. He never performs - he just practices."

"Does it ever get monotonous, you know, the same old same old?" I asked.

"No never. He never sings exactly the same way either. Each note, each word, is an end, in and of itself. Each song is new, familiar too and friendly. Only the words never change."

"Oh how sad. It happens once and then gone."

"Yes Davey." John added, "Life is so unique. Our words can never be said exactly as before. That's why it is so important to be careful in what we say, but not so careful that we fail to share love."

I then thought of Myriam. I was guilty of the latter more than the former. On second thought, I thought to myself, "I was guilty of both." I was too careful with words and also careless with words.

When I first entered the building from outside I had walked through a *narrow door*. I could never have imagined the wide space that opened up from the narrow entrance. This place was spacious yet delicate. There was a huge downstairs and four corridors leading into four wide stairways about sixty feet high. I decided to walk up the north stairway. When I came to the top, I could hear what sounded like scene study among actors. In the first room to my right in the hallway about 20 feet wide I saw the words on the door: Zephaniah and King David.

I knocked on the door only to see John motion with his left hand for me to just walk in. John put his right index finger to his mouth for me to kind of tiptoe into the room.

King David was speaking; I knew this because John was mouthing the words "King David" to me. "Create in me a clean heart, O God, and renew a steadfast spirit within me."

Then Zephaniah with his right arm around King David, again John mouthing his name "The Lord your God is with you, He is mighty to save, He will take great delight in you, He will quiet you with His love, He will rejoice over you with singing."

Again I heard the singing voice and the spoken word as one voice and one song. The house was filled with the presence of gentleness and power. It was a high volume of sound clarity, and yet with a quietness of silent silence as I never before knew. I was quieted.

I heard myself whisper in my heart, "He will rejoice over you with singing. He will quiet you with His love." I was being quieted. Yes, that's what it was. I now had a *quiet inside me* as never before.

John then asked, "Are you ready for Luke?" John suddenly broke into a huge smile. I was surprised to see John smile so broadly. Always pleasant and serious, but now suddenly he was beginning to laugh. Walking down the corridor I could now hear another voice and the words, "... and they all heard one another declare the wonderful things of God in their own tongue."

"What does this mean?"

And then I heard a huge outburst of laughter from someone and somewhere else. We walked to the end of the corridor and there were no more doors but an open space into a theater. John pointing ahead was then saying to me, "The other voice is Luke's voice."

John then broke out into laughing. John shouted out to Luke

"Yeshua Adonai," and Luke shouted back to John, "Jesu Christo," and John then back at Luke, who was now falling over with laughter,

"Jesus is Lord," only to have John now holding tightly so he would not fall, too, from loss of balance, holding onto Luke saying, "Joshie baby Messiach."

My observation was that they just said, "Jesus is Lord" In English, Spanish, and Hebrew. *Tongues in my estimation referred to human languages.* In this case, all being understood and all referring to Jesus' place in their lives as Lord for all of them. The same tongue meant the same language. I also figured *language* from their presentation was more than cognizant language but real communication with feelings happening. The feelings expressed were a language too giving nuance to the spoken language.

"We don't have the same tongue." Mine is better than yours, shouted Luke. "That's why you never have anything important to say," said John, and they both laughed some more.

Then Luke announced, as if making a campaign speech to a group of financial supporters.

"You are right. We don't have the same tongue because yours is wrong - mine is right" John then said, "No your tongue is not right - it's left!" Now they both lost all composure, laughing and rolling around the floor doing somersaults.

Then, as suddenly as they began their laughing dialogue, they now were quiet and, exceedingly happy. They hugged each other. They were all smiles as they looked up, and Luke shouted across the theater, "Hello David. I have been waiting to see you, speak with you, and..." He then suddenly broke into laughter and forcing some words from his mouth, "Improv with you." Luke then rolled out and did another somersault.

After getting these words out and finishing his sentence, Luke broke out into more joyful sounds without intelligible words and groans that only caused more laughter. Was he now praying in tongues? I had one actor friend, who had some experience in Christianity, who mentioned to me the distinction of praying in tongues as opposed to speaking in tongues. Luke was all smiles as he walked forward with his hand out to shake mine. "How are you Davey?"

David: "Hello sir. Great show and very funny. I like it."

Luke: "Oh we were just hearing from God from one another. It makes us exceedingly happy. It's fun to be happy. 'They heard from one another declaring the wonderful things of God in their own tongue.' Those words are right from The Script. This in one sentence describes God interacting among mankind and people interacting with Him. It's a perfect picture of His bride, which is His church. This is the Narrow Gate Theater. God is happy and funny."

David: "I never thought of God as either."

Luke: "Well let me assure you, He is both. The better you know Him the more you laugh, cry, mourn, and dance. I love my job. We get to change preconceived notions that our audience has. Come to think we change too as we do the play. We hate work around here because we love play. That's why they call it play. It's a beautiful day isn't it?"

David: "Oh yes, a really nice day."

John: "See you later gentlemen. I will walk myself out."

19

MORE THAN A DOCTOR

Luke: "When I write I begin to understand things better. I know that must sound strange. Doing improvisation with John our director is so much like writing to me."

David: "You know I once had a director who was a counselor by career. She got me to stretch as an actor through improvisation. She went so far as to say the written lines for the part were very secondary to the act of being *very* now in the moment. How does improvisation relate to acting for you Luke?"

Luke: "Well, you see the writer in me loves improvisation because in improvisation I do not know what will come out of me next. That's what both writing and acting do. In improvisation I get to do the two as one."

David: "This same director cast me as the wig-maker in Rashomon. It's an ancient Japanese story done to a play. It's four different takes on a crime scene that each teller was actually involved in. It's serious but more for laughs too. The funniest part is the way people make themselves out to be the hero of his or her own story."

Luke: "What was the wig-makers role like?"

David: "The wig-maker is usually played by an old man, crafty, selfish but sage like too. Our director, Kathy, was not into playing age but playing what the actors bring to the script. So my character was young, angry, very bitter, and with a very negative intelligence. He spent his time around death making wigs from the scalps of dead people. His take on the crime scene was the only one that was accurate. His view, however, was cynical and without hope. I loved what I was doing in the role. I played him lonely, pathetic, needing a friend but covering his need for fellowship by wearing a mask of knowledge, anger, and bitterness."

Luke: "How long a run did you have? Sounds like a fantastic characterization."

David: "I quit about two weeks before we opened. If I am wrong on the time, it may have been a week before the opening. I remember it as my *final straw* with acting. If you talked with Kathy and she said, 'David quit three days before production' I would not argue there either. The greater truth of not knowing exactly when I quit reveals how badly I feel about how far I would go in letting down my cast. I quit something I loved. I hurt the director and the cast. It was *devastating* to me. It's a strange pattern in me."

"For myself, I killed the final strain of life left in me that was fun and enjoyable. After this failure, I buried myself in work and I have not looked up or gone out to play in a long time. It wasn't the first time this happened, but it was the worst time and the last time. I, from that day on, have not worked in theater ... fifteen years ago in Hartford. I would not ever act again and do such damage to everything and everyone. With me Hartford is where things change for the worse."

Luke: "My heart goes out to you, Davey."

David: "Yes, but if I did this to you, would you still have sympathy?"

Luke: "Yes, but if you did it to me I would chase you down to get to the root of your issue. I would confront and care-front you too."

David: "What got me going on about this was watching you and Mr.

Stephens go on - reminding me of my best time in improvisation. I was not acting in that role as wig-maker but having fun as never before. The wig-maker was the *greatest part I never had*. My life is a lot like that too. The life *I could have had*."

"Listen, this is depressing me. This is not your problem but I have to go now. I mean, you folks shield the noise of the world really well here, but I'd rather have the noise - it keeps the feelings in check, if you know what I mean. The improv back with Kathy was too much for me too, and you folks are, well this is crazy theater. I mean you are very nice, really nice, but please let me go now, okay? *Please!*"

Luke: "David, let's change the subject for just a little while, okay? There are a lot of things I could say to you, but let's hold it in check for now. One thing I will say about you is I like that you're making a little time for us and with us too. It's good to have a change of pace for a few hours. Isn't it? Right? Besides, I have a ticket for you to see *Paul In Prison*. The show starts in about thirty minutes from now."

David: "Yes. I saw the marquee next to the Narrow Gate Theater Company. It helped to draw me in. Did you know that John invited me too!"

"Okay," I said somewhat tentatively "I will stay. Do you want me to wait outside?"

Luke: "No, absolutely not. You remind me of me in many ways. It took me many years to figure what I was about. I had varying abilities, but did not necessarily connect one ability to the other. Most people know me as a doctor but I see myself more as a journalist and as a news gatherer. I always had a knack for news coupled with a love for how the human body works. I still do. It was my medical ability that got me out into Galilee. I was a proselyte in Rome.

What that means is I was a gentile or non-Jew who wanted to be Jewish. I loved the whole history of Jewish people. So this love of history and keeping track of news events dovetailed with my medical background. You see I was in Galilee when Jesus was beginning His ministry there. I went to these events, as you may call them. I however did not attend these as a believer, but as an informer for the Pharisees. They wanted facts, information, and they paid me well as a doctor for their circle of Pharisees that resided in the Galilee region."

"Before I go into my story of hope, change and redemption, I just want to pause here to say I had varying abilities. I discovered I really am an actor. I am an actor in that my essence has more than one entity. I became an actor through living life. I played various roles just to get by in life. My acting never was *performance* based but *function* based. In our acting company Narrow Gate Theater, we teach our actors to not be self-conscious and also to let go. We call it *Holy-Wood not Hollywood*. We say, 'Do for others and not for yourself.' We say travel narrow, not broad, travel light and avoid the heavy."

David: "So I see. I came looking for broad and you give me the narrow. That's kind of funny don't you think?"

Luke: "Yes its very funny. Laughing helps us to keep focus on what is important."

David: "All the good teachers I ever had in theater tell us to be focused. They say that acting is not a philosophical exercise but the ability to focus in and do. Being specific is the key to the door of stage. This narrowness you refer to is really an attribute for life isn't it? Anyway I just wanted you to know the parallel is very compelling to me. We call what you are doing the inner monologue. Do you call it that too? It is as I explained to Mr. Stephens what Paul Harvey does when he says *The Rest of The Story.*"

Luke: "Thanks Davey I must admit I love to share my backstory and you are such a good listener. Yes, so much of Jesus teaching is inner monologue for life itself. I spent a lot of time, on my own, as a child. I was a dreamer. We were a wealthy Roman family and I was witness to Rome's cruelty as a conquering nation. My parents were familiar with the Jewish captivity by Romans in the Judean region of Rome's empire. My father was a doctor and he treated Pharisees in Rome. He saw my fascination with Judaism, as he was an educated man. My father saw nothing of value in Roman religion. He would often say, "Rome is great, but not for its understanding of divine authority. Greek culture would be an improvement for Rome, and the Jews, well, they made good clients for our medical practice. That was my father's take on Rome. So as a young adult I became a proselyte and of course, a doctor. Why not? There would always be a need for a doctor. The ability to make a living is always a factor, but my heart was in culture. I could go on for days analyzing people. The way they walked or spoke. I saw this through the eye of a medical man and as an enthusiast of culture. What I loved most in Rome were the different kinds of nationalities and customs in our city. It was so multi-cultural that, I could not have known this at the time, but I was becoming a *life actor*. Not a performer mind you, but a conversationalist and good listener."

David: "I have used the term *life actor* among the Woodstock crowd. I had never heard this term from any except from us. The term *Life Acting In Woodstock* was a real trend in Woodstock for a time. We created our own little media by having the locals share their backstory for the newspaper Myriam and I edited the Woodstock Wood Journal."

Luke: "Yes, that's good Davey. Was it fun doing life acting?"

David: "Yes it was. More than fun if that were possible, it was fascinating. I remember the bar restaurant in Mt. Tremper near Woodstock. We did improvisation with the attendees on Sunday nights. I remember once when our show *was over* they gave us a standing ovation. What was amazing is that we were all '*in character*' with the people there. Each of us was playing different parts. It was not as if we were doing a show on a stage, but simply relating with them. We did characterization with those at the bar at their tables. They were in *the play* too. *They got it and* we pulled it off."

"We reached audience and actor as one. We all knew we entered a very special play. Again, we were at play and also doing a play."

"We were the *Woodstock Life Actors* and those in attendance were part of the cast. Myriam was my partner and our daughter Sarah got involved too. We were divorced but wanting to get back together. It was a personal renewal of hope for us. *Life Acting In Woodstock* was one of those rare moments where the right brain met the left. In its place was something *spiritual* and *holy*? I do not know what that was or is, only that I miss it."

"I tell you Luke, it was way beyond any realm known to me. If I knew how to get to that place I would go back and never leave. If I ever got back to that place Luke, I would never want to return to the life I have now. My problem as leader of that movement was that I did not know how to lead because I was sure how I got there."

My hands were now in Luke's hands holding tightly over the rustic table near the stage of the theater. I was not aware of my need for Luke's physical presence but I felt the warmth of his hand in mine.

Luke: "I want to go to that place with you Davey with all my heart I want to."

David: "It was nice of you to say that Luke. Life Acting days were so profound I did not know who to give credit to. I only knew it was full of imagination. It was about doing *Woodstock State Of Mind*

Concerts. It was also Myriam and I as editors of the back-page of the local newspaper. We were facilitating people to write articles for us who had never written before. We covered the New York Yankees at Yankee Stadium too. I did regular reporting of games and Myriam was the photographer. I didn't think of it at the time but we interviewed many future Hall Of Fame ball players. Of course in Woodstock they always want a leader that they can eventually reject. I became that leader for a time. I was a reluctant, but obliging leader. They called me a guru and I rejected that. As open-minded as I was, I was innately too conservative to accept that designation. In other words if I became a guru, I would have to '*act*' all the time to keep up that persona. I was, after all, a life actor liberating people to be yourself. I was not going to be their idea of Buddha or hip capitalist, or '*the artist*.'"

Luke: "Yes, it's hard enough trying to be one who doesn't know who he is, and then having to be someone else's idea of *one who doesn't know who he is*."

David: "I like that Luke. Sounds like you would fit right in with the Woodstock search for personal identity, yet one who could actually take others to the *Promised Land*. There was for me something gentle there that I cannot find anywhere today."

I pondered this as I was now in that *dream state* that the witches hated about me. I *was suddenly adrift in conversation*. My mind was in the Catskills again as my conversation with Luke was engaging me with life as exciting and creative. Now with Woodstock in my mind I was remembering those Woodstock days as my getting back into a new kind of synagogue. The Zum Gali Gali's of Rabbi Fishberg were gone and replaced with a *Woodstock State Of Mind*.

The happiest days of my life were happening all over again. I was simply being happy. However even in those *good days,* I went into escape mode. What was most needed in my healing was not dealt with. I smiled a lot that summer of my life, more than one summer, but oh so short a time. I smiled until the fall. The fall I fell. Myriam and Sarah left me again in October of 1981 because I left them. That fall of 1981 was also when I did and quit *Rashomon*.

This was the *fall* where I knew I had something that I could not keep. It was beyond my willingness to stretch emotionally to recognize what I lacked. I did not know how to keep what I had because I did not know how I got it in the first place. I only knew that I wanted it back. Myriam and I were back together in Woodstock, and our daughter Sarah saw us together. We were all three making healthy choices in love.

When the Life Acting Company disbanded I got depressed. It forced me to deal with things that *activity* was preventing me from dealing with. I wanted the Zum Gali Gali's, but the only place I knew for them was in the past. The summer and fall of 1981 was the end of the Cohen family re-gathering. I was unable to re-invent myself. *Time machines don't work if you make the same mistakes.*

Facts were hard for me to deal with especially when the tragedy of my lost marriage unraveled. That which was missing in Life Acting is what was missing in my marriage. I still did not know what that was, so I was unable to keep it. What I was sure of is I still did not have it. I thought of Scarlett O'Hara in *Gone With The Wind*. She was not in touch with who she was either.

Suddenly I found myself increasingly tired. I thought maybe I had dozed off into sleep. How long that sleep was, was relative I suppose. It could have been one second or one hour. Things here at Narrow Gate were on a different time zone, to say the very least.

I was now in a Myriam state of mind. I was back at our apartment in Brookline near Boston. We were just married. I was 20 and she was 20 also. We were in love. We said we both, as 20-year-olds, had

20-20 vision. We loved each other. As the old song says, "I only have eyes for you." We often took long walks holding hands. Our favorite walk was along the Charles River. Our favorite activity was looking into one another's eyes. That's when I wrote the poem of my love *Those Lips Those Eyes*.

Myriam saved me from the sexual revolution of the late 60s and 70s. We did it right by getting married too. The pressure to perform sexually among strangers was very real and I was a guy. Imagine how much more it was for a woman. We were faithful to each other and wanted no one else and nothing else. We were married the day the United States of America landed on the moon.

This was the same summer of the famous Woodstock Music Festival. We noted the significance of the dates. It was another reason for seeing a love connection from a source greater than us. What that source was, was not important. All that mattered was we were in love and *would be together forever*.

All this re-connection to *Life Acting In Woodstock* got me back to a more lovely time only to remind me it was no longer happening in my time. "This is the second time today," I thought to myself, "that I am in touch with a peace and then *the peace is* racked with torment."

"David are you alright?" said Luke.

"Yes," I said. "I hope you do not think me rude nodding off like that."

"No," said Luke. "It was only a moment, a long blink of an eye. Are you alright? You suddenly seem so sad."

"Yes and no," I said. "Please let's get back to you and the Galilee region. I so love to learn history from a first person perspective."

"Yes," said Luke.

Luke: "History in the first person is the way to make history personal, and prophetic too. Increasingly we at Narrow Gate have observed that people value information and head-knowledge much more than heart knowledge. Much of Bible teaching today, for instance, is from the outside in. One is taught to seek the answer without experiencing the life of the answer. Think of this: E= mc squared. This is Einstein's theory of relativity. Everyone knows this is true, however how many who quote this have any idea of what that means? This is how Bible knowledge is generally taught. We refer to this as *'Objective Learning Disorder'* or *'OLD.'* We have meetings for people overcoming *OLD.*"

David: "You are joking about OLD meetings aren't you?"

Luke: "Well sort of. Not officially anyway."

David: "It wasn't until I took Acting One in college that learning became interesting to me. I could now experience history in the first person. I literally was able to act my way through history, literature, poetry, even political science. I could be subjective. I got to personally interact with information and its people. Learning was finally no longer dry. It's the opposite of OLD. My learning style became more personal and subjective. It was what I needed to learn in order to make learning interesting. Finally in college I became a good student. It all came into being by taking Acting 1."

Luke: "You bring up a great point. The Bible is prophecy and historical fact at the same time. It's full of imagination that is not a fantasy. In Bible time, one-time zone fits all if you will. Eternity is time not philosophy. The Bible is a He and not an it. The Bible is a book that is a live theater. The Bible is *Immanuel* or God with us. The Bible is not the manual? The Bible is so much more than a map-guide. The Bible is an ongoing journey alongside its Author. He causes fellowship with others along the way because He the Author loves people."

I started to get hopeful again. What Luke said was exciting to me, but every time I get hopeful at Narrow Gate Theater I am forced to face reality and it makes me miserable.

David: "Luke, please tell me about Galilee."

Luke: "All right, I will."

"In the Galilee I was the Pharisees medical man. I headed up a team of physicians. My passion and reason for accepting this assignment was to continue learning Judaism as a proselyte. What I could not predict was that my greatest assignment as a student was being a news reporter. I reported to the Pharisees any information I could gather regarding the whereabouts of Jesus of Nazareth."

"For instance, there were several big meetings in Galilee. You read of 5000 men in attendance. Well then, what about women and children that also were present. There was much joy and spontaneous healings among families. We should not ever minimize the healings and the joy of just being there. Things just happened in ways that brought people together. I liked Jesus teaching, too. I reminded myself that He was also a Jew."

"Part of my conversion into Judaism was to understand different expressions of Judaism. He made strong statements about love, real truth, and real justice. He definitely was not a scribe or Pharisee. His authority was in His humility, and in His humility was sheer boldness. It's not as if His preaching changed me, but it did change my view of Him."

"I was a non-believer in this Jesus movement. I reported to the Pharisees, my employers as a physician and also my mentors into Judaism. So when I became acquainted with Judas it was not as if I was linking up with a traitor. Judas was easier to talk to. First he was wealthier and more educated than the other disciples. He was more as we were socially than the other disciples. He had lots of mutual contacts in Rome too. He had the feel of a Pharisee about him. My perspective was that Judas was, as one of Jesus followers, my *deep throat* informer as a reporter for the Pharisees. I say *deep throat* from the Watergate investigation you as a contemporary man would know about. Deep Throat was in the Watergate investigation the *informer* into President Nixon's activities as Judas was our informer on Jesus activities. He was the guy who cared enough about his movement to get the truth out *or so I thought*. He was also a good interview."

"I saw Judas as a high ranking believer. Had I been a believer in those days prior to my own change, I might have clearly seen Judas as a traitor. Judas acted as Jesus' public relations man. He was very concerned that Jesus was failing to see the real enemy was Rome. Judas, tended to see all Jews though diverse, as having the same goals. Jesus was, in his mind, the most powerful of all Jews, but not united with the whole of Judaism."

"It's almost as if Judas was saying there is no real sin among God's chosen so let's defeat Rome. This way all of Judaism can rule and reign. Judas saw Jesus as not being a team player but Caiaphas of the Sadducees, the priests, and the Pharisees as God's champions. Through Judas, I knew events before they occurred and I was there a kind of: *Luke, Reporting To You Live At Mt. Beatitudes*."

"It all changed for me. Let me qualify this. It changed for us all, in one way or the other, on the day He rode the donkey into Jerusalem. It was the last week of Jesus life."
"His charisma was electric. Such a simple gesture to ride in on an untamed, now suddenly tamed donkey. The entire city was stilled by the simplicity of true power and the child-likeness of its King. They put palm branches on the ground. Their faith was not in a

concept in these moments nor was it didactic. It was genuine. It was now! '*Hosanna*! *Salvation Now We Pray*.'"

"Remember, I was a student of Judaism. I now saw the missing link for God's chosen. It was the Messiah. It was Yeshua. It was Jesus of Nazareth. '*I dare not say these thoughts to the Pharisees*,' I thought to myself. I then realized I was being trained into Judaism much like that of Jonah. That is, to know *about God but not to know Him*. On this day I finally 'got it' that Jesus was different from all of us whether Jew or gentile."

"As I said, the entry into Jerusalem that first day of that final week was everyone's turning point. For the Pharisees I was no longer in their minds primarily their physician, nor their student but one now called on to hate Jesus. I was to report this news from their perspective until the crisis was completed."

"Jesus turning over the money changers tables was very significant. This was the ultimate in money and religion as one. Pharisees loved money and they loved control. Money and control were one and the same power. For Jesus to show such passion and authority against their power was the final straw."

"Jesus could not live but He was loved by the crowds. What if Judaism changed from the Judaism of the Sanhedrin into Jesus' Judaism? Judas was shocked. Jesus did not come to save Judaism, but to destroy it. To be clear here, He came to destroy the system Judaism had become. I saw this, and though I had no more conversation with Judas I now saw he had been Jesus' betrayer for quite some time."

"In Judas, I see the same with many today. People who have a preconceived view of God. No matter what the evidence one maintains disbelief sometimes disguised as belief. Judas knew of Jesus goodness. He did finally have guilt about getting paid for his betrayal, but guilt in itself is not change. Judas had remorse but did not have repentance. He would not really change."

"Judas was idealistic and God's mission was *not an ideal but a real*. Idealism always ends in legalism, and legalism is the spirit of lawlessness craving power. The Bible refers to Judas and the antichrist as *'the son of perdition.'* I then remembered, when Jesus said these words, 'My body is real food and My blood real drink.' These words are too subjective for outer-based thinking. Objective Learning Disorder *OLD* will not grasp this. This is the deadly side of *OLD*. Judas way of processing belief fosters *unbelief* in those who think they believe. That was Judas' problem - he was attempting to *'think'* his way into belief."

"I was out and about the streets of the city on the night of His trial. I was interviewing at random all kinds of people in the streets. All of them Jews, come to think of it. These were the ones who saw the miracle of God's Presence on that palm day. These same people were now very critical of Jesus. Why? Did Jesus change? More to the point, why did *we the people* change against Him?"

"Then it hit me. It was the rulers. It was their media of information control that was controlling people. The only way around this skewed information power was to make personal *the new revelation*. The revelation I saw when Jesus was on the donkey. We sometimes call this *Donkey Day* and the revelation that Jesus was and is God's Messiah. This revelation was the only way to protect my heart from disbelief and the spirit of mendacity from the media's rebellion."

"I was amazed how all had forgotten Him from just days before. Palm day was real. The people rejoiced with Him, yet on this dark night no one believed anymore. My questions became more of a plea for all to know what was really happening. I wanted to show that the power brokers were controlling information. They were illusionists doing tricks before our eyes. My journalistic approach now was editorials and street preaching designed to wake people up to the mainstream media's biased against Jesus. This same Jesus they adored one or two days before. I was alone."

"The other observation was that all those I spoke to were now very unhappy. On that first day of the week, on *donkey day*, they were happy. Today in their complaint of Jesus' failures, there was unhappiness. An unhappiness not due to Jesus but due to changed expectations induced by the Pharisees and the Sanhedrin. The only 'sanctification' from the 'news media' was to *eat* the Word of God. *OLD* does not eat the food but only looks at the menu. It will not eat real food."

"We at Narrow Gate interpret this as *internalizing* the Word. In that moment of revelation, I hated working for the media I was with. The Sanhedrin were controlling the news and getting weak people to agree. All are weak."

"Being weak, I thought to myself, was not justification for the evil of hating this just Man. Ironically, if Jesus was the public relations Messiah they wanted, He would not be the Messiah. Of course they did not want The Messiah but only for him to be the *rescuer* who never comes. I ask myself has it changed in today's eschatology regarding His second coming?"

David:	"What is eschatology?"
Luke:	"It involves the end of things."
David:	"Funny how when you are checking out at a supermarket one can see on the magazine racks all kinds of end of the world notices like in *The Tabloids*."
Luke:	"Yes, but you won't hear it mentioned in most churches."
David:	"That seems odd. Just from a story point of view I would think the

Scripts version of the apocalypse would be better entertainment than the apocalypse theater I see in film or on TV."

Luke: "The Script and the church are not the same. The church is human the Script- Bible is Divine."

David: "I like a good script."

Luke: "The Script we are showing you here at Narrow Gate Theater is perfect, inspired, and written so to be acted upon by its reader. God wrote it so we can act it into our lives."

David: "I am all ears."

Luke: "Be careful in today's time to see where people are coming from when one does not believe in Jesus' soon return to planet earth. The question is less theological than one might think. The better question is: Does this mindset show that Jesus is not welcomed back? - A kind of *we like things as they are* mentality. Jesus' main theology on His second coming is '*Watch*' or '*Wake up.*' The *watcher wants Him*. Does the one who does not watch or want to *wake up* want Him back? Some presume to be awake because they espouse a theology. God seeks a practice not a theory. 'He who hears these words of Mine and acts upon them builds his house upon the rock.' Jesus the Bread of Life broke the mold. People love the mold. Would you eat bread that had mold?"

David: "No!"

Luke: "I had to leave Satan's media. I now had to leave his airwaves of mendacious lies and I had to report truth. I was now certain Jesus would die this very night if the Sanhedrin had its way. The bulk of my interviews were now held during the trial of Jesus. The final media being the famous words of Pontius Pilate to the crowds Do you want me to release for you Jesus Christ or Jesus Barabbas? The control on the crowds coming from the Pharisaic order was intimidating and discouraging at the same time."

"Barabbas," the crowds roared.

"Israel as a nation was sealing its destiny. Jesus warned them all, 'Not one stone (of the temple) will remain; everyone will fall to the ground.' If you go to Israel today, you can see exactly what history records. The temple was destroyed and the 1st century AD stones to this temple are on the ground in Jerusalem just as He said. Prophecy again becoming history. The nation of Israel is still very flawed, yet it is being restored in these last days. It's right out of Ezekiel's dry bones coming together bone by bone. It's another example of prophecy becoming history in news of our day. Ezekiel's dry bones can apply to any who read and receive to be restored. It's yet another way for history and prophesy to meet."

"After I saw from a distance Jesus on the cross, my interviewing of others was over. I was not asking questions anymore, as I did not need to ask questions to know the truth. I no longer needed the help of people to have a point of view. Public opinion was no longer what influenced me. Now a preacher in the streets of Jerusalem I was magnet to metal being drawn into the *good news*. I now shared this without asking permission from people. Overnight I switched medias. I remembered Isaiah words as I grieved, 'He was despised and rejected by men, a man of sorrows and acquainted with grief, like one from whom men hide their faces, so He was despised and we esteemed Him not.' I was grieving God's pain of rejection. The only one not affected by public opinion and new trends was assassinated. Jesus was the only one who was not sitting on the throne of selfishness. His death was the ultimate of *inside skin*. He was identifying with the captives."

"He who was without sin became sin. The Bible as *the Script* is live theater because its theater is always *happening now*. Today and tomorrow, too. Words on a page are being lived out and acted out in the moment. You and I are invited into to participate in this play."

"'*Enter through the narrow gate*' is where less is more. One has to be small to fit through. It's not coincidental that those that fit through are called 'the children of God.' The Script gives insight that its purpose is to *childrenize* the receiver of its Words. This gives new and permanent insight into what acting really is. Its acts of faith I speak of. David you can have what you had in Woodstock - only much better and forever."

"We can live many years off one '*God moment*.' This is how eternity and time meet. The incarnation of God in Jesus' birth is the moment that began this way of life. This very moment and thought in '*captive obedience*.'"

"Through The Holy Spirit, Jesus incarnates again through those whom He lives life through. That's how we get the word '*Christian*'. At Narrow Gate we call this *incarnational acting*."

David: *Luke was appealing to my actors sense. It was a lot like my one on one with Martha and Myriam in Mount Vernon Virginia. It's a much better way to learn, but Luke was relating this to God as happening now. Just like theater does. He even brings in current events with Israel being restored. Prior to my lifetime Israel was not a nation and for thousands of years too. I was experiencing God and history relating as one?*

Luke continued…

"These transition days of Jesus were my transition days, too. My transformation. Transformation lives today in the pages of the Bible and heard in the life of Narrow Gate Theater. It yours too, David, if you want this. He is happening now just as when He happened in history 2000 years ago. History and prophecy are in one time zone in the Bible. Get your news personalized from God and into your heart. 'Without prophetic revelation My people show no restraint.'"

David: *Luke is a journalist but he gets into it like an actor.*

Luke continued...

"I knew well the location of the upper room where the disciples met. I was with them when we met after the crucifixion. Ironically the whole Sanhedrin was scattered with fear about Jesus return. He of course was already dead and yet they knew it was far from over. 'What if He did rise from the dead? What if they steal the body?' They did not fear that they had murdered an innocent man, but *'how will we explain this to the public?'*"

"Another irony is that it was the disciples who did not believe that Jesus might rise from the dead. They as a group had no hope even though Jesus spoke often to them often of His rising from the dead. They were particularly gloomy. *They did love Him but* in their grief they lost hope. How can Life itself be dead?"

"It was Mary Magdalene who took her grief to another level. It's not that she was searching for a risen savior, but that even in His death there was an obedience and a kind of hope. She came to care for the dead body. Jesus rewarded her child-like faith by appearing to her first. She saw and believed."

"By this time the disciples recognized me as one of them. Because I was not close to Jesus until that very last week, I did not carry their heavy weight of burden. I was soon like Mary Magdalene in belief that He was alive. I was also among the Pharisees who ironically feared He might somehow rise from the dead. I was now, unlike the Pharisees, believing as a believer. Mary's example was filling my cup of belief. In fact, my cup was over-running with hope. I believed

Mary really saw Jesus! Cleopas and his wife shared also that they had walked with Him along the road to Emmaus. They shared and I listened with belief."

"Later that night He appeared to us all. In shock, awe, and hope we each celebrated. What was stolen was now returned to us, and He breathed out His Holy Spirit over each of us. *'Receive the Holy Spirit,'* He said over and again."

"Here I was among the particular Jews who were despised by Jewish authorities. I, myself not a Jew, yet somehow was no longer what I was. I was something we later referred to as *'one new man.'*"

"With this new humanity I was being welcomed in my new found faith with new found friends and family. When I later began writing my report of these things I am sharing with you, I never lost sight of this new family connection. It was more than a Jewish thing. For those who would believe it was not just the completion of Judaism but the completion for all humanity."

David: *I then suddenly remembered Myriam's words when she left for Jerusalem. She said she was a completed Jew.* How strange, all these years between Luke and Myriam, yet they have the same history. Luke a gentile and Myriam a Jew, both the *one new man and woman*. Prophecy and history as one. Suddenly too, I was feeling the timelessness of eternity and time as *One Time*. Myriam, my daughter Sarah, and Luke were having a common experience in the same place 2000 years apart. Today Myriam tells me stories from the sights of the Israel that Luke lived in. Myriam and Luke were so much the same. Time and eternity are becoming one to me here at Narrow Gate through a similar story in different historic times. *God's Time* I pondered? My mind was spinning, but spinning upward. Luke's storytelling was so encompassing. *Was his belief spilling over to me? This actor man is a superior performer and I am really engaged with his presentation.*

Luke: "When He suddenly appeared to us and breathed on us, it all changed for us. 'Receive the Holy Spirit.' He spoke in Hebrew the *Ruach* Ha Kodesh or literally Breath The Holy. We each personally, and all of us as one, received the Holy Spirit. This was the same day He rose from the dead. It was the Jewish Feast Of First fruits."

"Later that week Thomas had his moment. Thomas is known over time as the '*doubter*' because of not being there when we received the Holy Spirit. He wanted tangible truth and wanted to see the nail prints. A greater truth of Thomas however, was how he asked for the correct thing. He wanted authenticity and not an apparition of faith. He wanted proof of His death so he could believe in the resurrection. When Thomas saw and believed, he spoke the deepest truth we all needed to hear, '*My Lord and my God.*' He joined the powerful fellowship of the believer. Yes! Jesus is God!"

"I do not know if you know this David, but the prophetic writings were completed and are now referred to as the New Testament. I wrote about 30% of its entirety. Amazing that I, an outsider, would be called this way. After salvation my curiosity for people grew in love and *inside skin* empathy. I loved listening and accumulating what the disciples told me of Jesus." "It's ironic how people today, especially in this technological day, spend time and mountains of money to gain what they can have free of charge. It comes by connecting God's frequency and meeting Him where He spends His time. The Good News Channel happens when and where this happens. It's beyond technology. It is *wherever He happens*. Millions of dollars are wasted that do not connect with heaven at all. Some one person, on a street meeting and greeting in His Name can reach more than 10,000 attendees seeing a *show about God*. The delivery of His message and the content of His message need be the same. You cannot have one without the other."

David: "I watch these television shows as I surf cable TV. Sometimes I see what I call faith Christian shows. They often seem to be not what I get from Myriam's take on her faith. When Myriam and Sarah share faith it's all about their *journey*. When Myriam shares it's like eating *real food* versus a *cardboard menu* with nice pictures. I have never been an insider on these things just an observer."

Luke: "With the good news what's inside the envelope and what's outside are one and the same. There is a hard truth element to the good news. That's why the outside envelope and inside content cannot be two different things. You cannot have a worldly package and a heavenly message or its like saying 'the ends justifies the means' or vice versa. His way and His message are one and the same person. I am not saying all cultures are the same, but the gospel is the same. Just as He is the same. Humans share the same humanity. It's amazing if you go deep with what I am saying you realize how much all humans really have in common. It's not as complicated as it is made out to be. The gospel fills the human need and makes it so much easier to be human. Letting Jesus be Jesus is never a trendy thing. He by being Himself relates to all times and all cultures."

David: "It's a kind of buffer against OLD objective learning disorder."

Luke: "I can see you have been with Jonah. Maybe I can make him your sponsor for our OLD meetings."

David: "That's a good one Luke. If the Script is The Bible, well you make it sound like fun. I like the way you do it. The Bible as a Script really interests me. It's playtime! And yes Jonah would make a great sponsor!"

Luke: "We like this play thing you have going on too Davey. It's very close to the heart of our cast. We are constantly in the *Play of The Script*. The *Script* says it's 'children' who inherit the kingdom of God.' Again we see the intent of the entire *Script as* children-izing all participants."

"What I see today are crowds saying, "Jesus I love" you but we want to help you with what you stand for. This thinking is not love but children losing their childhood."

"You would think it would get old. Every day I mourn and I grieve over today's hypocrisy. On the other hand, every day I rejoice that the only media that is alive and true is what we have. He is True Good News in a world of lies, and lying to ourselves. There is no other Truth Davey, but what you learn here you can bring to where you live. Just learn as you share and never lose the joy of serving."

"No one speaks of the Holy Spirit as much I do. I assume that was God's way of distributing His words by having me anchored in the Holy Spirit in a special way. The whole script is written by the Holy Spirit. On the other hand, the way I am I could not write any other way. By speaking Himself through my uniqueness I see His uniqueness."

"The only Luke you meet is in The Bible Script. People die but God lives now. This conversation we now have is not necromancy, but God is alive and is now improvising through me to you. Sometimes when one reads the Bible his mind goes to places that are personal to him. That's what's happening to you this very moment. Eternity is not a philosophy about time. It's real time and it's Gods time."

David: "Jonah says it's like God playing you instead of you trying to *play God*. What a good way to hold your characterizations. I have never seen such concentration in actors as I do here."

Luke: "Narrow Gate Theater is a revelation that the Bible is God here and now through the characters in His Book. What's more is He pre-casts you before the foundation of the world. The key is to *want to show up*. His casts are by design meant to be a revelation of His character. History is not eternal. History happens once Bible Time is always here. Just jump into its Script. It's a river. It's a wet you may not ever want to leave. We sometimes call this 'the water of the Word.'"

David: "Thanks Luke. I so appreciate that you want me. What a story and interesting life you have had. You really get it about Life Acting. I wish I had you back in Woodstock. It's the way you integrate life and the importance of acting. You probably could have saved it from falling apart."

Luke: "It's more like I am putting it back together for you so you can lead it up again."

David: "No you can do it and I can join you?"

Luke: "Let's hold off on plans for now but thanks for wanting me in. I want to give you some of my notes from the Acting One workshops we do. We call these *Immanuel Acting One Workshops*. We base the workshops on the day of Pentecost just 50 days after Jesus died on Passover. It's from the Book Of Acts another book God wrote through me. The Holy Spirit was poured out among believers that day. The Holy Spirit baptized over 3000 that day alone. This day is commonly referred to as the first day of His church or His bride. On this day, 'they all heard one another declare the wonderful things of God in their own tongue.' The key to the workshops is taken from these verses. We in effect we hear from God from one another. Great fellowship among the actors comes from this much like you saw from John Stephens and I when we played out those verses together."

"This is what you are invited into Davey. It's not as if all people want in, but the invitation to know - this is for all people. So many who have been cast do not show up *for the practice. On* the other hand, we find the more the audience resists Him, the more power we receive from Him. There is one thing that God cannot do and that is to fail."

I found myself sitting alone again. I of course knew I had been with Luke, but exactly when we separated I am not sure of. I remembered he said something about the featured play for this evening, Paul In Prison. 'Yes, that will happen soon,' I thought to myself.

I then began to measure myself with Luke. We seem about the same age - 45ish. Of course Luke lived a long time ago, but the Luke I just spoke with is my age. The actor I spoke with is anyway. I am not speaking with Luke (I had to remind myself). These actors hold their characterizations exceptionally well.

Nevertheless, Luke in life made a great transition for the better. We call this in theater the *character arc*. He, with all his abilities, saw himself as a life actor and as one who adapts roles into his life. He is a kind of news gatherer with a skill to keep himself employed as a physician.

He saw injustice and made things right. He became a great man. Aside from his greatness, I liked him too. He made great use of the instrument that was his life.

As a life-acting teacher, I marveled that Luke was a *great lifer*. He used what he had to be more than the norm. More than me and my norm that's for sure. I never did anything great. My Dad was always saying how he wants to be great. Well here's a guy, Luke, who was great without trying to be great. He was just taking care of what was before him. He did not destroy others by staying on a task. He was not ambitious - he was faithful.

When I was an actor in New York, I was ambitious. I wanted no one to steal my throne of great expectation. I was, in my mind, already great before I was great. In my mind, there were three words: "Me, Mine and I. This is my space and no one is able to take it from me."

That was a drill I learned at The Actors Studio. This acting drill was my mantra. Myriam and our daughter Sarah would pay the price of admission to my play. It had a long run. Its name was called *David's Ambition*. The giant monster in me was having its harvest meal.

I know it's not good to compare with others, but Luke's good choices and character change were worth taking note of. Luke met his cross-points too. Getting through each gate of challenge was worthy of my copying him.

I then thought of my choice of the word *cross point*. Is that a coincidence or is that exactly where I missed out and Luke found out. *The cross?* I knew Isaiah words too. "*He was despised and rejected by men, a man of sorrows and acquainted with grief.*" Why was that verse in the Old Testament? The rabbi and I had a talk about this once.

What did we say?

My mind went back to Myriam. We met at the Center Stage Theater in downtown Boston. They called themselves non-equity professionals. It was an alternative theatrical choice for me. I could have been in the company at Northeastern University, and Myriam too at Boston University. Without knowing one another, we both the summer of 1967 met at an audition for *The Dark Of The Moon.*

There was an eerie magic in that first production. The play is actually anti-Christian, which I didn't fully notice until just now from my moments with Luke. It dealt with magic spells. I will never forget at a Red Sox game just when the sun was setting in August 1967. I was on my first date with Myriam and I thought she was putting a spell on me. I of course was falling in love. I had no other point of reference to explain this phenomenon. Loving Myriam was of course not a spell but love. I also remember Tony Conigliaro (of the Red Sox) was hit by a pitch from the opposing team. Jack Hamilton was the pitcher that fateful night. It was very scary as a truly rising star was never the same after the crash with a baseball against his temple. A silence suddenly came upon 30,000 plus fans at Fenway. A chilling moment in such a warm romantic evening. A dark side of the moon kind of evening. A dark foreshadow of the dark magic of tarot cards I would later dabble in, that destroyed that summer of love in Boston. Life is so fragile isn't it?

Many thought Tony Conigliaro to be dead on the spot. It turns out he survived after over one year out of baseball. He almost made a complete comeback, but fell short. He died a very young man of a heart attack as a sportscaster in San Francisco.

The summer of the Impossible Dream for the Red Sox and also for us the dream come true of 67. For Myriam I was the first and only man she ever trusted. The two of us were what I call middle class homeless people. I say *homeless* not due to living in the streets. I say this due to a lack of values at home. Values that would make a person not anything more than rootless with regard to being able to foster commitment in relationships. Unless of course one changed. I of course did not understand very much of anything at the time. I only understood that I wanted to be with Myriam forever and she with me. Each of us filled the big hole of lack we each had accumulated over time and tears. I needed her to fill that desperate heart-shaped hole, and she in her way was desperate and needed me. I then heard a knock at the door.

Dennis Stephan Cole

20

PAUL IN PRISON

"It's John. I want to know if you are ready for the show tonight?"

"Yes," I said, "please come in."

John entered. He was wearing a brown tapered sport jacket and corduroy dress slacks pleated and roomy. John was a well-trimmed man about 5ft.- 11in., say about 180 pounds. I hadn't up until now going back 20 plus years, seen him dressed up in anything but a white shirt and designer looking blue jeans. As far as dress code for theatergoers goes, I had no preconceived notion of what to expect. "Just nice to see some conventionality," I thought to myself, admiring John looking the part whatever part he played.

"Well, I am ready and thanks also for the new stylish clothes "I said.

"You are with us for the weekend I hope, please," said John.

I followed John down the main hallway near the huge staircase that resembled a mansion home more than a theater building. I was feeling in my back legs behind my thighs a slight muscle pull. A *marathon* walk today?

I then saw crowds of people with tickets in their hands. I assumed it was from the box office they had just come through. What I saw in attire was something somewhat less than a shock, but almost a shock. What kept it all in the realm of normal *theater dress code*, were that people were in dress up clothes. Biblical clothes, if that's what they were, were the norm. Some were dressed contemporary too. Also, and this really got me, some were people dressed in clothes from other eras other than modern or Biblical times for that matter. 19th century top hats were common here, men in wigs kind of British looking. Others were in gowns. Women in long dresses. There was complete acceptance of one another.

"Was this an example of time and eternity at the same time? Am I meeting people from different eras of time?" I began to laugh at myself sounding so Narrow Gate Theater like. "These people are crazy and I am sounding like them," I thought to myself, and started to laugh aloud only to catch myself putting on a serious face hoping no one noticed I had seemingly laughed without a reason.

I know New York City as a fashion capital, but this was beyond fashion. These were clothes from culture groups throughout history. Each in ones own world and yet part of one another too. Also they, without being cold, all were not caring what others thought. Ironically the atmosphere waxed quite warm. I liked it. I could even feel my mouth widen with a big smile. Sometimes when I smile wide my nose will crack. I was having a *nose cracking good time.*

I entered with John. Luke was with him and he was dressed in 1st century garb. I looked behind me and tagging along was Jonah and he was wearing a loose white gown from neck to ankles. He also had some beautiful sandals that were made of what I thought was leather the likes of which I had never before seen. Jonah whispered in my ear, "I am wearing the actual gown that I wore in the belly of the big fish, only now it's clean and pressed." We bring our clothes to 54th And Broadway Cleaners." He then started laughing and suddenly laughter was happening throughout the theater. We were then all seated and we began to hear the orchestra in the pit just below the front of the stage.

A magnificent sound reverberated throughout the theater. My body was feeling as if it were an instrument, and that something or someone was playing me. I was not in the orchestra, but was somehow of the orchestra? How can that be? *It was a great way to get into the music* I thought to myself.

John then whispered into my ear, "We all are music and instruments from the Master. We are being played by God in this place," he said, and He is making music from His masterpiece. This is how God plays. He loves play."

I then said, "John, what do you mean?" John then put his finger by his mouth and pointing toward the actor who is playing Paul, I whispered to Luke, "Who is the actor playing Paul?" Luke looked back at me and smiled. "Why it's Paul, Davey. Paul is the actor. It's Paul playing his play again and also for the first time. I love opening night, don't you?" The play began. What does he mean, *again and for the first time? The play began.*

"I speak the truth in Messiah, my conscience confirms it in the Holy Spirit. I have unceasing heaviness in my heart for I could wish that I myself might be accursed and cut off from Him for the sake of my brothers, those of my own flesh, the people of Israel."

He then looked up from where he was writing and noticed people seated in his living space - that is we who were in the theater audience.

"I was just remembering my loved ones. When I start writing, I want to put things down on papyrus. I then forget time. Have you been here long? So glad you have come to my home, apartment, alas my prison. Do you know how I know this is my prison? I am not allowed to leave. So where are you from? From around here?"

Then an amazing thing happened. Some from the audience answered Paul. I heard one say Briarwood Queens, another Manhattan, another Zimbabwe, another London. There were various accents, which seemed to make Paul happy. Paul asked we of the audience "have any of you ever lived in Brooklyn?" I then found myself blurting out. "Yes I lived there twenty-two years ago." What was I doing talking to the actor in the play? Paul looked right at me and said, "Watch you don't get lost in Brooklyn as it's a hard place to find your way out of. It's a big place I am told. You can say that again," I thought almost out loud.

I had an on again off again flirtation in recent years attempting to write my autobiography called *Lost In Brooklyn*. It was in Brooklyn where I lived for just a few years and where I lost all I had found in Boston.

'Is this guy reading my mail?'

Then Paul said to us all "Are you citizens from where you live? Well I am a citizen of Rome. There was one who gave me 40 lashes minus one (a famed Roman torture) but was not a Roman citizen. I of course am a Roman citizen and from birth. Of course I have another citizenship in heaven, which is why I am sure you have come to visit me. Isn't it? Thanks for coming. Would you excuse me please? I want to write this down right now so I can keep it forever with me."

"Theirs is the adoption as sons, theirs the divine glory, the receiving of Torah, the temple worship and the promises, theirs are the fathers and from them is traced the human ancestry of the Messiah, who is God over all, eternally blessed. Amen."

"Hello *mishbuka*. That's *family* in Hebrew. Thank you for filling the hole I have in my heart for my family by being family while I wait for my natural family to be family the way you I are family. I know you too, do not have family the way you and I are family. We can help each other. You know me as the Apostle to the gentiles. I know me not only as chief of sinners, but also as The Apostle Of Murder. Yes, murder. I earned that distinction. I not only persecuted Christians, or as some say Messianic, but I was a murderer. Without my approval the murder of Stephen would have never happened. I remember how much I wanted to control things. I was a leading Pharisee of pharisees. Control was my way for power. I gave the signal and the execution began for this outrageous false teacher of our Bible. It was the way Stephen looked into my eyes, just before his execution, that so offended me. He did not fear me. Who was he, this lightweight theologian whose very life was on the line to not fear me and to not beg for his pathetic life? I remember the stoning. Rock after rock stone after stone, and the terrible pounding. I remember the fatal blow that killed him. (Paul pointed to his temple to describe the location of the final stone) His body finally betraying his countenance... contorting and shaking. I was certain he was looking straight at me when he looked up to God and asked, 'Father forgive them do not count this sin against them'. Against him? I tell you he said it to me. Who was he to ask God to forgive me? Who was he to forgive my sin! He was the sinner. I should be the one to ask God to forgive him for his many sins against the Almighty One whom I had come to defend. I now despised him. As Stephen lay on the hard ground dead I despised him even more!"

I started to think to myself have I ever despised anyone? Have I ever even hated anyone or anything for that matter? This Bible guy Paul has great passion. Hate to me would be way too inconvenient well maybe I do hate Robert Sterling, but I would much rather just dislike or ignore him. Passion takes a lot of energy. Since Brooklyn I have not experienced any passion? Passion is too painful.

Paul continued... "Inspired with rage and how my following loved my rage. It showed my power. I was at the height of my prestige and how I loved it. I had man's approval and God was on my side. In rage we began arresting more from this Jewish sect called Messianics? Great turmoil and stress came upon these false believers throughout Jerusalem. In rage we gathered papers to arrest and torment more false believers in Damascus. Maybe find ourselves another Stephen to stone to death. I was so proud. I was loved by my people and I was doing God's work for Him. We headed for Damascus in a parade of self-righteousness. What I remember next was a bright sun that burned my eyes into severe pain. I had to close my eyes, as the stinging sensation was so real. I was thrown down into the ground. I then opened my eyes and all was so dark. I was blind and in a panic! The ground was so very hard and my body ached from the fall. I was also humiliated having been seen so out of control by my following. I heard my men say, 'Saul, Saul, are you alright.' I was as vulnerable as Stephen had been. I thought I was in hell as I was completely without hope. I was absolutely alone in my personal Sheol. I was afraid and oh so lonely. I suddenly had thoughts of Stephen.

It was in these moments of fear and blindness I learned two lessons that I will never forget. One was that I cannot control God. Here I was a man of control, who was not in control. Lying on the ground I was humiliated before my following. The god I thought I had served was not helping me. The second lesson I learned was I did not know God. I then heard the words, 'Saul, Saul, why do you persecute Me?' My response: 'Who are you Lord?' His response: 'I am Jesus whom you persecute. If I knew who God was why did I ask, "Who are you Lord?"

I knew of God but I did not know Him. I thought I did. If my life had ended there it would have been the most tragic of lives. I was just one of many who followed God but did not know Him. I thought I did.

For a moment I was intensely lonely, lost, and oh so afraid. I thought I had died and was meeting my maker in judgment. The same judgment I had so recently placed on that good and righteous man, Stephen. But my life did not end there. God was giving me what I failed to give to so many others.... mercy.

Well my entire life changed radically. I now had more power than before. It took me many years to understand this power, but over time I through weakness grew in strength.

You see it was not a controlling power but a power that came by surrender to the One I had formerly persecuted. I now had the Person of God, the power of His Might, and the purpose of who He is. Yes, 'if you believe in your heart God raised Him from the dead, and proclaim with your mouth Y'shua Adonai, Jesus is Lord, you will be saved. For its with your heart that you believe and are justified and with your mouth that you confess and are saved. As it is written anyone who puts his trust in Him will never be put to shame. For there is no distinction between Jew and gentile the same Lord is Lord overall and richly blesses all who call upon Him for everyone who calls on the Name of the Lord will be saved."

What is he saying? Is this Broadway or some kind of Christian synagogue?

Paul continued... "Of course from my former life I lost all I had before: prestige, money, and respect. I now had from my former companions much worse than disrespect, even more than hate. In fact, I was so despised by the same group who so adored me before; I had become to all of Judaism what Stephen had been to me. *The scum of the earth.*

Because my theology changed? Well yes, it radically changed but the new issues behind it were so very personal. I was hated because what I now knew and what I now had in me, was so personal. It was passion for something lovely.

This passion was a threat to their power and they hated what they could not own and control. Yet in all the persecution, I now walked in a greater power.... not from this world. From a broken spirit I discovered true boldness and a new family...You. This is not Bible study this is Bible reality. This is Immanuel - not the manual. The Saul they knew was a master of Scripture as *the manual*."

"Oh, I shared how this faith in Jesus was so very Jewish and the fulfillment of the law and Passover. I then proclaimed to be a true Pharisee because I believe in the resurrection. They, the Pharisees were okay with that. The Sadducees, who are the priests of the Sanhedrin, who do not believe in the resurrection will discuss this among themselves and sometimes ask me to arbitrate among them about the resurrection. I am glad to do so. I advise all that "I am a Pharisee and believe in the resurrection. That Jesus is the resurrection and our Passover Lamb that rose from the dead. He is God's sacrifice for sin." When I say this they agree together again against me. Religious entitlement is my caution to all who study the Bible. Study cannot take the place of relationship with Him. The One I denied over and again. True study enhances relationship and in this better doctrine too. God with us. So they told me I was insane. They told me all my learning was making me like a madman. They said 'Saul you are insane how could you walk away from all you had to become a madman?' I told them I was not a mad man. I was happy man. I used to be a madman but now I am a happy man. Happier than I had ever been. Finally, they said, 'You are a fool.' I said, 'Yes I am a fool.' They agreed! Then I said, 'I am a fool for Christ and Who's fool are you?' I tell you, pure hate came my way."

"You see; I have come to visit you even more than you me. When you read Scripture, it is God who visits you. When you read Paul, Moses, David or the Lord's own brother James, you hear and see God's Voice. The Holy Spirit demonstrates and reveals Himself through flawed human beings in Scripture. From Him I say, 'I have come to visit you.'"

"In your time, the spirit of the 'anti-Christ' is worldwide. It's not local to Jerusalem only but where you live too. There are many 'Saul's' as I was. Saul's that want to control you. Remember, control is power to those who want to change God's laws and make them man's laws. For Jew and gentile alike and for Israel and all nations, it is God's laws that are being dismantled. God's laws are being replaced with man's laws and men want the glory due God. The sign of anti-Messiah is one who wants what belongs to God for himself. These anti-Christs want themselves to be the standard for what is right and what is wrong. 'Because of the increase in lawlessness the love of most will grow cold.' Jesus warned us about these days of your time.' He also said that 'Satan is the *ruler* of this world.' The fulfillment of his position and of sin is now coming to closure.

New controlling lawmakers in governments, religion, and finance. The one who controls commerce controls governments and the standard for religion. Worldwide players are playing out their agenda of control right where you live. They are not counterfeiting just any god but the one true God. Yeshua Ha Mashiach."

"You see the end is very much as when Jesus first came on the scene. You have heard me speak of grace and yes 'by this grace one is saved.' But if we replace His law with man's law there is no grace. Only lawlessness disguised as grace. Without the Torah, the law and in particular the Ten Commandments, there is no standard for right and wrong. If you do not follow this standard one denies that there is a right and wrong. When this occurs we then have lawlessness disguised as grace. The new lawmakers are really lawbreakers and want to take God's place and get His glory too. I hope they do not come for you as we did for Stephen. If you give in to this lawlessness or if they force you to break God's laws, then what was said is now spoken again. 'we must obey God rather than men.'"

"Do not be afraid. When you see all these things know that His return is very near, 'right at the door.' Some of these are false prophets, as I was, will speak about God, yet other false prophets will claim no knowledge of Him at all. Whatever their starting point into power, what they have in common is they all want to rule you. They do not want God. Only what He has. They also want and need followers. You! You need not be as passionate as these leaders. They prefer you to be passive. They just want you to follow them. They want you hungry for what they give and angry that others have more than you. They want you to not have much, but see their rule as your provider.

Government, religion, and money, all loving what is His but not loving or wanting Him but to replace the living God with themselves. This is anti-Christ. One antichrist to lead with many little antichrists and you following along. Passivity is the common evil of all times and especially in your time. Passivity always follows the norm. Most people like to hide in the middle but in truth the middle is exposing the deceptive lie of its ruler. Satan! The middle of the road only appears to be safe but it is where people crash."

"Come to Jesus and to His way. Come now into the last day's ark that is being built. It sanctifies you from judgment and the consequences of sin. To be for Him is to be with Him. This will cause you to be against common thinking. They will call you haters if they have not done so already. 'Love your enemies', but know who your enemies are. Do you have any questions? We have time for one question."

I was again surprised by Paul's question to the audience. I was however now much more acclimated to theater at Narrow Gate. I was really liking this theater too. The acting was great. I saw in Paul's character some great transition. He was mean as Saul but sweet and funny as Paul. I saw also how he became Stephens' essence. A kind of humble and yet bold too. The other thing I got from the play was the act of forgiveness. When I say 'act' what I was seeing was the act of forgiveness taken by Stephen to Paul and Jesus to Paul too. I saw in Paul his forgiveness for all who chased tortured him and beat him throughout his world. He had love for his captors. I had never before experienced that God forgives. It's not that I was taught of a merciless God, but I had never quite even considered that forgiveness from God was something that happens. I also saw the power that people of faith can have too. Could it all somehow lead to a new beginning for a person? Someone in the audience then asked a question. He was an older man tall blonde greyish hair. Lots of hair too wearing a black vest, cowboy boots and dark blue jeans. He had a nicely trimmed grey beard and thick red hair on his head and as he stood up he seemed to be 6 feet four inches tall. A Texan accent?

"Mr. Paul? I would like to know what was going through your heart and mind over the years after Stephen's murder. Did you talk about him much to your contemporaries? We do not read in the Scriptures any comments with regard to this."

"That's a good question," answered Paul. In the early days of my new faith and family there was great anxiety toward me and much was because of what I did to

Stephen. Stephen was beloved among his friends. Over the years the Stephen murder became as you might say the *elephant in the room*. I also learned over time I could talk about Stephen but by then I wanted to keep Stephen to myself. So much of all I have to say in Bible insight comes from the transference of Stephens story into my story. It was so very personal to me. I felt that if I spoke of it less perhaps his life could live out through mine even more so. I also hoped my Stephen memory could heal me from the hate and revenge I carried. Stephen so clearly had forgiven me. His memory helped me to forgive those who tormented me. Stephen was in my thoughts all the time and his living example to me was my healing. The murder of Stephen was so cruel. I did not want to draw attention away from his act of mercy toward me the chief of his execution. It was his martyrdom and not mine." Paul continued with his monologue...

"Oh the depth of the riches of the wisdom and knowledge of God! How unsearchable are His judgments and His ways beyond tracing out! Who has known the mind of the Lord? Who has been His counselor? Who has ever given to God that God should repay him? For from Him and through Him and to Him are all things. To Him be the glory forever and ever. Amen."

"Yes, yes, mishbuka. Be family. This is what we have and no one can steal this, so do not give this up. Be family to one another and extend family through love, and the blood of our family is Jesus' blood. Our *'true'* genetic connection. One Family!" *Suddenly Paul spoke to another character in the play.*

"Hello, guard? Yes. Did you listen in...? Please just a few minutes more?" *I looked back to where I saw Paul's eyes go and sure enough there was a man in a plain dark grey gown walking up the center aisle and he was shaking his head and saying no without using words.*

The audience all looking back at Paul saw his right hand raise with two fingers up saying "two minutes?"

"All right two minutes" the guard said loudly but friendly too.

Paul's smile was so broad that all of his teeth showed. Okay I'm exaggerating, but I saw how happy Paul was to be with people. I saw it in his 'smile button' type of smile. He connects with people.

Paul continued... "Keep the fellowship sweet family. It's our greatest blessing in these last days. Remember the Bible as your Immanuel - not your manual. There is great fellowship in the Scriptures. 'The Lord is with us'"

"Give that guard a big hug too! Remember your inheritance, sweet family. Remember your citizenship in heaven. 'On earth as it is in heaven.' 'Pray in the Spirit,' especially for all the saints everywhere." The Lord's return is very soon, so be happy!"

The next moment was amazing to me. Instantaneously every person in the theater stood up, myself included, with all hands clapping. "Bravo. Bravo. Blessed be the Name of the Lord. Adonai! We love you Paul."

Paul then raised his hands and looked up. He began waving to us, his audience. Then he looked at me. I could not hear his words but I could read his lips. "Hello Davey. You are welcome here among us you are family!"

The ovation went on for several minutes and we spontaneously broke out into song. "Praise God from whom all blessings flow. Praise Him all creatures here below. Praise Him above the heavenly host. Praise Father, Son, and Holy Ghost." I was made aware by John that our song was a tradition in churches, but that our singing of this was not traditional in the least. The sound of music and the acoustics at the Narrow Gate were like nothing I had every before experienced. We sang for the longest time.

The music was happening in me and through me. I had never felt more cleansed and morally free. I lost myself in song by expressing words of passion I did not know I had. We sang many songs that I had no way of knowing the words too and yet I knew all the words. All songs went straight up into heaven? They must have.

"*Is this worship?" I thought to myself.* Luke then said, "Yes Davey. We are one with our Creator. We have broken through the time barrier and all its restrictions. We are on heaven's time zone now. 'On earth as it is in heaven.'"

"I did not ask you a question," I said to Luke.

"No you did not, but I heard you. We are family."

Luke then began to laugh, and so did John Stephens and Jonah. The next I remember was that all in attendance broke out into laughter and joy. It was more about joy than a particular joke. It was joy even with tears.

Laughter was the manifestation of the pure feelings that were being expressed.

Laughter at Narrow Gate came from pure joy that all was good. The theater space was now crowded with excitement. We were crowded but not cramped. I was reminded of the Broadway area street scene prior to entering the theater. There were crowds but I was never crowded. We were in the center but we were not the center. There was no pressure to *perform*. The center was *Adonai*. *Adonai* means *Lord* in Hebrew. Adonai was the first word I remember learning in Hebrew school. If this was Hebrew school for adults, I surely liked this Hebrew school.

Declaring the wonderful things of God in their own tongue, Luke said to me in a whisper and then he broke out and laughed, clapping his hands up to God. 'The heaven's declared His glory', Luke shouted! I wondered to myself or out loud, "Did I die today and just now go to heaven?"

"There's no difference," Luke blurted, I then wondered *how did he hear me?* Then he and John laughed and hugged. Jonah then came over and said, "Group hug," then Luke, John, Jonah and me all hugged. *I was in the middle of this, and I was as happy as I had ever been. In a flash I thought of Myriam and Sarah. For the first time since I could remember, had no regrets in my memory of them. In fact it was not a memory that I was having but a now thing. I was experiencing love for them without remorse. I was in the midst of family, and my Narrow Gate family was expanding my family outreach by Narrow Gates in reach. Yes, these were mishbuka, my new family. I love these people.*

John put me up in the hotel sleeping quarters of his house theater. As I said before it was really more like a bed and breakfast. He also provided some nightclothes, not to mention a hot tub, shower, and exquisite bathroom facilities. He said he was preparing a breakfast meeting for James and me at 9am the next morning, Saturday. "It will be the time of your life. I am certain David," he said smiling. "*Shabbat shalom*! It's so good to see you again son."

I noticed he called me son, again. '*Why was I so offended by this before?*' I like John's fatherly way. It's comforting to me. What would my life have been like had I not turned him down before. Tonight, I do not have the same angst about all my bad choices. I was truly at rest. I laughed myself to sleep.

21

JIMMY

When I woke up I was still laughing. The sun was shining on my face through the window. I had to peer out just to see if the walking mall was still in effect on 52nd and Broadway. Sure enough there were the walking crowds without noise. There was a quiet in the streets the way a snowstorm can oh so gently fall to the ground. Then in the background I heard a new sound of music in the streets. A familiar sound and words to a song I knew: It was the song of Tevye and Golde from *Fiddler On The Roof* singing *Sunrise Sunset*. It was our wedding song from 1969. "I am remembering my wedding day with Myriam" I thought to myself "and it's not making me sad." I decided to not analyze why, but enjoy the morning's moment.

I laughed again. My laughter came from pure happiness.

I then heard a knocking at my door and I said, "Hello."

"Room service sir, for you and for the apostle James," said the man.

"Yes, thank you. Please come in." As he entered I noticed he was wearing dark blue jeans and a black turtleneck sweater with white tennis shoes. His dark jet-black hair was apparent to me. He appeared very energetic bright, and about 30 years old. "May I ask your name?" I stated.

"Yes David. My name is Stephen," he said.

"Oh" I joked, "any relation to the Stephen that Paul documented in his play?"

"Why yes sir. I am Stephen, '*the*' *Stephen*, if you will." He began to laugh but held himself in check and then smiled broadly and said, "Welcome to Narrow Gate Theater."

Just as he was speaking, I saw out of the corner of my eye a very distinguished man wearing a maroon colored robe now entering my room. He was wearing an oversized white prayer shawl with Hebrew words woven in color blue into the garment. I recognized it as a *tallit*. His sandals were full of dust, but somehow not dirty.

He put his hand out and said, "David. I am Yaacov, a bondservant of God and of the Lord Yeshua, our Messiah. Greetings. Mishbuka blessings to you, and shalom."

"Yes Yaacov. Will you be joining James, perhaps Stephen and I, too?" I stated.

"No, I have to run along," Stephen said. "I asked for the honor of serving you, David. Thank you."

"No, thank you Stephen" I said to Stephen. I then remembered I was speaking to the actor who was playing Stephen, a man who is dead for 2000 years now. I stopped short of saying "good improvisation" to the actor. I settled for saying, "I am honored to be in your presence." Stephen then quietly exited.

I then looked at Yaacov as if to ask him, "When is James coming?" He seeing through me said, "David, allow me to introduce myself. I am James. James is English for the Greek translation of the Hebrew Yaakov. Of course Jacob is the English translation of the Hebrew Yaakov. If you like, just call me Jimmy."

"No, yes, I don't really know what to call you but can I call you James?" I asked.

"Yes by all means, call me James," said James.

James: "So what did you think of last night's play?"

David: "It reached me on many levels, be it personal, political or theological. Funny that I would say theological as I do not see myself as having a theology but I suppose I do."

James: "We all do in one way or another. What I got from the play was that in these last days there is no in between. All entities are connected. A non-theology is the theology of ignorance. Or let me break it down: ig-nor-ance. In other words, it is not wise to ignore what is happening."

David: "That's good, Jimmy! I mean James."

James: "Again call me Jimmy. We find serious things as humorous too. We do our Bible plays worldwide and find lots of humor. Sometimes our audiences will laugh but most times they miss our humor. God's humor. Yes, the *good humor man* is much more than ice cream."

David: "Are you saying God is a Good Humor Man?"

James:	"Well, I am saying that the Good Humor Man is better known for ice cream than God is known for His humor."
David:	"Can you give me a few examples of humor in the Bible Script?"
James:	"Of course I can. The scene has Jonah complaining to God about wanting to die because he is so uncomfortable. The whole Nineveh world has spiritually collapsed and is repenting into a real fear of God. On the other hand Jonah wants to die because it's hot outside and the plant that shaded him has wilted. To a contemporary person his air conditioner broke down. Jonah appears so small and self-involved. The audience relates to this with a healthy laugh at themselves. It identifies with Jonah who spitefully indicates he wants to die because of a current heat wave in Nineveh."

"When Jesus says 'pluck out your right eye,' does He mean cut out *your eyeball?* I do not think so. He is using exaggeration to make his point. Yet when we do this scene, we show one plucking out his eye and then closing his right eye because it's now gone. Now with his right eye closed to show it is out, he begins to explain why he should cut off his right hand. We do not typically visualize Jesus with his eye closed. Think of the cartoon character Popeye. We show its better to look like a one eye closed Popeye than to be a well-conditioned man headed *for hell.* God is using exaggeration to make his point and it's funny as all heaven. Young children in attendance laugh."

"Another one is explaining why all these grown men are so happy in the Book Of Acts whose human author is your new friend Luke. What happened was that on the day of Pentecost 2000 years ago the Holy Spirit invaded Jerusalem's space. It was about 3000 people receiving forgiveness for crucifying Jesus. Just before Peter's great sermon they were so very happy. Childlike joy was soaking in God's forgiveness. Jews from all over the world were finally understanding one another. Over the top joy was happening among adults in a way they had never before experienced. Real communication was happening and hearts were open to others as never before. Those who did not engage with the Holy Spirit's presence, the outsiders, said of them that, 'They have had too much wine.' Peter's explanation? 'No, no, they could not be drunk.' So what came to Peter's mind was the following. 'No, no, they could not be drunk. It's only nine in the morning!'

"With all that God was doing, still all he could explain was that it's impossible to be drunk at 9am? What was he thinking? Do you want to know what I think he was thinking? *I do not think he was thinking at all*, but having a wonderful time. They appeared drunk because they were so happy. In '*Truth*' they were free and forgiven. They knew it down deep especially after Peter preached their need to repent. Heavenly jokes are moments of pure happiness and the inner knowledge that all is well. On Pentecost 2000 years ago it happened and still does today. You know I will have to ask Peter about this one. You should ask him too."

I then got quiet for a moment and began to access what was happening for me at Narrow Gate Theater. I woke up this morning and I was literally laughing. When James gave Peter's explanation for why the people were so happy at Pentecost, I started to laugh again. I must be happy!

David: "Maybe audiences miss the humor because they do not understand the joy that I have seen from your cast."

James: "I appreciate that insight. For you to see that joy is connected to laughter can only come from The Holy Spirit. The Ruach is not far from you son, not far at all."

David: "I remember an old highway in Brooklyn. The Belt Parkway that connects Brooklyn with the boroughs of Queens, Manhattan, and Staten Island. Years ago in the 70s, there were apartments built by

Fred Trump. In those days we did not know Donald Trump but his father was locally famous. Trump apartments were being built in the boroughs of New York City outside Manhattan. Their buildings gave hope to middle class people for a better Brooklyn, or Queens. When you drove east you would get one message on the huge sign for us all to see. It said, '*Brooklyn* As *It Used To Be* Heading west it said, *Brooklyn As It Never Was.*'"

James: "Brooklyn was a big small town, very famous for its baseball team, The Brooklyn Dodgers. The ball players were super-famous, but in those days professional baseball didn't pay much salary. They had second jobs in the winter. The fans loved them and they were neighbors among their fans in the streets of Brooklyn."

David: "Yes. Paul's opening and closing comments were about *mishbukah*. Being here is bringing me to the best of my family. Did you know my brother Mansfield and I were at Yankee Stadium for Roger Maris' 60th and 61st home runs? He broke Babe Ruth's record on October 1st. What a great family week we had with Dad and Uncle Joe. Maris hit number 61 into the right field bleachers. I was there in the right field upper deck with Dad, Mansfield, and Uncle Joe. Had Roger hit it harder or on a slightly different part of his bat it would have carried up to us. There is film footage of this one-time event when Babe Ruth's record was broken. I am in that footage for a fraction of a second. The ball lands in the lower right field stands. The camera shows the ball's trajectory downward into the lower deck. The camera shows the ball's height parallel to us in the upper deck. There I am in clear sight. Anytime the tape to number 61 is shown, I am there with my family. It is a wonderful memory for me. We are etched into human history."

James: "Immanuel Bible Theater is also etched forever into human history. In Bible time without changing facts things can happen again. Have you ever read a passage in scripture for the first time again and then again? With Immanuel you can re-experience a good moment. With a more difficult moment you can repeat its scene until you get it right too. Have you ever had a dream where you redirect the scene of the dream to get the outcome you want? The Bible does not change but you can change. It's new every time. People worldwide enter the pages of Scripture and then into the pages of their own lives. We in effect engage with the lives of those in the Scriptures just as you are doing with me now. It's one heaven of a family album we have here. We can, for instance, add a new family member into the picture frame any time. There is always time for new beginnings. Bible acting is the most fun thing in the whole world. Learning the lines is better than a roller coaster rides for adults and children alike. Actual history is once but for the participant in Immanuel it occurs when one is ready and wanting to to experience the Bible Presence now and new. Pentecost 2000 years ago happened once in human history but its reality is for us now. If you want it He is ready and willing. Bible time is happening now without violating history. This can be very healing for we who are here now. That's how we can change those bad scenes in life by doing them differently now. When you want Him as much as you know you need Him you hit a homerun. The *manual* always misses this joy. *Immanuel* never misses."

David: "Paul's message was that we can be that family. I hardly know the Narrow Gate people, yet you are family to me. I know this because it's family, as I have never known family to be. It's upward. We help each other along the way. I have never known actors to share like this."

"I wrecked my family and you have welcomed me *the family wrecker*. You have been family to me. Mishbukah is so simple and yet oh so deep. They tell me you are Jesus brother. I bet you can write the book on family. Right?"

James: "Thank you for your kind words, but you are wrong when it comes to me as a family man. I struggled greatly. Not a little bit but a lot.

I struggled with Jesus as my brother. It was not fun for me with Jesus as my brother. It's not that I have an exposé on the real Jesus. No. He was nicer, kinder, more mature and yet more childlike than I can explain. He as my brother was so full of life. He was funny yet sensitive to every moment that mattered."

"Ironically it was His goodness and my being his *little* brother that I hated. I hated being inferior to him. He was good at everything. He knew my struggles, and loved me anyway. I hated His love yet I wanted His love. I needed His love. I resented that I needed Him more than He needed me. Maybe I was judging Him on that one too. He was so good He probably needed me too."

David: "My father and brother had the same name, Mansfield Cohen. When we attended my father's funeral and I introduced myself, people would openly say, I didn't know Mansfield had another son. I think that statement covers a lot of ground, wouldn't you say?"

James: "Well yes, it does. Your Dad had your brother on his mind. It's like having a pure passion to love all but also a burden keeping the family name. Passion is personal but obligations block the joy of passion. Your Dad put an unnecessary burden on his family. Most people spend more time doing their self-obligations than their passions. God gives passion people prefer tasks."

David: "Are you saying Mansfield was a burden to Dad?"

James: "Not Mansfield himself, but the burden of carrying on the family name was his burden. Dad's burden to complete what he wanted for himself and the family name was put on your brother. You of course were left outside the door without an explanation. It's very hurtful and I am sorry this happened to you."

David: "They would talk all night and into the early mornings. Dad wanted Mansfield in the family business. He wanted Mansfield into the Harvard Business School too. He followed up on all Mansfield did. Dad even spoke into the girls he dated. He followed him on his paper route. Me? I had almost two hundred sports events in high school and Dad missed every one. It's as if we had two sets of families. My brother was the Varsity and I was Junior Varsity. When Dad got a girlfriend, and Mom went into severe depression, Mansfield became an absentee brother and son to Mom. He barely graduated from high school as a result of his take on Dad's hypocrisy and Mom's depression. He resented Mom for not understanding Dad's need, but intuitively saw Dad as a hypocrite. As I think on it, my brother suffered greatly."

James: "So when I say passion, I am sure he had passion for both his sons but his time was spent focused on Mansfield. He missed out on having you both. The burden for the family name caused his time to go to your brother but you all suffered. Mom suffered the most."

David: "I have resented my brother for many years now."

James: "I resented my brother. I could never have a normal childhood. Talk about a family burden. My parents loved us all. There was joy with each child born. There was also the human burden of raising the Son of God. Their passion for each child was having the same love for each, however the full time job for my parents which was worrying about Jesus, was thrust upon the entire family of Joseph."

David: "One would think your family would somehow be exempt from family dysfunction."

James: "Just the opposite was true. We were special but we also had a special burden. The entire Joseph family had to make a decision."

David: "My brother died in 1990, six years ago. He got Hodgkin's disease. We all flew out to Los Angeles for his final two weeks. Mansfield's wife Rachel and children (my nephew and niece), Ronnie and

Esther, were also present. Myriam flew in from Israel and also our daughter Sarah. It was family time for us. I did not expect this but I would have a decision to make. It had to do with the living Mansfield, not the one who was dying. I with my continuing journey would have to live with what was decided."

James: "I had a family decision to make too. Yes, my brother was murdered and, to say the least, treated very badly. It was shocking to see this. The lies said about Him. The reality that He was hated and despised to the point of a phony trial, all designed to kill the very entity that I despised in Him, too. His deity. God was my brother."

"What I hated, and what we as a family struggled with, was who He was and is. Why could he not be normal like us? This was our unspoken criticism of our family toward 'Shua' as we called Him. The burden for Him to be so special was inconvenient for all of us especially me. I did not completely realize this. Then we saw Him losing His life for the same things we despised in Him too. Our family unbelief was put to the test. He was being accused, beaten, and broken. Why? For the same jealousy that we had for Him!"

David: "Jesus was a divider to my family too. This is amazing you and I would have this conversation. This is similar to the contention our family had just before Mansfield died. Myriam was the leader of all this. Myriam was astoundingly beautiful. Her now and newly blonde hair was long and thick as ever. Her fingers and arms so long and thin. She smiled so brightly. She was not dressed to show her figure but her modesty revealed her beauty."

"I had not seen her since 1987 when I visited her and Sarah who were living in Israel at Ruach Adonai. Myriam was a teacher of acting and painting. She did 'live' plays too. She was also a director. She had incorporated art with faith. Her philosophy is so like all the actors here at Narrow Gate. She must have had many male suitors but was still unmarried. She seemed somehow fulfilled in marriage. She showed no interest in me as husband but gave me love. She had a personal confidence I had never before seen in her or seen in anyone. She was not needing me but wanting for me."

James: "When I saw my brother dying on the cross I saw what I lacked. I lacked love for Him. I could not even apologize to Him. I wanted to see Him with my mother but it was too late, he was dead."

David: "It was my brother Mansfield, still my big brother, reaching out to me."

Mansfield: "Hey little brother."

David: "Hey, Big Man. Why are you faking it like this?"

Mansfield: "People are believing me. Do you want to know why?"

David: "Why?"

Mansfield: "Because I always was a better actor than you."(I always loved his sense of humor.)

David: "Well do me a favor and I will give you credit for being the better actor. Stop faking it and get better, Ok?"(To my surprise my voice cracked.)

Mansfield: "Ok. I will tell them I was faking it because it's kind of true. Really true. Listen, Davey brother. I have been healed."

David: "Well you look pretty sick to me."

Mansfield: "Not as bad as your last job as an actor!"
David: "Ok, you bad actor who can't even die right!"(We both laughed

and hugged. I was leaning over his hospice bed.)

Mansfield: "My last will and testament to you is, you listen to me, Ok? When Dad left Mom, I always wanted to be a surrogate father to you and I kind of failed so thanks for listening to me now. Ok?"

David: "Sure. What's on your mind?"

Mansfield: "You know Myriam is one amazing woman. I know you two are over as a couple. I am not to get you back together. It's just that she knows something. She's shared something with me over the years. She has sent me dramatic presentations of what she does. She's reads to my family and me when we are together. She was with my family yesterday. I have received a healing Davey. I'm ok. I am going to heaven, brother, and I want to see you there. It's all coming to a head and an end for everyone, very soon. I am simply checking out of planet earth kind of early. I am saving a place for you."

James: "What did you feel when you heard Paul speak of *mishbukah*."

David: "I immediately thought of Mansfield. Mansfield was like Paul in the play. Family waiting for his family to be family. The way you are here."

James: "Mansfield spoke to you about Yeshua, didn't he?"

David: "Yes, of course. He went on about how he Mansfield was an overcomer because Jesus overcame sin and death and that his life finally made sense to him. He said "our being Jewish was not enough" and then I got the drift. Myriam had brought Jesus to yet another family member. *'So why, with all the warmth* I was now experiencing *with Mansfield? Why am I now going numb?'* I asked myself. Suddenly it was like a curtain came down and the play was over. What if I did join in with the old family as a new family?

"What if I did?" I thought to myself, 'I would then be the second son again, *second place once again*.' Mansfield beat me to the punch. Figures! Now I would be *number two* to Myriam, Sarah, my sister-in-law Marianne too. I don't even know about the nieces and nephews?"

"I politely let Mansfield finish. He saw something in me turn off. Yes Big Man. I will consider what you are saying, but look bro... I do not want to buttonhole you from everyone else.' I hugged him and told him I loved him. I walked away. He died one hour later."

James: "I am sorry Davey."

"I was now suddenly among Shuas believer family. Sure, their faith was weak, as they did not believe that He would rise from the dead. They however, honored Him as one they adored. These friends of Jesus were men and women who loved Him. There was a family connection among them that we did not have in the Joseph family. This hidden family of Shua strengthened my resolve that evil had triumphed over good and that hate had murdered my brother. Ironically in grief I was experiencing family with my brother by being with the family that knew Him and truly loved Him. *I finally have Him as family and now He is dead.* All was lost. Evil had triumphed in the end. God was dead. I became exceedingly sorry for my sin, but I had no outlet. I was getting physically sick. Our sin killed Life. Death without hope had won."

"We were the core family of believers. Finally I was one of them. I was the chief of sinners because I knew Jesus best, yet intentionally did not know Him at all. To all these followers, He was Lord. To me He was my brother. My older brother, who was the favored one. I was now ashamed."

"If Jesus truly was the Lord of the earth, then that would mean my own flesh brother was my Lord too! I began to process this as an honor but "I learned too late" I openly spoke aloud these grievous words to my new family."

"When He did rise, my faith rose above all the strongholds that held me in doubt. We had the celebration of life over death. The worst became the best. Our love for Him was born in the furnace of deep sorrow. He was dead and now He was alive. With Him dead, there was no hope or outlet. When He rose all hope was reborn"

"People today celebrate His death and resurrection in symbols. There is little despair and therefore little victory. The story's life is not played out. For us His death really happened. It was so final."

David: "Well even as a non-believer I know that as the story goes He rose from the dead. How can any contemporary person have the perspective you had. People in the last 2000 years simply were not *there* as you were."

James: "You can have this too by seeing the bad choices in your own life. He is there for you to redeem all these bad choices. As long as you hold to your own success or failure it's *as if Jesus is still dead.* This mindset will not see its own guilt because it will not approach God as he really is. Sin is death and in sin there is an element of pure hopelessness."

"I became aware of King David's words 'there is none that is good not even one.' People of all times can come to this place that Paul came to when he said of himself 'oh wretched man that I am who will save me from this body of death?'"

"I finally saw myself that day as one who was totally selfish. I never did anything without my own well being in mind. I was pinned down with pure guilt and sorrow, but I had no outlet. This reality settled deep into my being for a few days. He was dead and I was the guilty one."
"When my brother rose from the dead it was a relief from the guilt I

153

stuffed away. When He breathed upon Me and said 'receive *Ruach The Holy Spirit.*' I knew I had His forgiveness, mercy, and His grace. I was truly unburdened, not only from my sin but from ever having to perform again. I had bottomed out and saw myself for who I was. I still see myself as I did that day of the cross. Meeting my Messiah doesn't change my understanding of me, but it allows me to come to my God knowing he's ok with me. From this lowly place I can say 'humble yourself in the sight of the Lord and He will lift you up.'"

"This is how you and others who did not live in Jesus generation can find what we of His time did. Come as you really are to Him as He always is."

David: "I want to have hope."

James: "When people ask me what is the greatest criteria to be a Narrow Gate Actor I tell them its repentance. Then say, "what's that got to do with performance?" I say "absolutely nothing. Repentance cures the actor from ever having to perform again. This reality plays out in the Script. You can overcome a symbolic faith and replace it with *real faith*. Life is more fun that way. He is giving a casting call for actors not stars. His call is for doorkeepers, water holders, and all other such non-performance entities. Repentance is a gift from God and those who receive this are His doorkeeper - actors."

"You can see the cruelty my family did to my brother by seeing the insensitivity you have toward your own family. He reveals Himself in all close relationships. Mourn and grieve your wrongdoing as I did over my brother. Mansfield is not the Lord but the Lord is in the midst of your conflict with your brother. The Lord is in the reconciliation of that relationship too. This is how you 2000 years later you can go through *the Passover* as I did. Go through your problem, not around your problem. Religion is about making reality into *symbols*. We want to avoid the pain of facing pain, to be healed of sorrow. Do not let anger or fear cover-up the necessary grief needed - for your own wrongs to be healed. 'There is a time to mourn and a time to dance.' The two work as one. God is *active* and ready to heal us. He is not a statue without interaction and life. Do not turn away from the things that block you as these block you from Him. If you hate your brother you in effect hate my brother as I hated Him once too."

David: "Mansfield was my brother and certainly not the Lord. Yet it was my brothers greatest request that I would believe whom you both came to."

I was suddenly jealous of Mansfield and hoped my face did not reveal this to James.

James: "Your brother was something greater than just your brother, David. It's what he finally had that so offends you now. He became a true believer. He in a different way than before has a father that you do not have. You reasoned but resisted the revelation you were offered. What I am saying now transcends human reason. Formulas can be sold. They offer symbols as answers and negate true Truth. Man's experiences alone are not the basis for Truth. Experiencing Jesus is the basis for Truth."

"Man falls short. Jesus is the God-Man who takes us through the narrow gate. God's law shows right and wrong. Jesus forgives wrong and He alone is right."

"This is what Mansfield won and what you are still trying to figure out. Unfortunately *figuring it out* is not finding it out. What your brother offered you was reasonable but it transcended reason. You need to discover as Mansfield did. Drop your guard son. In Narrow Gate Theater we practice not wearing a mask."

David: "I am sorry to let you down. I really love everyone here. Your story is amazing."

James: "Yes David. When my brother became my Lord, He was no longer my brother but my Lord. When my brother becomes your Lord, your brother will finally be family. You hold onto things, David, until your hold strangles its life from your grasp. We are praying you will see my brother as Lord of life, and Mansfield no longer lord of your anger. Jesus can break the stronghold the past has on you. The new makes the old family new family. Mansfield knows this now."

22

THE WRESTLER

James then excused himself saying he wanted to bring a surprise guest into our conversation. He would not tell me who he was. James was not being capricious or secretive. Maybe he just wanted me to be quiet with my thoughts for a while.

It is amazing that with all my ambition to be the actor of the family that it was now Myriam who was living out *'my* destiny.' What she was doing was not my vision, but she, not I was the performing artist. This kind of theater was not her vision in the early days of Boston, but she changed. I could always have an effect on her, but now no one had a hold of control over her. She was no longer discouraged by other people's opinions. She was *bought by Jesus.* She once said to me, "*Jesus the Passover lamb, is a love story.*"

It's true! I was jealous of the Man Jesus, as I was jealous of Mansfield. Yes, her Yeshua is God to Myriam, but He was also the man who stole the heart of my love. If she was the love of my life, why did I leave her and Sarah? I'm still jealous. Jesus had entered my family and I wanted him out. James was jealous of Jesus and I was too. He's a guy who was born in a stable and died without a following on a cross. He's a man who never wrote anything or left any work of art, yet he sure has a way of getting into the middle of family life.

I love it at Narrow Gate but it's too intense here. The actors get into their parts too much. Where is the separation between actor and audience? Are they training actors or are they training activists and preachers? Are they storytellers or are they prophets using theater as a means to an end that has nothing to do with what Shakespeare is all about. Even Shakespeare said, "All the world's a stage." Where in this place are the 'union breaks?' When in Narrow Gate land do you get time off? This is what I hate about being here.

On the other hand, what they say is learn to not wear a mask. The mask they say is a heavy weight.

Take off your mask. John Stephens told me *hupocritos* means hypocrites in Greek.

Literally, it means, 'those who wear masks.' And they tell me Jesus says in the Sermon On The Mount "(Mask wearers) take the beam out of your own eye, then you will see clearly to remove the speck of sawdust that is in your brother's eye."

All these years I was thinking the two witches had no effect on me. I walked out on them and showed them up? Now I am thinking, 'wait a moment.' Something really changed in me after I met the witches. What is it from them that I have with me now?

Paul in his play says false prophets don't have to be false believers. What all false prophets have in common is *they want to take God's place*. The witches wanted to replace their prophesies with the things people go to God for. Did I replace a God I did not know with an anti-god who was aware of the God I was being offered? John Stephens was offering me more than a part in a play. I turned him down even though I loved what he offered. I loved him too. *I love him even more now.*

Was I being neutralized by my own passivity? Was the *curse* the witches had on me *permanent passivity*?

Is passivity aggressive disguised as being victimized? I used to have what I called 'Davy's dictionary.' "A cynic is an idealist turned inside out." I was sensing both cynicism and idealism were ways of passivity. Both go around the problem and not through the problem.

"Oh the tangled web we weave when first we practice to deceive." I then thought of the witches in Macbeth. They were prophesying into Macbeth's ambition to rule. They were active in the opening scenes of the play Macbeth and then gone. It was very similar to the white and black witches in my life. *Gone but not gone.* Like Macbeth, my witches appealed to my ambition. As in Macbeth, I sought to enact their vision for my life. I, as Macbeth, sought to rearrange my life and force things to happen. In my Macbeth, my wife and child were sacrificed to the god of witches. Were they the sacrifice gift I failed to bring the witch Natalie?

"It's about me. I am the one it can be said, 'Oh the tangled web we weave when first we practice to deceive.'" I went to a true seer, John, and rejected him. Myriam once said to me when in Israel, 'David, you are being deceived.' She was correct. I am not ignorant. I am arrogant. Passivity is my way of staying the same. Am I afraid to not be passive? Is this my way of controlling and yet am I not being controlled by an unseen spirit?

Suddenly I heard the door knock. "Can we enter," said James in his brusque but friendly voice. "I want you to meet a good friend." Then I opened the door to let hem enter, and there was a small man with a narrow face, bright eyes and a beard. He appeared to be very old although I cannot tell age here. They are all in such good physical shape.

"This is my namesake Jacob, otherwise known as Israel," said James. I reached out my hand and Jacob, looking at my hand, bear hugged me instead.

"Mishbukah, brother David. Such a blessing to see you." I reached forward in a hunching sort of way. I was feeling in my shoulders that strain I get from forgetting to pull my stomach muscles in on long walks. Jacob was much older than me and I was also aware he was in better condition than I. I thought I was in good shape especially after my walk yesterday but this guy must walk that walk every day.

David: "Blessings to you, sir."

Jacob: "Jimmy came by and wanted me to talk with you about wrestling. You are a wrestler, are you not?"

David: "Yes. Well, I was a wrestler in high school."

Jacob: "That's good. High School opened a door into a high calling, didn't it?"

David: "Well aside from winning most and losing a few matches, I never thought of wrestling as a calling."

Jacob: "Do you get spontaneous recollections of certain matches without warning?"

David: "Well yes, these moments come to me and often I do relive the matches. The ones I lost however are difficult to re-live."

Jacob: "Yes I understand. They called me '*grabber*' - that's what my name means. I grabbed my brother in the womb. Not that I remember doing this, but I was born a wrestler."

David: "I was a reluctant wrestler. If I had not gone out for wrestling, I would have had done baseball and football only. I often dream that

I do high school over and skip wrestling."

Jacob: "Ever notice the wrestlers on your team were different than the typical athlete?"

David: "Yes. We would get scientists and nerds as well as popular jock types. Sometimes the criminal types too. In those days we called them *hoods*. They would refer to wrestling as a '*fight*' and never as a '*match*.'"

Jacob: "Now I had the attitude of a grabber, which is great in wrestling. But my body was built like a chef or a painter."

David: "That's easy. We would put you into a lower weight class, like 95 or 103. Another category for bigger nerds was to make them leg wrestlers. They could wrap their legs around their opponent, hold on and win."

Jacob: "A true sign wrestling is a calling from God was the non-athlete people who joined your wrestling team. Could the nerdy legman or the 103-pound high school senior play in any other sport? Of course not, but wrestling is a calling. People who cannot catch a moving ball become good wrestlers too." *Jacob was now laughing at his own joke. He had an odd sounding higher register to his laugh.*

David: "There was one guy who was bigger, stronger, and faster than me. I could beat guys who were bigger or stronger, but this guy was as fast as me too. His strength and speed made it so I could not hold him. He beat me 2 years in a row in the sectional tournament. He made it so I could not enter the state tournament. When I got to read his local newspaper the second time I lost it helped soften my shame of losing. 'Bill Seasons Defeats Number 1 Seated Cohen.' I was glad for him, as he was a hood who made good. Winning a match, and not a street fight got him acclaim."

Jacob: "I was at the turning point in my life. I was challenged with facing every demon I had stored away in the very back seat of my memory. I had to face my brother. My bigger, stronger, faster, and angrier than me brother. I figured he was motivated not only to beat me but also to kill me. After all, I tricked him and got what he had in birthright and in blessing. My killer instinct was not to kill him but only to win. Not to pin him but win by points (Jacob began that high register laugh again). *Winning* was to still be alive after seeing him. My win goal was to see him, and continue my journey from Laban. All with the family name intact."

David: "So I take it you heard of my brother having the family name as you had your family name."

Jacob: "I was second born too and where I come from second place is last place. It's a kind of no win or being pinned at birth."

David: "Yes it's a disgrace to be pinned. It happened to me once and there was a hush in the gym. People were shocked that I got pinned. It was a surprise move by my opponent and I fell into its trap. I am shocked to this day when I remember it."

Jacob: "My stakes were more than shame. For me it was life and death. I was at the river Jabbok and I had learned some lessons. God had sent a bigger deceiver into my life than I had ever been. He sent me my father-in-law Laban. I was escaping from him after 20 years of hearing how fortunate I was to have him as a father-in-law and proprietor. It took about 20 years for my two wives to become more loyal to me than to him too. I stole Esau's birthright and inheritance through trickery. I would never have imagined finding one who could steal back from me what I stole from Esau."

James: "You see the family dysfunction? As they say Davey, '*oy ve es mere*'"

David: "That's good Jimmy. I didn't know you did vaudeville here."
James: "Very good Davey. There is a part for you in our company. It's just

that you are so *meshuganah yourself*. I don't know what part He has for you but I know God has a place for you with the *crazies*."

Jacob: "So here I was, having heard that my brother and his army were following me and I was to see Esau at dawn. Then in prayer or was it meditation. I suddenly got a call from the One who calls wrestlers into wrestling. You might say that's when I received my call into wrestling."

"I wrestled with an angel who was not only bigger than me but smaller too. He was much stronger. One who was so fast I could not see him. He had a strangle hold on my hip too. He could have pinned me in 3 seconds, but the one I wrestled was going for endurance. He was testing my endurance by being so tenacious himself. God's wrestling matches are God's way of testing us into greater character. God wanted this to be the match of the century. My surprise was that it was the match that took a century. It went on all night! And then the angel said, '*Let me go.*'"

"I thought to myself maybe this opponent of mine thought somehow that I was winning? Good, I thought to myself maybe it's just like the old Esau days. Maybe I can trick the angel? Maybe win through intimidation?"

James: "Still the grabber! To your credit Jake, so many just quit in the middle of a good work. You held on. You weren't smart enough to do anything else. (*James began* laughing *at his joke*.)"

Jacob: "Give me my blessing, I insisted. I needed to know I had God with me because I was planning to wrestle with Esau in the morning in a different kind of match. Esau was not going for the win or the pin. As I said he was going for the kill. I needed to know no matter how wrong I was that I still had God's blessing. I was demoralized by Laban's persistent *hold* on my life for 20 years. I did not see this at the time but Esau was really not my problem. *I was my problem.* I was at a loss to know what to do. I did not want to beat Esau as much as I wanted to be alive and with my family the day after our encounter. That's it! Knowing I had God's blessing was all I needed. 'Give me my blessing' was my main line in the Jabbok River Script."

David: "By preparing for Esau you got the match you never expected. That's how you got your new name, Israel. You earned it, "Right?"

Jacob: "He named me Israel because I had striven with God and men. I finally had my triumph over fear and guilt. I won the one I absolutely needed to win. I won by losing. I won by losing my fear of losing what I knew in my heart that I never really earned. After my match I fully accepted that I had stolen and cheated my brother Esau. I also began to see that from the beginning the only thing I did right was to want something good from God. I wanted what He had to offer and Esau did not want it enough. I lost the match but won something better. I won what I only could have won *by losing*. I lost the fear that I did not have God's love and support. I lost my need to cheat, steal, and be a *fast talking man*. By facing my match and showing up for it I could now see that in all my sinning God always wanted me as I was. I never had to be what I was not. He wanted me to be Israel too. Ironically my new name Israel is a statement for every man and woman, boy and child. It's for everyone who has overcome battles with mankind and God. The name (Israel) is for an entire people and I was the first of its kind under the new name. Even if I was the second born I was finally who I was supposed to be. Davey this was an amazing revelation for me. My victory was I no longer wanted to be anyone else but me. I was finally free. *Winning is facing your greatest obstacle and overcoming your greatest fear*. Facing death is finding life. Winning is not what defined me anymore. I learned to be free is to not be defined by losing or winning. My reward was simply to be one who loved and was loved. I loved my family and my Lord. He was the One whom I wrestled that night and for oh so long a time. He could have killed

163

me but He let me win. I wrestled with God and I won because I lost my fear of losing what I always had. I limp to this day but you see I am in good health. With each step I am reminded of the success that failure brings. Healing comes by facing and going through the hurt. Going through the hurt is the open door into the narrow gate."

"Esau never was my problem nor was he my opponent to God's blessing either. I was my problem, and my attempts at controlling things and people were my obstacle. When I met Esau the next day, all we could do was hug, hold, laugh and cry in each other's arms. It was the friendliest wrestling match in the history of wrestling. We were immersed in hugs."

David: "I have had extraordinary ambition, Jacob. I never had a River Jabbok. I have avoided it every time. You crossed over and you changed. You acted and you to wrestled through to the other side of the river. *The Other Side Of The Jabbok* is a good title for this great chapter in your life. Thank you Jacob. You are a great wrestler. I had ambition, but I have not replaced it with a new victory. Victory over defeat is a beautiful thing. I still lack the courage to lose. I won my wrestling matches out of the fear and humiliation of being defeated. I never won the ones I wanted to win most because I was motivated by the fear of losing. If I could overcome this fear, maybe then I could have the peace that brings confidence."

Jacob: "That's good Davey, and I might say, *His Peace*. In essence one needs to change the reality he identifies himself with in order to receive the call he always had. Change your name into *His Name son*. When you take on God's character, you take on His Name. Act on faith son. Wrestle through the things that bind you. God has His team. Do not turn him down when He is ready to give you in the match of a lifetime. It's participating in your match for life or death that brings you victory. Walk over the *River Of Fear* and hear His

Voice in your voice 'I will fear no evil for thou art with me.'"
(Jacob was then gone)

James: "We have made a remake of Charles Dickens' *A Christmas Carol*. We call it *Ebenezer Scrooge*. The key line in Scrooge's transformation is a calling out to God, '*I can't change what I have done but I can change who I am. Touch me and change who I am.*' Jacob was always showing he wanted what God had. He lied and cheated, but still wanted what God had to offer. To want what God has is not selfish. Esau was indifferent to what God had. Jacob was a person coming to the end of himself. The end of me is the beginning of He. 'Touch me and change who I am.'"

"Esau, as strong as he was in body, was passive with what God had to offer. It is God's character that God offers. Esau wanted man's product and gave up God's promise for one meal. Being on the fence is the problem. Most people are *on the fence* and are lost in the *crowd* of Satan's lies. 'Satan the ruler of this world rules from the middle because he owns *the fence*.'"

"People hide behind neutrality and call it wisdom. The passive will fear making a mistake. Often, one does nothing as if nothing were actually a non-choice. The passive chooses to not decide. Can one be an extrovert and still be passive? 'Yes!' Jacob was one who came out of hiding. He won and lost, but he showed up to play. At last he was no longer in hiding. He benefited greatly by his act of faith and so have many others, because one day he came to *the play*. The act of faith I refer to is the work of the Holy Spirit in a man, which actually brings *rest*. The wrestler need be readied, focused, and at peace as one move."

David; I was alone in my thoughts again. I have been passive. Even in my ambitious days of seeking stardom, I was neutral in what really mattered. I have been Esau in my choices. Jacob wanted what God has. Even Dad and Mansfield wanted the priestly name. I was jealous but I did not want the name. I just wanted what they had which I presumed they stole from me.

Suddenly I was so very lonely. I had been operating in secret. My sins were secret. Had my secret now become exposed? I hoped no one knew. I need to keep my secrets. With my head down I heard James say, "Shalom."

23

THE MARY YOU NEVER KNEW

I think I then fell asleep. When I woke up I found myself in the main theater where we had just seen Paul In Prison the night before. I was seated in the first row when an elegant, contemporarily dressed woman appeared on the stage.

Mary: "Hello David. My name is Mary or in Hebrew Myriam. I am from Magdalena. There is a boat that tourists take on the Sea of Galilee. They will pass my city of Magdalena and my name will be announced. Mary of Magdalene is how I am best known. It is my pleasure to meet you. Jesus cast out seven demons from me. That's the other part of how I am explained."

David: "Well it's my pleasure to meet you. I do apologize, as I am very unfamiliar with the New Testament. I was not aware that you are part of... of... ahh... *the cast*. Come to think of it Luke mentioned you to me."

Mary: "Yes, (Mary now laughing) I understand. I do not take your lack of Mary Magdalene knowledge personally. In fact, I enjoy the comfort of anonymity. I am much more famous or infamous than I had ever intended to be in life. It's nice to speak with someone without preconceived ideas on the subject of me."

David: "There was a time where, if you had told me my name would not be a household known name to masses of people by my mid-40s, I would be devastated with disappointment. I would have failed to be great. In the ten conversations I had with my father being great was in all ten."

Mary: "You are funny David. You are becoming famous among all the

	actors at Narrow Gate."
David:	"You all hold your characterizations so well here. Can I ask where you got your training? Funny how I am meaning to ask the others this question, but there is so much activity going on I never get to theory."
Mary:	"We really don't have a lot of theory going on here. We are dedicated to the craft. In order for our audiences to understand our story, we consequently are changing their view of what acting and theater is. Who God is too. The *what* and the *who* of the Bible is our passion. Finally, that without *acting*, humanity has no knowledge but only theory. Acting is true faith. It's the end of the assembly line of thought."
David:	"Now you are getting me into conversation … as you all do. Please, before we talk, tell me something? Am I on an audition? Is this a screenplay? A live play? Are there cameras recording this conversation we are having right now? I am serious."
Mary:	"We are not being cryptic David. At Narrow Gate we make all things *one thing*. Story and theory are as one. People are normally trained to separate reason and revelation as two different entities. At Narrow Gate we use Ecclesiastes chapter three as our model for integrating extremes into one revelation from God. 'There is a time to mourn and a time to dance' or 'A time to build up and a time to break down.'"
	"Yes, we are being recorded but not in the technological sense. It's much more spiritual. The ultimate vision for Narrow Gate acting is repentance. It's about going emotionally to ground zero. Things are being recorded not for inspection, but for introspection and inspiration."
David:	"I feel since I have been here that I have lost something I once

valued. The little amount of personal confidence I had prior to coming here is gone. I don't mean this in a criticizing way. Truth is it feels good."

Mary: "Did you know that true learning is unlearning? Ask yourself 'What have I unlearned today?' This is what you have learned."

David: "I have learned to laugh again, and I have also experienced great sadness. What have I unlearned? I feel as if I were dropping a heavy weight I have carried over my shoulders for a very long time. I am wanting to remember Myriam as when we first met. I am letting go of something. There is the weight of *being me* that is going away and a new sensitivity is taking its place. It feels lighter somehow, and I like the way it feels. I like it very much."

Mary: "The mask of humanity is a heavyweight David. One cannot be reached while wearing a mask. There are many masks in the world. Shakespeare spoke into this when he said, 'All the world's a stage.' Unfortunately, all the world is wearing a mask."

David: "I am learning at Narrow Gate that life is the teacher to the actor. There is a '*director*' and lots of direction happening all around us too. We are not alone. I also am learning that wanting to act is not enough. Something must be lost in me and that I need to be willing to give it up. I need to carry a lighter load."

Mary: "Less is more, Davey. Life is too big. It needs to be made small so we can see how close God is. He needs to be close or He's just the *big man upstairs*. The close up God is personal. That's why God makes Himself so close. If we get close, we can see how close He is. It's here (Mary's hand was on her heart) where we value that He is a big God who makes your problem small and fixable."

David: "Tell me the story of the seven demons cast out of you. Can you?"

Mary: "Do you know I love to tell stories? When we Narrow Gate Actors travel, we always ask for children to be present. Children love stories. We call this children-izing our audience. We want our plays to cause a new childhood. We want light to replace the heavy weight that grownups have to carry."

David: "Why do grownups, as you put it, carry weight?"

Mary: "Because grownups are too '*grown up.*' When I was a grownup among grownups, I was an angry and bitter woman. I justified my anger as one who felt 'entitled' to my anger."

David: "You have come long way Mary. You don't seem to carry any weight of anger. You appear light. I know that's an odd way of giving a compliment."

Mary: "Thanks! That's an encouraging observation as I was not like this before. I had no father in my life. I never knew my father and my mother hardly knew him too. I was not a leper but I might as well have been one. To put it better, I was a '*cast out*' as there was no place for fatherless children in Galilee. Was I a Jew? Who was my father? Who was my mother's husband? What responsibility did the synagogue have with a non-Jewish or Jewish family that the Romans did not want?"

David: "I am so sorry."

Mary: "There is one moment in time, you might call it my 15 minutes of fame. It's when I came to the empty tomb to visit Jesus body. I was not seeking the risen Jesus but I wanted to care for His dead body. Before I comment on what has been recorded in the scripture, which we commonly refer to as the Script, ..."

David: "...Yes, excuse me for interrupting. I have heard this said before. Why do you Narrow Gate Actors call Scripture the Script?"

Mary: "Can an actor act without a script?"

David: "Well, no. Even if he is improvising, the improvisation becomes a script."

Mary: "The same with us. What is unique with us is that we know the Bible is the Script. The words need to be acted out. We at Narrow Gate are in process of changing one's view of theater so to understand the Bible. The Bible is not commonly thought of as an actor's script, but it is. All humanity is called to act and to not perform. We are changing the preconceived notion of what acting is too. The Bible really is live theater. I might add that it is theater that does not require a budget. Just let it and Him happen wherever you are. Read it quietly, read Him aloud, read with others aloud, learn the lines and experience eternity in time. Live in eternity and time as one. Do you see why we love it here? Our acting is not a lie it's Truth. Acting on its Truth sets one free."

"The Bible, or as we say the Script, is improvisational. The lines are unchangeable, but the life of the unchangeable words are God breathed. *Ruach* is Hebrew for breath. Breath is the author of the Book - Script. The Holy Spirit is Breath the Holy."

David: "I thought God was the author of the Bible?"

Mary: "He is. The Holy Spirit is God. God's very nature is Spirit. 'God is Spirit and we worship Him in Spirit and in Truth.'"

David: "God as close up?"

Mary: "Davey, He is very close. What we do best is that we know He is close and do not treat Him as if He were far away. Many who say they know God act as if He were not in the room as we talk about Him. God is not theory but *The Actor Himself*. He interacts with us and through us. Our passion is to show the world how involved He is with us. 'Let your light so shine.' Is His inreach to us and His outreach through us. As actors of the Script we reveal His character by receiving 'every Word from the mouth of God.'"

David: "What about the Big Man Upstairs?"

Mary: "He's not upstairs He is right here. (She again held her hand on her heart.) The close up God is so close you can spend forever getting closer. That's what I am doing with you now. God is huge to us when seen through a microscope's lens. '*Infinity*' in the close up is Him moving closer."

"Of course, as I walked to the tomb the god I sought was far away. Far away even though I was sure his body was nearby. I was seeking life in the physical only. It's ironic that I was doing this. The only life I knew from Jesus was spiritual. I had not yet put the mystery of Him together into my heart."

"On that empty tomb day, I was about as lost and lonely as a human being can be. I had never known a man that gave back as He did. His love was pure. His love was full of attention to every detail of need. I never knew a man as a giver, only as one who takes, and always expecting me to give all. Men demanded that I give my body, my time, my works ... but never my heart. For me to give my heart would require the man to give something of his heart in return. Men do not pay back ... they only take."

Those words "men do not pay back they only take," really stung. I felt nausea in the pit of my stomach.

Mary continued... "Jesus was different. You see, I was demon possessed. A legion of demons possessed my body mind and spirit. I later became by profession a card reader with a following. I made a living giving prophecies that came from demons. It was my angry way of leaving prostitution. I also enjoyed having power over

	people, and particularly men."
David:	"I had two card readers in my life. They were sisters. Please forgive me but I called them witches."
Mary:	"I was a witch too and a sorcerer. The abandonment I had internalized from my life as a child grew into a monster of isolation and bitterness. My life as a prostitute cultivated anger in me that was only satisfied by more anger. It was a dark satisfaction. The demons in the cards make you pay many times more than you receive. I was demon possessed and demon oppressed."
	"My entire spiritual being was scarred. Imagine a person scarred with third degree burns from fire. That's a picture of my emotional and spiritual appearance. The Script says 'Rebellion is as the sin of witchcraft.' I was an angry witch seeking to inflict on others, particularly men, the evil that was done to me."
	"We have learned at Narrow Gate that we have God Himself as our scriptwriter. He is our Author. The fact that you and I are speaking together is a scene written a long time ago. It is also a scene He is writing now - for us this very moment. You have come to the narrow gate, but you have not gone through it yet. You are deciding if you want to continue."
	"We learn His character as He expresses Himself through us. We need to be willing. We humans commonly *play God* in one way or another. We cannot succeed at playing God. To play Him requires wearing a mask and His actors do not wear a mask."
David:	"I have experienced great guilt, even remorse. I have never had satisfaction."
Mary:	"That's an example of one who plays God but fails. Even atheists play God. In a way, atheists especially play God. Atheists replace

the true God with a non-god. Their non-god has no life and the atheist has to wear its mask by taking Gods place. Humanism is a common substitute for God. Most people are functional atheists some of whom these see themselves as *believers*. Playing God is simply not your role to play. What we do best here is that we embrace this kind of surrender. We know our boundaries and when we let Him play out His passion through our lives, we discover our passion through His. He is the creator of humanity so it stands to reason that we can take on His character. It is the way humanity was meant to live. 'Lose yourself in Me and find yourself.'"

David: "John Stephens said that to me, too. It's so simple yet so deep. So how did you resolve this?"

Mary: "Well as I approached the tomb, the loss I was experiencing was for the only man I ever loved and the only man who ever loved me. 'How can I live now,' I asked myself with each step closer to the tomb. My only hope was cut off from my grasp."

"I did not process resurrection. I was at a funeral for God. I too was functionally an atheist. In the old days of my anger, I was living a life without hope or love. I asked myself, 'How can I live that way again?' If I were to go back, I would never return. I saw only one direction. God was dead and there was nothing for me but a return to life without hope."

David: "I have seen this sadness in Myriam and in my mother. I hope my daughter Sarah has been spared. I am not certain of this."

Mary: "Your family has to make the same decisions as you do. Extraordinary pain has the potential for extraordinary healing. Most people stop in the middle of a healing."

David: "Why?"

Mary: "God is not a magician but a healer. Magicians do tricks but Jesus heals the whole person. There is a necessary pain needed for healing to happen. Most are trained to be impatient. The way it stands, only the *rich and famous* can win. They offer a quick fix for their following who lack patience. They offer a kind of *poster* - product that their following can identify with. We call this losing at the losing game. We say 'why do you go to the experts to do for you what only God can do through you?' The quick fix doesn't heal, but neutralizes passion for the real thing. In this mindset only the well endowed can be successful people. At best the *successful with the following* are winning at the losing game. Have you noticed the number of young people in their 20s who are homeless? Passive and angry they walk the streets seeking a *something* without hope. Do you see why so many are drug addicts? There is little imagination or even desire for what is good and for what can heal."

"There is a ladder people climb to be better than the other. The ladder has to go, Davey. There is an adage that the one who is climbing a ladder to the wrong house needs to start over and climb the right house. I say lose the ladder and win. Climbing the ladder *is the wrong house*. The ladder looks like it's going up but it's really going down and hell is its destination. Jacob's ladder is not the ladder of status but of humility going vertical into the heart of God. Jacob's ladder also brings you down to ground zero where you can humble yourself in God's sight and be lifted up '*ascending and descending.*'"

"If Jesus lived through every person on planet earth there would not be a clone of God. There would be seven billion persons liberated into being people alive and without masks. There would be no poverty. All economies would be providing services that come from a *calling* and not from a *career*. People would be creative through the giving of love. Different services to others would manifest love. It would be demonstrated in the products we offer."

"Killing babies in the womb and then saying this is *good is the culture of death* at work. Much destruction has occurred from this justification of the murder of those '*with child.*' Ironically, to call murder a good thing is an even greater evil. There is no hope if sin is no longer sin."

"There are other hypocrisies also that call *evil good* and *good evil*. The Holy Spirit according to the Bible is The Spirit Of Truth. Blasphemy of the Holy Spirit is saying Truth is a lie and a lie is the Truth. Believing from the heart that *evil is good* and *good evil* is blasphemy of the Holy Spirit, and the only sin our forgiving Lord will not forgive."

I was uncomfortable hearing this. This was the first time this weekend where Jesus is characterized as not forgiving.

Mary continued... "The ruler of this world is Satan. He has his minions in the culture and masses in the world systems mindset. When you buy into it, you are fed by his world. It's a spirit that is not only in drugs such as heroin but in *itself is a drug*. It's a drug that *numbs* one to the spiritual- practical influences the world has on you. It changes your heart and causes you to change from who you once were. Its an evil spiritual drug that goes into your flesh and he seeks to own you. Watch what you let your eyes to see. That's Hollywood's demon. Watch out what you allow your ears to hear too. The mainstream media and Hollywood work for Satan big time. Some are well aware they are working for the evil one and some not yet aware. Toleration is preached into the world about all things. All things except *for the things that are from the heart of God*. There is an aggressiveness in Satan's media against the things of God. Big corporate and political money goes into television to teach people to *not think critically* but to react to what *they* are selling. Its Satan's agenda to destroy one's moral conscience and his number one enemy is Jesus Christ and His Script."

"Yahweh God has created His own media and live theater. The Good News is where *information meets transformation*. His Script is a revelation from Him. He said to Joshua, 'Meditate on it (my law) and keep these in your mouth.' It's about internalizing Him and His Script. That's how we know our lines and never forget them. You might say *we eat them*. It's more than visual, it's a vision from His heart into yours."

"Believing the lies and supporting its product cause the typical person to buy into the lie. Discernment, which comes from God, is diminished by the lies one believes. Davey you need to love the truth and leave the *drug of your slumber*."

"There is a great line in the Script. 'Hate evil, love good.' This cuts to the core. This is actually a wonderful expression of a loving God caring for His creation."

"Seeing right as wrong and wrong as right is the common insanity of our time. People will not critically evaluate what is clearly happening. The believing community has what we call *normalcy bias*. It stems from an unwillingness to accept that there is a spiritual collapse happening now and in the heart of the denier. As long as it's not happening to me *it's not really happening is the mantra*. It's the way it is Davey. The world has always been evil, but in these final days evil is reaching its closure. Satan works night and day. Most people have stressful sleep not discerning why, but refusing to be healed. 'Why?' There is a refusal to see the signs of our times."

I could not help but ponder that I did not have a theology on Satan or on God either. I thought myself an innocent bystander in life yet I was actually quite involved with destructive forces.

Mary continued... "Have you noticed all the horror and filthy creatures that are bought and sold? The world is filled with *Mary*

Magdalene's of demonic possession. There are many *Mary Magdalene's* today who live in a world without hope. I see these *Marys* as I was, and I say because '*He has risen*' there is hope for you to rise too."

"People are sick and do not know they are ill. That's why there is so little healing. The sickened state is considered normal. This illness is from the denial that there is an illness. *Healing begins when one quits the game and joins life 'on earth as it is in heaven.'* When I met Jesus I quit the game. I was delivered. There is little healing today because there is so little desperation for healing to happen."

This is what Myriam did too. No she wasn't Mary Magdalene, a prostitute or in the occult, but she came to the same conclusion. Mary and Myriam live in different times (or do they) but their decision and the place of heart are quite the same. The solution is the same too. My life in occult has me play the part of the observer only. That means I am still in it because I refuse to act upon its effect on me. Am I still quite active in the occult? If so, how? I play the observer!

Mary continued... "When He came to my city of Bethsaida I followed Him from a safe distance. I followed as one who sought to embarrass Him among His following. He was among about 6 or 7 others of His apostles I assumed. He was walking with such ease. As far as I knew, He had never been to Bethsaida yet He seemed so comfortable where He had never been before. I saw this as arrogant. I hated His confidence. He, in my mind, acted as if He owned our town. Then I shuddered in thought, 'What if He got some convert's?' Come to think of it, He and I are in the same business! 'What if people come to Him instead of me to have security for the future?' The other thing I recollected as I looked at Him was He had real confidence. Much more than I ever knew or saw in any one else. He had peace?"

David: "That's why the two witches in my life were so threatened by John

Stephens. Threatened by my marriage to Myriam too."

Mary: "That's so true, Davey. I too as your witches had never known peace. So when I saw His peace, I was intrigued yet jealous too. I wanted what He had. If He had what I wanted, what did that say about what I had? My anger was reaching new peaks. Besides, he was a man and I hated men. Suddenly He turned. I thought He might get out of town. I was relieved. Then He took another turn, and was now headed toward me and my place of business."

"He walked straight at me as if He were a customer coming for a palm reading. I was about to scream; in fact my body and mouth were in a coordinated dance of defiance and demonic power. I opened up and released my scream of vengeance, but nothing came out of my mouth. Instead I saw His face. He was now in my space."

"I then heard His voice and He took my hands and said, 'Myriam. Myriam. I release all that has come upon you. Every lie you have believed. I release every lie you have spoken and every sin you've committed with your body, mind, and spirit. I cast out the legion of demons you have carried. Begin now! Come out now!' Suddenly Jesus smile was so very wide. I noticed the slight space He had between His two front teeth. 'Begin a new childhood. Now Myriam. Now and Forever.'"

David: "That was it? Such a short discourse."

Mary: "That was all of it. I looked into His eyes and His eyes smiled again. His face was like a child's face. His hands strong and yet lean. I saw the lion and the lamb. He had perfect Love. No man or woman can give this as He does. 'A cord of three strands is not easily broken.' He is the missing link in marriage and in all human relationships. He is our friend and redeemer. He destroys man's wanting to beat other men because He loves us all. He loves me. He loved me and all the hate that I had attained was gone. Hate's scar was healed in me."

"When He rose from the dead, all that I had before came me back to me. I was now more sure than ever that all was right. Shalom was my closure from fear, doubt, hate, and revenge. I was forgiven and I had forgiveness to give. When He breathed His Holy Spirit on us that evening, I was even more at peace and more certain. On and on through time and eternity, I am more sure. I live in Love. A place of forever learning."

"He was and is for now and for all time. He is… He is the only One. He has joy and in this He desires to have play with you, David. He is so childlike yet also warrior like victorious. He wants you as family. He wants to extend His family to you and through you. He wants through you, to redeem the world of the angry and oppressed Mary Magdalene's. He is the new beginning and the forever farewell. He is…"

I had my head down in prayer as Mary was praying. I felt a warm hand on my head. This warmth made my whole being relaxed. Peace went through my body. I was immersed in warmth and love. It was more than physical. It was all encompassing. I remembered in those moments my mother's lullaby to me when she put me to sleep and me as a boy. I had not thought of this in oh so long a time. It had been so long since I was in prayer. I remembered the last time I prayed was when I swerved from the tree I intended to crash into. This was different. There was a perfection to this prayer that far exceeded my own understanding. I heard myself whispering, 'Yes,' even, 'Amen,' as she continued on. Then I looked up. I was in the theater and I was alone.

24

MYRIAM MEMORIES

That was an amazing monologue and prayer she gave. I was in the same theater where I had seen Paul's play. I was now alone.

As an actor and a news reporter (that's what they are telling me here), am I also called to be a kind of first fruits? Getting the news first hand? That's what a good journalist does as he gets the news first and then reports on it. What if my passion for acting was really a call from God? What if I had then surrendered to what John Stephens was saying to me in 1974? What if I surrendered now? Acting was my chosen career and *I owned it.* I was also frantic about losing what I had. What if I had what Myriam has now and what these Narrow Gate people always have?

Does God come to us or we to Him? If the Bible is eternal, is the Bible still happening now? Have I tapped into time and eternity now and while I still live on the earth? Do I know what I just said to myself? Does God live in time, eternity, or both? Am I being invited to enter a Bible scene that happened 2000 years ago because the Bible always happens? *Does* the *Bible play in the town I live in? Does it play* today *and wherever I am?* Are the Ten Commandments being offered in my living room as well as Mt Sinai? Are they offered right now if I open my heart to Him? *Right now?*

There is a British director named Peter Brook, who wrote *The Empty Space.* His point was theater happens where it happens. It happens now if you want to *play.* All it needs is for the actor to fill the space. Is God inviting us into His sphere? His space and stage? Is my life the empty space that He fills - if I will play? Is God's theater child's play for grownups so we can all grow into a new childhood?

Is this what they mean when they say, "On earth as it is in heaven?" I remember the Broadway Theater Guild saying, "Will it play (our play) in Peoria, Illinois?" God wrote a book, which the actors here call *The Script.* Did Jesus mean to say it needs to play 'on earth as it is in heaven?'

Why did I walk away from John twenty-two years ago? He offered me a part in a play. What he offered would have saved my marriage. My marriage would have saved my family. My mother saw this. If anyone knew what caused a family to break up it was Mom.

My Mom's Mom committed suicide. Mom was raised by her step-Mom who preferred her children from her first marriage. Mom meets Dad and they fall in love, but unfortunately there are no guarantees. When people get off track they literally get on the wrong rail. Other people crash because the engineer had a bad day, week, year, and there are many casualties in a train wreck. One wrecked life does not wreck only one life.

Dad left Mom because he got on the career track. So being great meant having lots of money. He unfortunately crashed when his girlfriend left him for someone else who was greater at not having guilt for causing his family to crash. The father I hardly knew, in his last days on earth, was a stumbling homeless person who still lived in an apartment in Mamaroneck, NY. These are the homeless who live in houses, but do not know what home is.

Mom was super sad for years after my 12th birthday when Dad left home. When we sang *Daddy's Home To Stay*, I think God's Name was mentioned. It's common for people who on the one hand do not believe in God to call on him. I remember once that she broke into singing *Love Makes The World Go Round*. I asked Mom, "What is love?" She said, "Davey honey, God is love."

People have hidden faith. It's often more than we can put into words. It still needs to be drawn out but it's there in each of us. If there is something I hear from the Narrow Gate crowd it's that faith is much more than a cognitive knowing. It's an experience with God. In fact, a cognitive understanding of God is what so often blocks a heart from the *understanding of who God is*. This is what I am synthesizing into the melody of my soul. That prayer of Mary was an original, certainly never before given. I liked it. *Prayer is improvisation. Its script comes from heaven. We people are its actors if we show up for practice.* It's *the Practice of faith. I like that!*

My Dad's bad motivations, ironically, were revealed in his final moments on this earth. He was crying in my arms and crying out to God. Sobbing how he lost his love. "All I want is ham and eggs (not very kosher) and the peace of a hommmme, and I want your Mummm."He had a stroke and his last words were so slurred from his condition, "Gaud, puesasse forgiveee mehhh." Then he looked at me ... no, he looked inside of me.

I tell you he had such kindness and full attention on me. *He loved me.* He looked at me and his eyes were saying, "I love you. I missed out on you. I missed you Davey my son."

He continued his look into and through my eyes. He was saying *hello* and *goodbye*. His face said, "I love you. I love you and I am sorry."

He smiled love into my eyes. He was doing to me what I had never before seen from him. He was so kind and gentle toward me. It was a glance for a lifetime or eternity. This happened over twenty years ago but I am realizing now what happened then. So it's *happening for* me *now. This very moment!*

I remember I then loved him back. I was loving him for the first time. This time *knowing he always loved me*. It took me to Dad's last breath, but I got a Dad. I just stayed with him until he loved me back. Like Jacob, I was holding out until I got my blessing. My Dad was the blessing I never had. Unlike Jacob it took me years to understand what I got then, but I Have It Now! All these years later *I receive* what happened before.

Its history and personal prophecy as one?

Myriam would always say to me *David I love you now*. I would say what about tomorrow and she laughed her laugh and said but I *love you now*. Now is forever, she always said to me. Time can help bring home what happened before and make it a now thing. God is Love and His Love plays out later on as much as today.

My Dad Always Loved Me. All these years and now at Narrow Gate I remember my last moment with Dad. I could now hold a jewel from the past. I pondered this in my heart. "This is good," I said to myself. "This is very good."

Dad then smiled and breathed, his mouth now open and his eyes now widened. He then stopped breathing, and that was the end. The year was 1970. It was the year after Myriam and I were married. The year Sarah was born. He died in his apartment in Mamaroneck. I was the only one there that night.

Mom came to Woodstock to our rented home. It was 1980. Myriam as I said before attempted a new home life while she lived in Brooklyn full time and I in Hartford Connecticut. Mom was so fragile.

She never remarried but she was now no longer homeless. I had visited her at a homeless shelter in 1979. She was there only a short time. I thought it was a Christian shelter, but did not give it much attention. Being nice to poor people was a '*Christian thing*' I figured and did not explore beyond that. With us in Woodstock she was now physically sick, but spiritually glowing. She loved Sarah. She gave Sarah her most personal possession, which was a *heart shaped necklace*. It had an opening with the Bible inscription inside: "I will never leave you nor forsake you."

I asked, "Who is that a quote from?" Mom said, "Its Yeshua Ha Messiach. I am married to Jesus and I have a home. In fact, I have a mansion coming to me very soon. Don't worry about me anymore, Davey. When He is master of your house, you will find home too. "Don't die Mom!" I pleaded for a moment sharing emotion.

"Embrace the me that is dying Davey. Then you can know *life*. I am going to a better place."

Myriam was very moved. She said, "Momma tell me more," but Mom, who had Parkinson's disease, could not say more. Her life was failing. "Maybe she *got religion?*" as I put it then. I was pained knowing Mom was so soon to die, but I had to minimize anything real. It was very personal for me to lose my mother. *I had pain but no outlet.*

Oddly, Myriam and I had little conversation about Mom's faith. Let me be clear, we had no conversation together. We just thought about it in our own mind and hearts.

I know I did. Mom died in her apartment one month later. Hospice was there and so were we.

I had this very strange encounter the hour she died. It was about 5:00 in the morning. I was exhausted from the night. Mom was (to use a hospice term) actively *dying*. She had said her goodbyes with that glow again. It was the same glow I noticed that other time in our necklace moment at the house in Woodstock. In her last moment before her coma, she was with Mansfield and I. She smiled. She never was one for words. I always trusted her. She and I were always there for each other. She particularly glowed for Mansfield. She knew he needed that and I was not jealous. I was never jealous of Mom's love because I was *always sure she loved me.*

Sitting on that chair at 5 am, I dozed off, but was not quite asleep. I then saw a face. It was a man's face with a soft grey beard and wide smile. I looked into his smile and I smiled back. Then he vanished. His momentum was toward Mom's room. The moment gave me so much peace, and then I fell off into sleep. Moments later, say 5 minutes later, the hospice nurse came to me saying, "David there has been a change."

I knew this was it. I was surprised to be so pragmatic in a moment like this. I mean, I was there for Mom's last heartbeat. I had her hand in mine and I felt her last beat of life. Mom was the most perfect relationship I had ever had. She was as fair and kind to me as was Myriam. The only difference was me. Myriam and Mom were family and friends. I was family to Mom, especially in her depression years before and after Dad left. Unfortunately, I was not fair to Myriam. I did to Myriam what Dad did to Mom.

The funeral people came one hour later for Mom. They put her tiny body into a zipped bag. They took her away for cremation and that was it. The only pure relationship I ever had was shipped away forever.

My mind went back to Mom's last minutes of life. What of the face of the man who came by and energized me? I had not thought about this all these years until just now. I then took a walk to my bed and breakfast room at the home section of the theater. As I walked down the hall I heard the worship music, and again I was moved. I was moved to tears about how I *missed out* on years of joy.

"I could have had all this if only I listened to John's words for me." I re-remembered Mary's words regarding her career in witchcraft. "It's totally demonic," she said to me.

Did the black witch put a curse on me when I took back the $1000.00 dollars? Do curses have to be direct or can one just slip into a curse. One thing is for sure. I walked out on both John and the witches and what was the net result? The witches succeeded at their mission, didn't they? I walked out on the three they so wanted me to walk out on namely, John, Myriam, and Sarah.

When we had our time in Woodstock back in 1979-1981, I had a palm reader join our writing staff. I later added an astrologer too. They would speak about *the force* and I thought I was being open-minded. Myriam did not hate them, but hated what they were about. She begged me to not report on *forces* in our newspaper. She said our dealings with them made her *'physically sick.'*

The other thing she had trouble about with me was that I was doing transcendental meditation. She could not articulate why I should not do it, only to say, "When you do your 'resting exercises,' you leave Sarah and I out. It's as if when you do this a *force* surrounds you and it enters your personal space. What it says to Sarah and I is '*get out.*'"

I told her that TM was a harmless ritual with a touch of science too. "If it's scientific," she said "then why," she asked "did you have to make a sacrifice to them by bringing a gift?" It's true I did have to bring a fruit basket as a ritualistic gift to begin TM. They kept saying the meditations were relaxation exercises. I later also remembered my card reader Janet insisting I give her sister Natalie a sacrifice gift. In her case the sacrifice of cash was not enough. I conveniently forgot to bring the gift. On the other hand, how many times did I make the sacrifice gift of cash? If my sacrifices were not to *the only God* who then was it to? To which or what god?"

Mary Magdalene would say it was to 'demons.' In TM they said your mantra is a word that really is a sound. If it's a sound, who or what is the speaking the sound? They never said I was to make a sacrifice to hear myself talk? Was it not a demon speaking in the first person through me? Myriam heard that voice too, and it said, 'GET OUT.'

They advertise TM as a neutral. The witches advertise their tea leaves the same way. They are not neutral but they do *neutralize*. They destroy passion and put passivity in its place.

The world is so without passion. My world was in crisis and yet it seemed I was so *relaxed*? *What I did not see was Myriam's need for my love.* I thought we were doing just fine. She said to me when our Woodstock experiment came to an end, "David you hate me? I said, "How?" She said, "Because you ignore the obvious. You are ignorant and ignorance is not innocence but arrogance. *You drain me David.*"

I had one other major encounter with Miriam and Sarah. In 1987 they had been living in Israel for four years. Israel Leiber, their mentor had a strong connection with Lapwood Theological Seminary in Boston. The seminary did an annual trip to Israel for three weeks in January. Israel was their tour guide and he encouraged Myriam and Sarah, now sixteen going on seventeen, to be helpers in creating dramatic presentations at Biblical sights. They encouraged me to come. I was glad to be invited. I still did not completely understand their faith in Jesus, but I was lonely for my family. What I really did not know was how faith in God was so encompassing. Over a short amount of time I grew to understand just what they had.

They prayed and sang songs to God. They also did what they called *messianic dance*. By the time the first Sabbath happened on our trip, I was also getting into the fun side of worshipping. There were lots of laughs. I was also amazed at how the Israelis really took to the Sabbath. They did not work on Shabbat - they had family fun. They would come to the King David Hotel in Jerusalem where we were staying, and they played and sang with family on Sabbath.

I could not help but notice that Myriam had her eye on me. I reasoned at the very least her heart was for us to be family. She never had another man and I never had another woman. We were the only lovers we each had ever known. Long standing married couples cannot usually say this. It was family and this happy thought, of course, only increased the tragedy of our situation.

Israel however was different for us. It had the timeless feel that we were never separated. We had in Israel all the advantages of love's purity. Sarah so wanted us to be back together and we had all our meals together. We each loved all the sights together. The Old Testament and the New Testament felt like the same book. It was easy for me because I was not asked to make decisions. Myriam seemed pleased that I was open to new things. Sarah would say grace and so would Myriam. Once I volunteered and I thanked God for our family and for food. Sarah laughed and concluded my prayer saying "In Jesus Name. Amen." I was fine with that. I said, "Yes!"

Two unfortunate occurrences happened maybe three days before our tour was coming to an end. We all three were a bit antsy knowing our good time was coming to an end. *How will we close this chapter?*" we each thought in our personal musings.

The first incident was when my hotel room door was open and Sarah walked in. Our rooms were near each other so I kept my door cracked to give us a feeling of family life. I did not completely notice as I was doing transcendental meditation, but Sarah walked into my room. She reported back to Myriam saying "Dad's meditating."Myriam then came into the room quietly so I did not notice her either, or did I?

Later at breakfast, Myriam asked me if I was still doing TM. I intuitively knew then she had noticed my meditating time. I had noticed my door was open and thought maybe they were in the room for different flashes of time, but in meditation I did not want to be disturbed so I ignored my intuition. I said to Myriam,

"Yes, it was very relaxing for me."Myriam then put her head down without anger but with disappointment. Myriam was not the kind of person who acted out. She was one who communicated real feelings but not necessarily with words. I saw *she was visibly disappointed.*

Later that same day we went to the Mount of Beatitudes. This is the place where Jesus gave the *Sermon on the Mount*. Myriam was the speaker for this Bible sight. In 1987 you could go to the Mount of Beatitudes and it was an open field that extended to the Sea of Galilee.

There was no church there at that time. There were no fences cutting off the timelessness of Bible events. When Jesus gave His famous sermon, it could well have looked like what we saw that morning. Myriam saw things in the spirit realm. She shared with us.

"This message is for the pure in heart. The same God, who spoke then, speaks now through His Holy Spirit who is present right now. Listen, hear, and see the Sermon on the Mount."

Then she, Sarah, and the students all spoke words from Matthew and the Sermon on the Mount. Some said them aloud reading from the Bible and others internalized them the way that they do at Narrow Gate Theater. Myriam then said,

"The Holy Spirit spoke life into Matthew and today we have Matthew five, six and seven. She said that he was God's human vessel to speak what God is saying to us *right now* He the Holy Spirit is demonstrating *The Sermon On The Mount* right now through me and through us. The Lord is demonstrating these words with us this very moment."

The word '*demonstration*' was emphasized. Myriam asked us when the words to *Sermon* on the *Mount* were finished that we should walk the Mount of Beatitudes. She then took me by the hand and walked the small mountain with me. She smiled at me. She smiled through me. She was giving love and taking emotional risks. I noticed this. I loved the attention. I smiled back.

She then broke away and said to me, "David, let's we three walk down the mountain and experience Jesus speaking the sermon to us. Then let's walk up the mountain and say the words. You can read them from the Bible, but let Him speak the *Sermon on the Mount* through you. She handed me a Bible and opened it to Matthew.

"Just receive sweetheart."

I noticed out of the corner of my eye that Sarah and Myriam were a *walking poem*. They just flowed and were in dance mode. I so wanted what they had. Unfortunately I had a block they did not have. You see, you can't act Jesus. The actors here at Narrow Gate have made that clear to me now. *I now understand what was missing in me then.* I was using all my acting ability to *play Him*. I was sweating from my forehead. My teeth were gridlocked and my jaw was tight.

It was so uncomfortable for me. Somewhere in time, say 10 minutes later, I simply said loudly and with a performer's frustration,

"I cannot do this!"

My timing was horrible. I blurted this out as Myriam and Sarah were in song. I tell you they sang like the choir from heaven. My words were a shout of frustration.

I broke the moment with something very ugly. I interrupted something special. That I was the one to interrupt their *epiphany* was a moment from hell. Myriam just looked at me. She never was one for negotiation. She was so very honest about everything. I did not say too honest. Her words were soft and forlorn, "*It's not about performing, David. It's about letting go.*"

I also saw in that moment how painful it was for her to be her. She is so real. She could no longer give herself to me. I was a *risk no longer worth taking*. I now saw how the 'good Jesus' was a barrier between us. It was so clear to me that day.

There were no more conversations. We, in the last two days, had no meals together. I took Sarah for a walk. We spoke about colleges she might want to attend in the United States. That was nice even if somewhat formal. Myriam was very quiet. I was certain she had held out hope for us in Israel. It was a kind of audition, and we both lost because I failed once again.

When I returned to Manhattan and my law practice, within 6 weeks I fazed out of transcendental meditation. I had done it for twelve years. I gave up smoking pot too.

With what I have learned from Mary Magdalene, and remembering Myriam's reaction, I am glad I had finally left the occult world, *but the occult world had not left me. Its effects were still in me.* Sometime later I moved to Albuquerque New Mexico and began my law practice in the great southwest. I had to get away from my law partner and besides my family lived in Israel. Anywhere in the northeast was a painful reminder of my loss.

It's been 9 years since the Mount of Beatitudes. I have seen Myriam a few times, such as when Mansfield died, but we have not had a heart to heart talk since. I have had good times with Sarah. Her first semester at NYU in September of 1987 she lived with me. When she transferred to Hebrew University in January 1988 is when I moved to Albuquerque. The short time we had together was wonderful for me. She seemed un- hampered by my bad parenting and betrayal. Myriam and I gave her away at her wedding in 1992. She was 22 when she married Peter. They pastor a church in New England.

I still laugh to myself, "Whatever happened to being Jewish? I have nothing but *goyim* in my family." Myriam laughed when I said that to her the day before Sarah's wedding and she replied with humor, "No David. She has never been more Jewish than now. Even with her husband who is *goy*." She laughed that laugh I so love her for. I then said, "*goy veh.*" We laughed again.

Myriam is married to Jesus. I pray every so often that Jesus is the only husband she ever has. It's impossible for me to ever forget her.

I had walked through *bed and breakfast* part of the theater. I had hardly noticed that people had gathered into the main theater where I had spent so much time with Mary Magdalene. It was Saturday night already and *Paul In Prison* was ready for show.

When I got to my room there was a covered hot meal at the table. There was also an encouraging note from Stephen letting me know it was important that he be at the play. In the rendition of tonight's *Paul In Prison*, he was playing Stephen. I then thought to myself, "Oh he's playing himself, no, he's the actor playing Stephen."

I, for the first time, wanted to believe he was Stephen and that God was demonstrating through him.

Whoever they are, they are the soundest people I have ever known. They are also the kindest. They are surely taking life acting to where it can thrive.

I heard a knock at the door.

25

THE HEART OF DEATH

"Hello David? It's John. May I come in?"

"Yes, of course John, please come in. Please share the abundance of food Stephen brought me."

The timing of his visitation was divine. I was so very glad to see John. He, sitting at the table, was in particularly good spirits. "I know him best," I thought to myself.

I know I am leaving tomorrow. Some closure with John, who so impacted my life, would mean so much to me. My thoughts were not racing but were comforting my mind.

Unusual for me. Am I learning to relax? I thought to myself, now sitting on the wicker rocking chair that was so comfortable to my body *and so comforting to my soul.* My lower back gets stiff easily and the chair was like tiny fingers massaging my bones. The cushion helped make the wickers breathe into my middle back up into the shoulders. It was better than the massage therapy I used to get from Norman Goldstein in Woodstock and he was really good. He had helped heal the chronic physical pain from the broken collarbone I had suffered as a child. This chair was lifting my body soul and spirit. Maybe it was the company I was keeping here with John Stephens. I was ready to talk, but more so to listen.

John: "You have done well here, David. The cast adores you."

David: "Thanks John, nice of you to say. What is it that they adore?"

John: "The way you go along with the things we do here. You are often startled, but you are always ready for new things."

David: "I have done lots of thinking in my alone time. I find myself in meditation on personal things I simply have not thought about for many years. My pattern has been to push unpleasant thoughts away. The only meditation I had ever before done was transcendental meditation and that is not the kind of meditation I do here. In this place I have sought to remember all my bad choices. My heart has been broken, yet here I also have found contentment. Thank you, John, for providing the environment that fosters such... such ..."

John: "*Mishbukah?*"

David: "Yes, mish - bu- ka."

John: "Introspection is essential for inner life. Jesus is a type of Shakespeare only much greater. Shakespeare said of the artist, 'The poet gives to airy nothing a local habitation and a name.' God does this for His creation. His poem is real life. Your life can be a *masterpiece* of His '*workmanship*'. 'All of Scripture is God breathed' and it has His stamp on every comma, semicolon. His Word is more than words as all the silences between each word are His Word too. When we do these live presentations one can see and experience His Breath between the words. Just reading it and receiving is what I am saying. These spaces are His Holy Spirit at His improvisational best. We want you to come join us and be in His Word with us."

David: "You know me as an actor and I know you as a director. There was not one day these past these last 22 years where I did not think of you. You so reached me, but I did not realize how much you reached me then until this weekend as your guest. Whatever you say now I will listen to and will apply to my life. You are giving me great acting lessons and are using the Bible as the basis for acting. If it was not coming from you I would have never conceived that acting and the Bible are an actor's script."

John: "You were called to be an actor and you intuitively knew this the day you took Acting 1 at Northeastern. We are showing you the right way to act is the right way to live. The Script is taking Acting 1 and making it *Acting One* for you. You are finally seeing beyond the career trap and into *your calling*. Others will benefit, as you are willing to grow."

David: "This is what Myriam has done. She left the *performance of it* from what she saw it was doing to me. She is doing Holy - Wood in Israel and is living out her forever calling now. She skipped the career trap, she's making a living too. She is forever at play. I have not told you about Myriam and you have not asked."

John: "I still am not asking, but I see Myriam and Sarah in you and through you."

David: "To be free of people's expectation yet to serve others. That's how I see Myriam and Sarah. I also see how much I miss them."

John: "They miss you too. If you see the *Scripts Words* as His food and eat them like candy to a child you can be *free of self-absorption*. His theater can restore your life."

"We call this the *new reformation. It's for* we people in our time of human history. Martin Luther did this in the sixteenth century when he lived. He and some others too re-established that the Scriptures are the primary place for where we can know and find God. Luther also translated the Bible into common language. The priests and pope were not the final authority anymore for the reformers. This is what Luther taught when he said '*Sola Scriptura!*' We at Narrow Gate say '*Only Script*! It's not about a translation. We need a '*demonstration*'! His Word in His Script is the password to Him. It's the key to His identity. All of Bible teaching is to reveal and deepen relationship with Him."

"His Script is actable whenever it happens. It happens when He happens. The Bible is God seeking fellowship with His creation. We affectionately call this He- Mail. This is what you have experienced with us at Narrow Gate. The new reformation is a *demonstration of the Bible with the Holy Spirit* interacting with people through the *Script*. In the *'new reformation'* we seek new actors to demonstrate His Word through their presentation. The Script is the password into His essence. It needs be heard again. Again for the first time too! We want all to know we need to rediscover *'Sola Scriptura'*. This includes the spaces between words in the Scriptures. Actors as *Bible Demonstrators* can show a better way to read the Script."

"Many when reading the Script rush through the words. We are also commonly taught in Bible study to give the result of His Word, but not the *playing out of His Word*. The alongside God is the way to learn scripture and fellowship with God too. This improvising with Scripture causes fellowship among the participants. Today Bible verses are commonly tossed around and offered the way a doctor writes a prescription. This approach is the Bible is as a *'manual.'*"

"God is demonstrative and passionate. The Bible is *Immanuel* God with us. He wants fellowship with people. The new reformation is *The Bible* as God interacting with us as we read Scripture. This carries over into real life. Reading the Words aloud and teaching Bible by reading it aloud is new to our time but not so in Bible history. The Bible was sustained orally through Israel's tradition of speaking aloud the Word to each new generation. It's having people sitting around a table and playing the parts too. In Holy-Wood you do not need acting skills. Just read it and childlikeness will overtake the frustration involved in *'trying'* to act. All of God's Words are instruments in His orchestra, raising up *Bible Demonstrators*. There is a rhythm to His Words like notes in a song. This is where *Bible Acting* becomes so effective and relevant. The Holy Spirit is demonstrative and this shows why Jesus says, 'He who hears these words of Mine and *acts* upon them builds his house upon the Rock.'

Acting is not an elective in a college curriculum. It's the core teaching in the Book Of Life. *The key is acting from God and not for God."*

David: "I generally thought the Bible as irrelevant but gave it some respect as a book of ancient teachings. My view has vastly changed."

John: "Bible acting is theater that offers revelation into the ancient scriptures. Just as the reformers saw the revelation of scripture then, God today is raising a movement of many reformers. In effect saying '*revisit the scriptures as The Script*'! Bible time is always *now time*. See the Bible's chapters and verses as an actor playing a scene. Experience Bible verses as lifelines from the breath of God's passion. The parting of the Red Sea happened once in human history, but in the eternal Script it happens right now too. Read it aloud. Give sermons in churches where the preacher internalizes chapters and lets God demonstrate through the speaker. It's what we call *Bible Acting*. Taste the fish with Jesus in the Galilee. Be with Moses when the *Ten Commandments* come. Hide in the dark of the caves with King David. Enter as an actor only let the *Words play you*. Be affected by what you just said because what you just said are not your words but *God's Word through you*. Its Gods play and God at play with you. Remember only 'children enter the kingdom of heaven.' Play in His play, and the play will play out into your life. This brings out *imagination. It's fun Davey*. The new reformation can make 'church' organic in a way the sixteenth century reformation never did."

"We ask 'why do you go to Hollywood when you can have Holy-Wood?'"

"At Narrow Gate we play to an audience of One and are increasingly free of self-consciousness. Here our presentation and our lives are one. We are not stars seeking fame or fortune but what we have is contentment and constant creativity. It's so simple and close as in *one* times *one* times *one* equals one. That's the Godhead Davey. The Father The Son and The Holy Spirit. The One God."

David: "That's what killed acting for me. *Making it* in the theater became my passion and I lost the love of something that was fun. The star syndrome ruined my life. I lost much more than career. I lost my creativity and my love of life. You show me God is my casting director."

John: "It's not over! What was lost was lost. But though lost it can be found again. The value of getting back that which was lost gives greater value had it not been lost. Be brave David face your error and come through the narrow door of opportunity while the door is open. Remember in *Sartre's No Exit* the door opened but the people went into *overthink* until the door shut."

David: "I was in that play but in real reality I have lived in that scene for many years. I got stuck in rationalization overload. I wanted stardom. I finally saw through *stardoms* illusion but have not replaced its deadly effect with a greater power."

John: "The star system exists to create failure for stars and their following. Idolization of its stars is there to soothe its captives. The star system in this world is not hated but is considered a high value. It does not require a career in performing arts for its manifestation either. It's a deadly spirit that metastasizes throughout human culture. It does not require integrity, only outward success. Its followers glean the stars success by buying its products and worse being enslaved to its lie. You David never were a star but you are a victim of its disease."

"Narrow Gate was raised to destroy the desire to follow the *star of stardom*. The wise men were among shepherds, a humble husband, and a poor virgin to follow *the star* to its humble king. These are the actors of His Play. The Bethlehem Star draws His story into your story, *but only if you will come.* If you are wise you will follow *His Star* and not yours. I ask audiences can you name the names of the shepherds at the manger of His birth? One cannot name one of them. Why? Because they are stars in God's play and not slaves to the stardom that is mankind's power grab for acknowledgement by other men. God did not mention their names, and yet they were there when history happened. You don't know their names but know who they were. That's *Bethlehem's Star.*"

"Watch out for the scholarship star system too. The Greek and Hebrew scholars whose reputation says, ' You need what I have in order to find God.' Greek and Hebrew are original Bible languages, but there is a mindset that says the average shepherd in the field, watching their flock by night, somehow do not have knowledge. To God, these nameless ones were His first choice to share the life that would change humanity forever. He shared His Word in their language and in a way that they could understand His language. God confides in shepherds of all varieties. Relationship with Jesus is experiencing the person of God. This will cause a hunger to keep Bible learning simple, fun, and hungry for the knowledge of Jesus. We call this *relationship theology*."

"David, you will love not being rich or famous. Moreso you will love having no desire for it or have regret it never happened for you. God is a simple, humble, deep, king and the good ruler. True human liberation is to be as He is. The new reformation is nothing new with God but for we humans it's necessary to rediscover Jesus. To discover the Jesus you never knew by getting a new take on the Bible as He is. No One owns the new reformation it's a movement available for all humans."

"When one enters this, one has been stretched. Then you are not your own. I trust you have experienced fun, joy and play with us. Even in the pain!"

David: "Thank you John."

John: "So are you coming? Every human being comes to a crossroad and a most difficult door he cannot navigate alone. It's an invitation to go down into ground zero."

David: "You are asking me to choose?"

John: "Since we first met 22 years ago with the *Thespian*, yes I have been seeking this for you."

David: "You have done a more complete job this time, John. I never thought Broadway would be open to this kind of theater. I remember when I said to you, 'People do not want to come to the Jonah play at Greenwich Village to hear about God.'"

John: "They still don't Davey. *There are always some but it's always a few.* Broadway has not invited us - we just showed up. Satan is the ruler of this world, but we have 'entered through the narrow gate.' We have chosen to dwell in God's world and Satan does not rule in God's world. We are not making a better world on the earth, but we are taking those *who will to* come *out of this world*."

David: "You have not asked, but it's obvious. I am without family. I am worse than my father. If I somehow got out of '*the world*,' as you put it, is there a place for me here? Your actors are real people. I am only at best an actor. A bad one and I don't fit in."

John: "Nobody fits, until they change. Think of Mary Magdalene before and after. Paul, Moses, Matthew, Luke, and Jonah. The script is filled with character arcs. You were lost when you walked in yesterday and you are lost today. The difference is today; you know *for sure* you are lost. To learn is to unlearn. What have you unlearned is the question. To unlearn requires the act of unpacking what cannot fit through the narrow gate."

David: "That's hardly encouraging John."

John:	"I am not trying to encourage or discourage. I want you to assess who you are. When this happens you can re-ask the vital questions and finally decide."
David:	"I do not mean to change the subject. I am with every word that proceeds from your mouth. It's just that looking at your mouth, if you will, seeing you again after all these years, you have a distinct and familiar look to you. You look like someone I know. I am putting it together right now. You have the same face as the face I saw *in my mother's room just before she died.* The same beard too. Being here has reminded me of the face. I had forgotten that face."
	"You have the same face. I don't mean to interrupt this stimulating conversation, but if I don't just tell you I will be distracted. It's crazy but lots of crazy things are happening these two days. I know the face cannot be yours. It's the effect that face had on me that is so similar to the effect you have on me now. The effect your face has always had on me."
John:	"And what is that effect Davey?"
David:	"It's peace John. It's a desire for you to not leave me. It's something you have that puts all my missing parts together and makes me never want to leave you. What I am saying is making me *feel again.* It's the same face that so soothed me just before Mom died."
	"I know somehow you cannot be the face that visited Mom, but the reminder has reminded me how sorry I am for what I missed by missing your face. The face that reminds me what I have *not faced.* Please forgive me."
John:	"I was wondering when you were going to remember. Hi Davey. (He held out his hand to shake hands with me.) I am glad you like my face. I am the one who is that face, the face that met Mom when she died."

David: "Stop joking John. I mean this, you are being funny but I am serious."

John: "So am I." (John's face was without animation and now looked even more like that person with that face.)

David: "You cannot be an image I see and also a physical being. I can't believe I am explaining this to you. You are you, and that's enough for me. Please stop joking."

John: "I want to share a story with you, Davey. Have you ever seen the film *The 7th Seal* by Ingmar Bergman?"

David: "Yes I have. Maybe the greatest black and white film ever made. It's quite a message about death. It shows death as fair but very resolute on his mission. Death is a person, and you know he is going to win in the end."

John: "That's right Davey. *Death is a person.* That he wins in the end is a limited understanding of who death is. Have you ever noticed how when one dies, whether it be due to a lingering illness or sudden calamity, there is always a shock?"

David: "Yes I have. The feeling of loss is very strange. Death is a shock and death is so final. It's very strange. It's like death is not supposed to happen."

John: "That's right, it was never supposed to happen. People are not prepared for death because this was never meant to be for mankind. When a loved one dies, the one who is still living experiences a lack of control. 'This should not be! This cannot be!' *The loss is real because humans were not built for this kind of loss.* Humans were meant for forever and sin has altered mankind's destiny."

David: "Death is so strange. It's as if you never completely overcome the shock."

John:	"The film *The 7th Seal* and its dealings with the inevitability of death are very accurate. My story goes to a greater place. My story is how the person of death deals with death."
David:	"Are you referring to yet another character in the Narrow Gate cast?"
John:	"Yes, Death is a grieving person. To most people Death is trauma. There is great fear of death, but death and life are two sides of the same coin."

"Horror films with zombies and vampires glorify death. Satan owns this kind of death. The evil empire of dread. This death is glorified on earth. There is an arrogance about sin and this arrogance leads to more death. So death itself is mocked, ridiculed and minimized. Ironically, it is life that is not valued."

"Moses warned Pharaoh over and again that God was against Pharaoh's gods of satanic magic. The gods of horror, including the witches you would frequent, are gods of black magic too. Most of planet earth is under a spell. Pharaoh ignored God."

"Think of the word '*ignore*' and add '*ance*.' You get *ignorance*. To ignore is to intentionally make oneself ignorant. This ignorance is arrogance not innocence. In fact, ignorance is the partner to arrogance. Pharaoh was warned over and again until finally one more warning was '*ignored*.' Death to the firstborn of all he served. Like Satan himself, Pharaoh demanded servitude from the ones he served. He dared God one more time. One last time. He ignored God's passionate warning."

"On the night Israel was secured by the blood of a lamb on the doorpost of each of its homes, Egypt's homes were slain. Its god was Pharaoh and Pharaoh's faith was in his god of demons. There was total shock in Egypt. Children young and old, men and grown women were suddenly fallen over and dead. Death was never intended by God. This death, however, was now a masquerade of horror and Satan's domain over people. Death made entrance onto the scene. Death is inevitable as a consequence of the sin of Adam, yet this curse on Egypt was avoidable. It was a waste. It did not have to happen."

David: "I always thought death came to the Egyptians by an angel, the angel of death."

John: "You saw my face when I took Mom home. Death is my blessing to those who seek true life. The same was true with so many Egyptians when I came for them. The Script tells of the mixed multitude of Egyptians who joined Israel in fellowship and later on in circumcision. These were protected with Israel by the blood of the innocent lamb on their doorposts. They saw life and wanted life."

"Today, despite sin and a demonically oppressed world, I have come to show death as the way to life. Death is your friend. 'A friend that sticks closer than a brother.' I was myself then, and the same when you saw Mom come home to me."

"Eternity is not a philosophy. It's real time. In real time the cries of the Egyptians are in my heart and mind still. Their fear and agony is a forever cry in the universe of eternity. A cry that exists worldwide in today's world too. 'Why is this happening to me' is the question that sounds its cry in the halls of forever."

"I grieve not only over the shock of death, but over the waste. It never had to happen. Theologians speak of the sovereignty of God as if death and life were a game of chess, the way it's depicted in *The 7th Seal*. I grieve that death is now necessary for mankind. I rejoice in the Passover cross and blood of *Lamb Jesus*. This is the death that heals and brings life back through the Passover blood. 'The lamb who takes away the sins of the world.' This death is the doorway to life. This death is where our Script leads its audience and it's cast. After Adam's sin God improvised and had His Son make *His Death,* the way to life. Jesus, the 2nd Adam, came through great pain but with a far greater gain. *Death* was spared mankind in the original plan. Death ironically is now the necessary ingredient for mankind to have *life. L'chaim Davey.* Through death you now find life. In Yeshua's death you have life if you want life. The waste of Pharaoh's sin is made good through the blood of the '*Lamb Jesus.*' Don't waste Jesus death."

"Your Mom understood death as a friend. 'How precious in the sight of the Lord is the death of His saints.'"

David: "Am I going to die? I mean are you soft-selling me about coming with you into everlasting life? Are you coming for me now?"

John: "I am not soft-selling or hard-selling. I am not selling at all. I'm buying. I want *you Davey*! I have pursued you. You have already been bought. Now that you are bought, I will not force you to come. I want you to come."

David: "I remember a Twilight Zone feature with a young Robert Redford playing death. He took that old lady home to heaven. She feared death and would not let him into her house. She feared he was death coming to take her to *the unknown.* He was kind and helped her to give up control. He helped her to face her fear. Her fear was the end of things. Death was kind to her. He was a friend and a new beginning."

John: "Do you want to come, Davey?"

David: "I am afraid. Am I going to die?"
John: "I want to do a scene with you."

David: "You mean act in a scene before I die?"

John: "Davey, please stop your mind from overworking. Let's do play instead. You have watched lots of theater these two days. Now you can be in a live play with me and some friends. Right now!" Do you want to.?"

David: "Ok, yes, let's do it."

John: "Close your eyes for a moment. Closed? Now open your heart."

26

INSIDE THE SCRIPT

Luke: "When the hour came, Jesus and His apostles reclined at the table. And He said to them:

Jesus: "I have eagerly desired to eat this Passover with you again until it finds fulfillment in the kingdom of God."

I was *in the scene*. I was dressed as the apostles were. It was real. I looked up to see an audience and I saw and felt their presence. It was a core twenty maybe even two hundred and very intimate. My sense was that many more were watching. The apostles were *playing* to the audience too. Its as if the audience was there with us. I was reclining at the table with the apostles. I was so close I could hear their breathing.

Also Luke was not in this scene - he was a narrator. Of course, I thought to myself. He was not an apostle; he would not be at the Last Supper Passover.

What I can't get is *why is John Stephens playing Jesus*? I said to myself, Narrow Gate Theater actors are all in character because they are themselves. The Holy Spirit breathes His life into their beings. That's how God demonstrates through us. It's the ultimate in life acting. I get it.

But why is John Stephens playing Jesus? That's not Narrow Gate Acting. Maybe there simply is no way to get Jesus into the play and John is the right actor. The Jesus part has to be played by somebody. Right? Of course John is a great actor.

I then remembered when I attempted to play Jesus at Mt. Beatitudes. Myriam so clearly and painfully explained to me that no one can play God. So who plays Him?

We then were somehow transported into another scene I was now outside near a tomb.

Then I saw another elderly person, who I had not met, come forward into the scene. He looked right at me and said, "I am the apostle John," and he continued.

Apostle John: "Now Mary stood outside the tomb crying. As she wept she bent over to look in the tomb and saw two angels in white seated where Jesus body had been, one at the head and the other at the foot. They asked her, 'Woman, why are you crying?'"

Mary: "They have taken my Lord away."

Apostle John: "At this, she turned around and saw Jesus standing there, but she did she not realize it was Jesus."

Jesus: "Woman, why are you crying? Who is it you are looking for?"

Apostle John: "Thinking He was the gardener, she said,"

Mary: "Sir, if you have taken Him away, tell me where you have put Him and I will get Him."

Jesus: "Mary."

Mary: "Rabboni!"

Jesus: "Do not hold on to Me, for I have not yet ascended to the Father. Go instead to My brothers and tell them I am ascending to My Father and your Father, to My God and your God."

I remember noticing Jesus looked different in this scene than in the Last Supper. His voice sounded exactly like John Stephens but not his body. I remembered again that I was told that Cleopas had trouble recognizing Jesus after He rose from the dead. I then checked myself saying, "*David stop trying to figure things out. Go with the action and follow where it goes.*"

I found myself in another scene. I was now playing a different part, too. I was walking fast and I was now with Mary Magdalene. We were coming to the tomb. We then saw two angels and they said to Mary, "Why do you look for the living among the dead?" I then remembered Mary saying to me when she visited me, "I was going to a funeral to care for a dead body."

I was now transported into another scene. It was Mary Magdalene and I walking along the road. I assumed to the upper room where the disciples were hiding. I said to Mary with my soft voice as if talking with a child, "Listen to me Mary. *He really is alive. He is God.* God's not dead anymore. He had to die so we can live. We have to die too. We have to change to understand His change. We have to die to fear; so to understand death in a way that brings life. The suffering in the world and the sins of we humans all make sense through death. Death is a friend. Our best friend. He is alive. He is life."

She smiled at me. I could tell she was glad that I, as she, believed Jesus rose from the dead.

The next thing I remember is we were with the disciples. Mary then said, "I have seen the Lord."

There was doubt and cynicism coming from the men. I heard words such as, "Mary you are very emotional" and "what is needed is composure." Some other words I heard were, "Mary, I want to help you through this." And, "I know how difficult this is for you." Some said, "Let's pray for Mary." I saw pandering and it made me angry.

Then I stood out among them and spoke.

"No! *Mary knows better than all of us.* Perhaps we have not sinned in the way she has sinned. Perhaps, too, we have not received the amount of forgiveness she has received either. Why? Because we think we have merit? That's our arrogance. Mary has *no status* and she knows it. Her only hope is in the only One who did not judge her as we judge her now. She went to the tomb. Where were you? You missed the cross and now you have missed the tomb. How can you know anything when you just sit around and ponder the existence of God? Mary is involved while we sit around and philosophize. We cannot, no, *we will not see God*, but Mary has seen Him.

We refuse to drop the heavy weight of disbelief. We are too big with fear and pride to fit through the narrow gate. We are big in our minds therefore God is not significant to us because we do not value what is small, intimate and personal. Mary is *small* therefore her God is big in her life. She saw God, and thank God she is one of us. She is God's prophet to us. He is alive and He is risen. Hallelujah!"

I said that? It was as if I was scripted with lines memorized. I must have internalized those words. I was just improvising from what I have internalized from the *Immanuel Script*, and my time at *Narrow Gate Theater*.

That was amazing to me. It was *good acting, yes and it felt good* too. I had never before been so in the spirit of the moment. *I believed all that I had said.* I was acting

Truth. Was there an audience? I knew for certain that I was not alone. I was playing to God and my experience was *personal*. A child at play? It was all meditative to me. It was the opposite of self-conscious. I did not have a word for what it was. He was demonstrating through me? "I am a *Bible Demonstrator*, wow this is cool!"

I was also involved. I was not being passive. I was alive! I had been in a tomb and not for 3 days but 3 decades. I had risen as one of His disciples in a scene from the Bible. *Immanuel is God with us*. People internalize one thing or another. Usually we internalize fear and indifference. *This Word internalized was my healing as I internalized His Script into my life.*

I remember James telling me, 'If you do what the word says (improvise the word in life's situations), you will not forget what you heard.' The Script unchanging is also played out universally and worldwide. Its audience is also universal and worldwide. I let go, tonight, and *was involved*. We can be released from OLD - objective learning disorder! I laughed to myself saying,

"Hi. My name is David and I have Objective Learning Disorder."

John also said to me that most people today are consensus thinkers who copy common thinking so as to be accepted. It is common to lack a point of view. Overcoming OLD was being free to have a point of view. I am no longer a clone cloistered in a tomb of fear and passivity. I am liberated by being improvisational with '*The Script*' and its Author! *Scripture is Immanuel*. I am part of a new generation that rediscovers Jesus and again says *Only Script*. It brings revival.

Human history happens once. The Bible Script happens all the time. The *Bible* plays in *time* for our sake. When we enter in we join the ongoing revival. That's why John Stephens began *The Narrow Gate Theater*. He wanted to show that God's eternity plays out in time. This is what true '*life acting*' is.

This is how I can know Jesus as well as anyone who walked with Him when he had His life on earth. *He Is Now!* I can know Him as Myriam and Sarah do, too "This is better than a time machine," I thought to myself. I then laughed and laughed until I cried joy.

27

BACK AT MOUNT OF BEATITUDES

I then looked up and the apostle John stood before us. Somehow when he speaks, I am more aware that there is an audience. He is like a narrator gathering listeners to the *narrative* that is *Bible His-Story*.

Apostle John: "On the evening of that first day of the week, when the disciples were together, with the doors closed for fear of the Jewish leaders, Jesus stood among them and said,"

Jesus: "Peace be with you!"

Apostle John: "After He said this, He showed them His hands and side. The disciples were overjoyed when they saw the Lord. Again Jesus said,"

Jesus: "As the Father has sent Me, so I am sending you."

Apostle John: "And with that He breathed on them and said,"

Jesus: "Receive the Holy Spirit. If you forgive anyone's sins they are forgiven; if you retain the sins of any, they have been retained"

David: If I do not forgive sins *I retain the sins I do not forgive*! In receiving His *breath,* I immediately had a desire to release forgiveness. I was in effect releasing all the weight I carried. Passivity is a heavy burden. I was now no longer a reservoir, but many rivers pouring out through me into the ocean.

I was there. *'There'* came to me. I now understand *Narrow Gate Theater* is God happening now. History happens once but God's eternity is here to find humans like me.

All these thoughts and more were coming to me as He breathed on me. I was changing by His breath. Rabbi Fishberg once spoke to me about the Holy Spirit as God's breath. "When King David says, 'Do not take your Holy Spirit from me,' David is pleading for his life. If you do not breathe, how then can you live? The Holy Spirit is our life supply'"

I too *was* a *dying man pleading for breath so to live.* I was crying out for life and I was not afraid to ask. I was asking the One who loves. "Lord, please forgive me." I cried aloud. "Give me life. Give me purpose. Give me you, please!"

Jesus looked at me and smiled. He spoke to me without opening His mouth. He voice was John Stephens. He looked through me and tenderly breathed life into me. *'Receive!'*

"You have come home Davey. You are forgiven and you are forgiving. You are not blaming anyone and this shows you are forgiving. *You are forgiven by Me.*"

I was stunned by the lightness I was experiencing. I was without weight. I thought to myself. "I *am even lighter now* than when I was born. I tell you I am lighter than a newborn babe." I then heard Him say to me, "You have been born again."

It was the voice of John Stephens. *It was the voice of Jesus. John Stephens is Jesus*!

In an instant I saw something as clearly as I saw the angel visit Mom when she died. I saw an image of my two tarot card readers dissolve before my eyes. Their image was pure sloth and their grip upon me was gone. It was the their demon who had his grasp on me all these years. It was a clinging sloth like creature that had been sucking life from me for many years. Now it was all dissolving before my eyes. The witchcraft and its demon were gone from me. My body felt light as if it was no longer held by gravity. I felt like air itself. My muscles were soft and tight at the same time. I had a moment where I was in the sky *walking on a cloud.*

"You are the light of the world," I again heard Jesus say to me. "Light is the absence of weight."

I had never experienced such an extraordinary *unburdening* of things.

My very will was being led me to the back of the house theater. I noticed through the huge open window, in the huge open area in front of the main theater, that it was now morning. It was Sunday morning and the first day of the week. It was sunrise. I was hearing the music of Narrow Gate. The choir, the orchestra and the amazing acoustics. Then I saw a multitude of people walking out of the theater and into an open field. The back exit of Narrow Gate Theater led to a field?

How is this possible in New York City? Nevertheless there was a crowd developing. It must have been thousands. I saw men, women, boys and girls. I saw families and what I was sure was Paul's *mishbukah* of Jew and gentile. I saw people knitted by love that were obviously genetically different.

As I continued to walk, I remembered when I entered the theater there were huge crowds, yet we were not crowded. I had been in the center of a happening but I was not the center. I was free. This was the same, only it was not New York City anymore.

"This is *not Kansas*," as Dorothy would say to her dog Toto.

There was a grassy field that opened up. "This is not New York," I again said to myself. As I walked I saw a lake below us. "I have been here. When was I here?"

I was dressed in my contemporary street clothes, but others were in what I could refer to as *Bible clothes*. Others still in a different contemporary than mine. Different clothes for different times and cultures throughout human history? I must have died at The Narrow Gate Theater. The angel of death has taken me home. John set me up to not fear my impending death. Suddenly I heard John's voice and again it was the same as the Jesus voice.

John: "David, I am not an angel as you understand an angel. 'For I will pass through the land of Egypt on that night, and will strike all, the firstborn in the land of Egypt, both man and beast; and against all the gods of Egypt I will execute judgment: I am the Lord' This David is in *The Script* it's from *Exodus*."

"Listen to Me. 'I am the Lord I AM HE!'"

Then he began His message to all. I recognized *His* Words from the *Sermon on the Mount* from the time we visited Israel in 1987.

"Blessed are the poor in spirit for theirs is the kingdom of heaven.... Blessed are those who are persecuted because of righteousness for theirs is the kingdom of heaven... You have heard it was said, 'Thou shalt not commit adultery,' but I tell you if a man looks at a woman lustfully, he has committed already committed adultery with her in his heart... Our Father who art in heaven, hallowed be thy Name."

David: It then occurred to me, maybe I can find Mom in the crowd. Mansfield too. *Dad?* I started seeking for them. I now heard the *Voice* and knew I was getting closer. I had scrambled my way into and through the crowds. I was now so close to Him it felt like 90 feet away as close as third base is to home plate. I was so close, but all the 6 foot plus guys were in front of my 5ft - 9in.

It was Jesus Voice it was John's. Jesus to me was John Stephens. I did not recognize this until I could see Jesus as He is. It was much the same for Cleopas on the road to Emmaus. The unrecognizable Jesus was now finally *recognized*. I remembered the almost car crash. That was a horror averted. This time I did die and this was *my wonderful death*. Jesus took me home! Now I want to see Mom.

Then I heard another voice. "Hey Davey, nice going man," and I then heard many saying, "Davey, way to go!" There were thousands of people standing and cheering for me. I even heard a few bravos. I was getting a standing ovation very like Yankee Stadium and a Mickey Mantle home run to win the World Series. Only it was me and what I won was greater than the World Series

As I walked up to *the Voice* it all momentarily stopped. Sudden silence was everywhere. My movements in the silence were now in slow motion silence. I was in *slowmo* leaping like a deer through the woods as I flew upon home plate. I could not help that I was aware of a baseball analogy and that Home *plate was a Rock*. The Rock of Israel was my friend, John - Jesus!

I then looked up just as my feet touched the rock. John Stephens, who had stopped His sermon, took me by the hand and said, "*Welcome home Davey. I am He* and I have been on a long search for you." We hugged. *He is a good hugger*. He never hugged me before.

I finally came to be, so I could see. He was always Jesus, seeking me!

I in the hug was immersed into Love. 'My Lord and my God' I said to Him. I slipped a look back to look into His eyes. It was the same eyes as John Stephens. Only He was Yeshua, Jesus my Lord. He said to me in a whisper in the gentlest voice I had ever heard, "Think of Me when you awaken each morning. Remember Me early and always." I then was about to ask Jesus a question about Mom when He suddenly went back into His sermon.

"Do not lay up for yourselves treasures on the earth where moth and rust destroy and where thieves break in and steal, but lay up for yourselves treasures in heaven where moth and rust do not destroy and where thieves do not break in and steal; for where your treasure is there your heart will be also."

So I was again looking for Mom when I began to remember why this outdoor place was so familiar. *This is Mount Of Beatitudes where Jesus gave the Sermon on the Mount.* It was playing again because the Narrow Gate Theater had worldwide activity into its location. Of course! I was there. I was here. There was no distinction in time. I then remembered when Myriam, Sarah, and I were in this very place in 1987. I so failed here and throughout my life, yet now I was not distraught about my failure. I finally won my match. I lost my fear of failure. It was a *glorious failure*. 'Lose yourself in Me.' Here at Mount Beatitudes my great failure and now my triumph. My death and now God close up.

I can now see, the me, I was called to be.

"David," I then heard a familiar voice. The familiar voice pierced my heart with hope I dared not hope for. I then turned. It was Myriam!

"Myriam," I said in a loud voice. I fell to the ground in inexpressible joy. I was completely out of control yet focused into- her face. Her eyes so blue, so young, and fresh. I adored her. For all these years I refrained from fully absorbing the pain of my loss. My brutal loss was now my most tender gain!

I was with the one I loved *and there was no way I would hold back that I was so in love.* I touched my love's face and I looked inside her eyes. '*Those lips those eyes* I said over and again.' I then received her touch and our embrace. We each sobbed, sobs of joy, and pure happiness. There were few words. I was now certain that I would not find Mom, Mansfield, or Dad. Not this day. I was alive yet something old was gone from me. Trust was now in its place. I had died but not in my body. I had never been more alive.

Myriam: "We are on the same frequency David. We are on the same channel. We have come to the same place at the same time. Finally! And without all the airline fees to get here."

We laughed and laughed. It was so good to laugh with the bride of my youth. We hugged. It was the most fulfilling hug!

Jesus continued with His sermon... "Do unto others what you would have them do unto you, for this is fulfills the law and the prophets. Enter through the narrow gate for wide is the gate and broad is the road that leads to destruction and many enter through it; but small is the gate and narrow is the road that leads to life and only a few find it."

David; "I found the gate, Myriam. I found Love. I found Jesus. Now I have found you. We are here. There is nowhere else to go." Then hand in hand with Myriam, we heard the final words to His sermon.

"He who hears these words of Mine and acts on them builds his house on the rock. The rains came down, the floods rose, and the winds blew and beat against that house but it did not fall, its foundation was built on the rock. But he who hears these words of mine and does not act upon them builds his house on sand. The rain descended, the floods rose, and the wind blew and beat against that house and it fell with a great crash."

Myriam; "I so love you David. We did not *crash!* I have waited and you are my reward for waiting. My prayers for us have never left my heart or my lips. In prayer this morning I again cried my longing for you, and I now I am with *you. Now is a long time Davey.*

We laughed and whispered "*forever*" into one another's ear. We laughed the laugh of lovers and overcomers.

Those who have endured the journey through the Narrow Gate.

28

AT TIMES SQUARE

"David. David can you hear me."

Myriam was right next to me in Times Square holding my hand. Sarah and some of our beautiful grandchildren too, were nearby looking at me and very concerned.

"David, you just got lost in time. Not to be punny, but it's not funny to lose your sense of *time at Times Square*," she said, shouting over the horns honking and the ongoing shaking of Manhattan's ground.

"Hey, you idiot!" Someone walking by screamed in my ear, and pulling on my prayer shawl. Go into the desert where you belong."

"I still get lost in time." I shouted to be heard by Myriam.

Myriam has a way of bringing me back and then I never want to let go.

My mind began to muse again...

All that happened to me at *Narrow Gate Theater* was so very real. It still is. True imagination is not about make believe, but what is truly creative. God imagined the earth and then *created* it in six days. He is as practical, as He is spiritual, and supernatural. Creation of the earth is reality and imagination as one! I love creativity. It's like perpetual recess for a third grader.

These costumes we wear in street ministry are another paradox that is pure fun. You'd think the costumes were an external actor thing but when we wear the costume we are clearly *God people* and *aliens* to this world. I am often so sad when the outreach is over. It's very tempting to be invisible again and to *leave* who I really am. I spent so many years trying to be someone else. The costume protects me and us from wearing *the mask that masks we are different. A good different.*

I then remembered John Stephens.

Sorrow brings one to the door of the narrow gate. Hope and joy are the way through the narrow gate.

I suddenly realized I was *Time Traveling* again.

"I get lost in time Myriam," Is all I can say. I am sorry. I do tend to live on different time zones, but being with you is always the right time.

"It was only a moment but I saw from the look in your eyes that you were somewhere else David." She then touched my face and kissed me.

Man that felt good.

"Grandpa I want a hug," said Elijah, our 3-year-old great-grandson.

My son-in-law old Peter then said, "You are the high ranking old guy."

"Hugs never grow old," I shouted over the noise and smell of car exhaust coupled with Manhattan's vibration.

"Ok, we have done our work for the day. Let's go to our headquarters. We can change there and have a meal with our friends."

As we walked up town a few blocks, Sarah took my hand. Sarah was matched in beauty only by her Mom. Myriam took my other hand and we were complete. Sarah was holding her Hannah doll. The one John Stephens gave her. When we do these outreaches she always brings her Hannah doll. It makes me glad. I looked into Myriam's eyes. She was never more beautiful than now. She glows!

We know what we do is not popular. We also know it is what makes us family. We are family with those who join us too.

"It's not getting easier," I said to my two girls, "but we have each other. And thanks to Sarah, lots more each other's, too." Again we laughed.

"All those years when things in the world were difficult, we did not have each other. Now that things are horrible, we have real family. *"Figures."* We again found occasion to laugh. "I am *meshuganah* but always crazy over you, and you, and you." I kissed all our old and young grandchildren one by one. Finally by *'mistake'* I kissed Pastor Peter my son-in-law on the forehead. I was doing a little Tevye from Fiddler On The Roof.

We came to our destination, just a 10-minute walk. It was Narrow Gate Theater Headquarters on 52nd and Broadway. We then walked into the homeless shelter just as dinner was being served.

Even though many of the guests are transient there is always a core who know us well and are in recovery. I too am in a *glorious recovery*. I then looked at the cross and remembered our *family blood connection*.

Suddenly I heard the sound the of old satchmo coming from the streets. "Yes its him! *I hear Louis Armstrong.*

"Colors of the rainbow so pretty in the sky... friends shaking hands sayin how do you do. They're really saying I love you."

"Yes I still can hear."

Above the cross was a citation from the founder of the mission:
John Stephens Memorial Mission, Enter Through The Narrow Gate.

The End

Dennis Cole is available for ministry, interviews and public appearances. For more information contact:

Dennis Cole
C/O Advantage Books
P.O. Box 160847
Altamonte Springs, FL 32716

info@advbooks.com

To purchase additional copies of this book or other books published by Advantage Books, visit our bookstore website: ww.advbookstore.com

Longwood, Florida, USA
"we bring dreams to life"™
www.advbookstore.com

CPSIA information can be obtained
at www.ICGtesting.com
Printed in the USA
LVOW10s0424010817
543262LV00024B/1364/P

9 781597 554398